GOTH GIRL RISING

Also by Barry Lyga

*The Astonishing Adventures of
Fanboy and Goth Girl*

Boy Toy

Hero-Type

GOTH GIRL RISING

Barry Lyga

Houghton Mifflin Harcourt
Boston New York

Copyright © 2009 by Barry Lyga, LLC

All rights reserved. Published in the United States by Graphia, an imprint of Houghton Mifflin Harcourt Publishing Company, Boston, Massachusetts. Originally published in hardcover in the United States by Houghton Mifflin, an imprint of Houghton Mifflin Harcourt Publishing Company, in 2009.

For information about permission to reproduce selections from this book, write to Permissions, Houghton Mifflin Harcourt Publishing Company, 215 Park Avenue South, New York, New York 10003.

Graphia and the Graphia logo are registered trademarks of Houghton Mifflin Harcourt Publishing Company.

www.hmhbooks.com

The text of this book is set in ITC Legacy Serif.

Library of Congress Cataloging-in-Publication Data is on file.

ISBN 978-0-547-07664-5 hardcover
ISBN 978-0-547-40308-3 paperback

Manufactured in the United States of America
DOM 10 9 8 7 6 5 4 3 2 1
4500268219

For Molly, who told me I should.
And look, I did.

my hair my hair

my hair's gone brown

i look in the mirror

and who do i see?

a brown-haired girl

who is she?

ONE

My MOTHER AND I BOTH spent a lot of time in hospitals. Unlike her, I survived.

Before she went and died, my mom told me to stop bitching about my cramps all the time. "It's nothing that every other woman on the planet hasn't gone through," she said.

And besides, she went on, your period is a good thing. It's a sign that you're alive and healthy.

Easy for her to say—cancer was eating her lungs from the inside out, so what's the big deal about some cramps, right?

Still, I knew that what I was experiencing wasn't right or normal. It wasn't what other girls were feeling every month. (I know—I asked around.)

Weird thing, though: After she died, my cramps sort of got better. It's not like they went away; they just stopped being so intense and so consuming. I started to think that, OK, maybe *this* is what other girls felt. Like I had been abnormal before, but now I was somehow becoming normal, that now the world was working properly and everything was good and normal and usual.

Everything except my mom's *face* . . .

My mom's face before they closed the casket looked like a Barbie doll's.

A Barbie doll someone had left in the sandbox too long.

All plasticky and too shiny, but somehow gray at the same time.

And then one day after the funeral—it was a pretty nice day, too—I took a box cutter from my dad's workshop and slashed across my wrist. It hurt, but not that much. Not bad at all.

So I slashed the other one, too.

And that's how I ended up in the emergency room and then in front of a judge and then locked up in a mental hospital.

That was my first time in the hospital. And I got out and I covered up my scars and I went on with my life and I tried to figure out what it was all about, and I'm *still* trying to figure it out.

But it just gets more and more complicated all the time. Every day. The world doesn't slow down long enough for you to figure out anything; it keeps adding things in. Things like geeky guys and comic books and comic book conventions and effed-up teachers and . . .

And another stay in the hospital.

TWO

GOD I'M *DYING* FOR A CIGARETTE. I turned sixteen while I was away but this stupid state says you have to be eighteen to smoke, so they wouldn't let me smoke in the hospital.

When I got home this afternoon, the first thing I did was look for my cigs. But Roger had tossed them already. Now that *he's* quit, he's an effing cigarette *Taliban*, even though it's, like, years too late for that.

"Mom's already dead!" I yelled at him. "Who the hell do you think you're saving?"

And he just gave me his Sad, Tired look. It's one of the three he's got, the other two being Pissed Off and Blissed Out on ESPN.

"You, Kyra." Like it's some big revelation. "Someone has to protect you from yourself. From all the crap out in the world."

"Don't do me any favors," I told him.

He took a deep breath. "It's your first day back home. Can't you behave just a little bit?"

I went to my room. Home all of five minutes and I was already isolated in my room. Living with Roger isn't much different from being in the hospital. He's in charge, just like the doctors

5

and nurses are in charge in the hospital. I have no say. I have no rights.

To make things worse, I'm going back to school in the morning. I don't want to go back to school.

See, I haven't been to school in a while. Six months, which includes all of summer break, when everyone else in the universe was off having fun. Except for me. I got put away. Now I'm supposed to go back to school like nothing happened.

School seems like something that happens to other people.

Last spring, I met this guy. And I guess I fell in love with him a little bit, which was a stupid thing for me to do because it never works out and it's pointless. So I kicked him in the balls and walked away from him and even flipped him off over the Internet.

And then my dad started in on me because, see, before all of this, this kid—this *Fanboy*—had a bullet. And I guess I sort of stole it from him and he figured out I had it and he called my effing *dad* and then all hell broke loose at home because my dad was all freaked out, like I was going to try to kill myself again. And he spent all this time tearing apart the house, looking for this goddamn bullet, which he couldn't find because I'd already given it back to Fanboy . . . right at the same time I kicked him in the balls, actually.

And I kept my mouth shut, too. No matter how much my dad screamed and yelled and ranted and raved, I wouldn't tell him anything about the bullet. Not about where I got it. Not about where it went. Not about the kid who called him at work to tell him about it.

So Roger—my dad, officially—gave up. He sent me to the hospital again.

And now I'm back home. Because as bad as it was, I'm tougher than my mom.

6

THE LAST TIME I SAW HER

the room the room the room is rosevomit because

THREE

THINGS ARE A LITTLE BIT BETTER at home, of course—I have my *own* room, without a crazy roommate who got knocked up at fifteen and used to let her boyfriend beat her up. So I've got that going for me.

And I have my computer.

It's been *months* since I've been able to do anything on a computer. They had computers in the hospital, but we were monitored and we only got, like, fifteen minutes at a time, so I didn't bother.

I fire up the computer and log on to my chat program and there's Simone, like she's waiting for me. Simone's my best friend—I know all of her shit and she knows all of my shit.

So it goes like this:

simsimsimoaning: *welcom back!!!!!*

Promethea387: *Thanks. Already feel like I'm in jail or something. Roger is being a PITA.*

simsimsimoaning: *u need 2 get oiut*

simsimsimoaning: *uv ben cooped up for MONTHS*

Promethea387: *Yeah, I know.*

simsimsimoaning: *grounded?*

Promethea387: *I don't think so. He's just watching me real carefully.*

simsimsimoaning: *shit*

Promethea387: *So? Never stopped me before.*

simsimsimoaning: *lol*

Promethea387: *I'm dying for a cigarette.*

simsimsimoaning: *i can hook u up*

Promethea387: *Roger is still home. I'll have to sneak out tonight when he's asleep.*

simsimsimoaning: *meet me @ jeccas house big party 2nite*

Promethea387: *OK.*

FOUR

SPEND THE REST OF THE DAY in my bedroom, just sort of trying to avoid Roger *and* the thought of school tomorrow. I'm not real successful at either one.

I turn up some music and try to drown my own brain, but I only succeed a little bit.

Roger knocks on the door a bunch of times. I talk to him just enough that he won't get too suspicious and start coming in without knocking. He told me on the way home from the hospital: "This is how it's going to be, Kyra—if you give me enough reason to worry about you, I'll just come in without knocking." And then, as if he read my effing mind: "And if it's locked, I'll knock it the hell down."

He thinks when he busts out "hell" I take him more seriously. Yeah. Insert eye roll here. (Man, I wish *life* had emoticons, you know? So that when your dad pisses you off you could like click a mental button or something and just show him one of those rolleyes. That would rock.)

Anyway.

After, like, *forever*, it's finally nighttime. There are no nurses to come in and check on me. No one tries to give me meds or anything like that. No psycho roommate crying herself to sleep.

Just me. In my own bedroom.

Roger knocks and then comes in and sits down. I'm lying on the bed. He sighs because that's what Roger does—he sighs a lot.

He gives me Sad, Tired.

"Are you going to behave in school tomorrow?"

"I guess."

"I need more than a guess, Kyra."

"What do you want from me, Roger?"

He flicks to Pissed Off for a second before returning to Sad, Tired. "I want you to think straight for once."

For some reason I feel sorry for him all of a sudden. That happens sometimes with Sad, Tired.

"I'll try, Dad."

He nods and leaves. I hear him head into his bathroom, then into his bedroom. Pretty soon the TV's on, just loud enough that I can hear *something* but not loud enough to tell what it is.

I give him an hour to fall asleep.

Then I stuff a bunch of clothes and old stuffed animals and shit under my covers to make it look like I'm in bed. I get dressed for the real world for the first time since spring—all black, of course; minimizer bra, of course. In the hospital, my black hair dye washed out, so now I have this ugly brown stuff. Nothing I can do it about it right now.

I sneak out the back door because that one squeaks a lot less than the front door.

Outside. I'm outside.

I'm in my own clothes.

I'm free.

Freedom! Like in that old Mel Gibson movie they made us watch in history. I want to scream it to the night sky: *FREEDOM!*

I stand in the cold and shiver a little bit. It's OK, though. The cold's OK. It's better than being in the hospital.

The only real problem is that I have no car. I used to be able to boost one pretty regularly, but I've only been home for a few hours, so I haven't been able to sneak out and steal one. So I'll have to walk to Jecca's. Damn.

Oh, well. I breathe in deep. The air's cold, but it feels good in my lungs. Better than the air in the hospital, that's for damn sure.

I start to walk.

FANBOY

AND I CAN'T HELP MYSELF. Even though I try to think of other things—Jecca, Simone, the party—I keep thinking about Fanboy.

And his graphic novel. And the way he kept trying to check me out without really checking me out and how for the first time in my life that, like, totally didn't bother me or freak me out. Except it freaked me out that it *didn't* freak me out.

I don't get it.

I remember kicking him in the balls. And e-mailing him a picture of me flipping him off. I was so pissed at him. I was so angry.

There was this senior named Dina Jurgens, and she was this total *Maxim* bimbette with the tits and the ass and the legs and the tan and the blond hair and all that shit that makes guys turn into such jackasses. Against all odds, she even put the moves on Fanboy. I found out that at a party one night she started sucking face with him, which is so stupid.

So maybe I was right to be angry because I liked him and I

shouldn't have, but he shouldn't have kissed effing *Dina Jurgens* of all people, but she graduated while I was gone, so she's not an issue anymore, right? Out of sight, out of mind.

But he's just *scary* talented. I mean, I've read a lot of comic books and manga and shit, and *Schemata* was just totally kick-ass. I busted him a lot about some of the stuff he put in there, and it really pissed me off that his main character was just wank-bait Dina all grown up, but still. It was amazing. I read most of the script and saw like twenty pages of artwork, and it was phenomenal. I still can't believe that bald little shit Bendis didn't realize he was looking at genius. (Yeah, big-shot Brian Michael Bendis. Big-shot comic book writer. Whatever. Prick. He didn't deserve to see my boobs. Long story.)

Cute, in that geeky way only guys have, really. Geeky girls can't really pull it off. Not the same way. Geeky guys have this shyness that works because it's, like, so different from the normal asshole guy behavior. So when you see a shy guy, it makes you sit up and take notice. It makes you want to understand them or makes you feel like you already understand them or . . .

I don't know. Protect them? Does that make sense?

I hate jocks. I hate big buff guys who think they were hand-crafted by God to dispense orgasms to the world. They're more into themselves than anything or anyone else. And that's just bullshit. Because here's the thing: No one in this world is so great that they're worthy of self-obsession. Believe me, I know. It's just the truth. We're all flawed, broken half-people. None of us is complete or even worthwhile. We all suck.

But Fanboy . . .

See, for a while there, I thought of him as just "fanboy." Lowercase. It wasn't his name—it was just his description, you know? The way you'd call someone in the army "soldier," or the way obnoxious pigs call guys "sport" or "son."

But somewhere, somehow . . . while I was *away*, it changed. It became a *title*. It became like a proper noun, you know?

I guess he wasn't so bad. I mean, it pissed me off that he was obsessed with Dina, but *all* guys are obsessed with her, so I should really let that pass. And he kept messing up stuff about women in his graphic novel, but I realized something while I was away—he *tried*. He was a fifteen-year-old *boy* from effing *Brookdale* and he was trying to create a graphic novel about women and their problems.

I have to give him props for that.

And a part of me . . . a part of me thinks that maybe I can help him. Maybe I can help make his graphic novel even better. I mean, I was the only one he showed it to. The only one he trusted. He never even showed it to his "best" friend, this super-star stud jock who's like a secret geek or something.

He showed it to *me*.

But I really treated him like shit. I shouldn't have done that.

My shrink in the hospital—Dr. Kennedy—told me that every day is a chance to start your life over again. Which is bullshit, really, but not *total* bullshit. I guess we *can* make changes. Things aren't always set in stone, right?

Fanboy didn't call while I was in the hospital. He couldn't— he didn't know where I was. So I forgive him for that. But he also didn't send me any e-mails, which sort of pisses me off because he could have e-mailed me at least once, right?

But . . .

Look at it this way: He didn't e-mail me, which is a mean, shitty thing to do. But I was mean to him, too.

So we're even.

So everything is cool, then.

Yeah.

This is what I'm going to do: Make it all better.

I can do that.

At school, he'll be excited to see me. I'll apologize and then he'll apologize (see, I'll even go first) and we'll pick up where we left off and this time . . .

This time I'll try really, really hard not to eff it up.

FIVE

ECCA LIVES ABOUT TEN MINUTES AWAY by car, but it takes me a while to get there on foot. That's OK—all that time walking and thinking is good for me.

There's a bunch of cars parked along the road, but the house is dark.

I walk into the middle of a "quiet party." Everyone's in the living room, all the furniture pushed into a circle. There's like twenty kids, all dressed in black, some with white makeup like I wear, some with exaggerated black or smoky gray eyeshadow. I'm the only one here without black hair. I feel like someone should revoke my Goth Girl membership card.

There are some candles lighting the room, but that's it.

Most everyone ignores me. They all know I've been in the loony bin for six months. Word got out. Only Simone and Jecca knew *which* loony bin, though, because even though I know almost everyone here, Simone and Jecca are the only ones I would actually call friends.

Jecca squeals and jumps up to hug me. Simone slips me a pack of cigarettes. Bless her.

I get this weird minute where I can't talk. It's like I'm totally overwhelmed. I realize: This is the first time in six months I've been with a *friend*. Six months of nothing but doctors and nurses and whacked-out mental patients and visits from Roger. I talked to Jecca and Simone on the phone a little bit, but that was it.

"You're back," Jecca whispers, still hugging me.

"Yeah." It's the only thing I can manage to say right now. How do you talk to normal people?

"Let her breathe," Simone says, prying us apart. She gives me one of those little one-armed hugs and then pushes a guy off the sofa so that we can sit down.

"What took you so long?" Sim whispers.

"I had to walk."

Sim frowns. "I'll take you home later."

I hate that I have to bum a ride from her. I should have my license by now. I should have a car—my own car, not a stolen one—by now.

The air's thick and sweet with pot. A bong is being passed around. The guy Simone pushed moves that slow way stoned people move. The word is *languid*, I think.

It's weird because I figured I would have all of this shit to talk about when I finally saw Sim and Jecca again, but now that I'm here, I don't want to talk. I don't want to *think*. I'm really glad that the party is "quiet." It's like everyone just sits around and gets mellow and stays quiet. And you have to turn off your cell and shit to come in and it's pretty cool to be in the dark and the quiet for a while. You can talk—you just have to talk *quiet.*

So we all just sit here and smoke and relax and it's cool. The chatter's low. No one's talking about anything that matters.

But then someone passes the bong to me and I take a hit and it's not a cigarette, but it's great, really. God, it's been so effing long.

My lungs go all orgasmic with it and I hold my breath so long that I think maybe I've figured out how to never breathe again, how to survive without exhaling. God, would that be cool or what? That's what it feels like, like I don't need air anymore, not as long as I have the sweet smoke in my lungs.

And then my eyes start to spark. That's the only way to describe it—they spark. I start to see little bursts of color. I close my eyes and they're still there and I exhale, letting all the smoke out in a cloud. The whole room's a cloud.

God, this is what I needed. I needed to be with some friends and just ease my way back into the real world after being in the hospital for so long. Now I can go back to school tomorrow. Honestly. I can. I really can.

Simone giggles at nothing and takes a hit and passes the bong along.

Bong along. Heh.

"What's so funny?" Simone asks.

I didn't realize I actually laughed.

Across the circle, Jecca waves to me, slowly, *languidly*. She's totally blissed out. Her parents travel a lot and she has these great mellow parties for the goths in Brookdale and Canterstown, even Finn's Crossing. No one's allowed to eff with any of her parents' stuff, but that's cool because we're all just here to get away from the rest of the world anyway.

And then it's time for hide-and-seek.

The hide-and-seek we play isn't totally like the old kid game:

You get all stoned out of your mind first, and then you go hide and someone has to find you, and it's awesome because you're just blitzed unbelievably.

Last time I played was *months* ago, before I met Fanboy even. I was the seeker and everyone scattered while I sat with my eyes closed, counting to a hundred. And when I opened my eyes, it was like the rest of the world had just vanished, just gone away.

And I loved it.

I mean, I knew deep down that the world was still there. That I wasn't alone in the house, that there were, like, twenty kids hiding just around the corners and up the stairs and all that. But the illusion of complete aloneness was there and that's all I cared about at that moment—the illusion. It worked for me. I didn't question it.

So I had counted to one hundred and I was sitting there on the sofa all by myself and I was supposed to get up and go seeking, but instead I just sat there. Just sat there, slightly stoned, completely alone in the dark. I didn't think about anything, didn't want anything, didn't really even *feel* anything. I just absorbed the solace and the solitariness of it all.

And did nothing.

I don't know how long I sat there. Could have been five minutes. Could have been five hours. Time stopped meaning anything.

Eventually, people started to get antsy and move. I didn't care. I just sat there as they slowly began to drift back into the living room.

"What the hell, Kyra?"

"You suck at this."

I ignored them.

"You're supposed to come looking for us."

"Leave her alone. She's totally stoned out."

Still ignored them. Grasped for just one last moment of peace, of alone. Clung to it. Wouldn't let go. Couldn't let go. Can't let go.

Six

So needless to say, this time no one says I should be the one to seek. Which is fine by me.

I don't know what's happening to me. The whole time I was in the hospital, all I wanted was to get out and be with my friends. And now suddenly all I can think about is being alone. Maybe it's the pot. Maybe it's just, like, culture shock. I don't know.

Some guy I've never seen before closes his eyes and starts to count. Everyone steals away, sneaking off into the darkness to hide. I creep away to the kitchen. The pantry is a big walk-in, and there's a spot under a shelf where I can tuck myself in if I lie down. Since no one is allowed to turn on lights, if I stay very still you can't see me even if you walk into the pantry.

After a minute or two, I start to drift off, buoyed by the pot and the silence. It's all peaceful until I start to think about Fanboy. I feel really bad for him, like he needs someone to touch him and hold him maybe, someone to—

The pantry door creaks open just a bit.

I lie perfectly still, my heart hammering.

"Kyra?" It's Jecca, whispering.

"Yeah."

She slips in and closes the door. Then she's next to me, lying next to me, the heat of her radiating to me, her breath a hush between us.

Her hand finds my face. I'm holding my breath for some reason. I let it out against her fingertips as she leans in, following her hand in the dark, and her lips touch mine.

SEVEN

THIS HAPPENS SOMETIMES. WITH JECCA. It doesn't really go any further than kissing, which is no big deal, right?

Jecca makes a little noise down deep in her chest. I've been holding her out. I open my mouth and she sighs her relief between my lips and I realize that I sort of feel sorry for lesbians. I mean real lesbians, the genuine article. The women who truly feel love and passion for other women. Because it's like *everyone* is doing it these days. It's like their very sexuality, the core of their beings, has become a . . . a *fad*, something they throw into soap operas to up the ratings, or something girls do to turn their boyfriends on. It's like it's been made meaningless.

I mean, I don't love Jecca or anything. And she doesn't love me. It's not like we're gay. Because we're not.

I don't think.

This just happens, is all.

She kisses me. I kiss her back. It's no big deal.

Except it does feel good. It does feel nice. When it happens . . . sometimes when it happens, I can forget things. Big things. Little

24

things. All kinds of things. Her lips are really soft; her tongue's soft, too. Sometimes she licks my neck or nibbles my ear, and that's great.

I guess some people would call this "experimentation," but that's not it because experimentation is, like, indicating that you would do something full-time after trying it out. And I don't think I'm a lesbian or anything. I like boys. I know this because when I fantasize, I think about boys all the time.

But I also think about Jecca. Not other girls. Just Jecca.

This is just . . . God, it's just comforting. And safe. And I *never* feel comfortable or safe, so these times with Jecca, when this happens, it's like a vacation for me, like being sent away again, only this time being sent away somewhere I *want* to go, somewhere I like.

It's looking for a touch, warmth, connection, heat, anything.

"What's wrong?" she whispers, which is weird because she usually doesn't say anything.

"Nothing." And I lean up a little bit to kiss her. I've been thinking the whole time. Stressing. And she could tell. So I shut off my brain for a little while and just let the safety and the comfort take over.

EIGHT

$\mathcal{L}$ATER. I'M STILL STONED. *So* STONED. And smoking my way through my first pack of cigarettes in *months*. God, it feels good! I lick my lips and imagine I can taste Jecca's lipstick, which I can't, but I imagine it, which is just as good.

I'm in the kitchen, giggling with Simone as she tries to open a bag of potato chips.

"I think I need scissors," she says, pronouncing the *c* so that it comes out "skissors," which for some reason makes us both convulse with laughter until we're giggling right there on the kitchen floor.

"Skissors," she says again.

"Suh-gar!" I say, spying the sugar bowl on the counter.

"Skissors!"

"Suh-gar!"

"Va-*guy*-na!"

I snort laughter. "No, it has to start with an *s*." I don't know why, but it's funnier that way.

She licks her lips and tries the bag again. She gets it open without making it explode all over the place.

"She-mata!" she says, holding out a handful of chips.

I stare at her. The chips are wavering right in front of me and my gut is telling me to eat them so fast that she doesn't even know they're gone, but my brain is thinking, *What did she just say?*

"Huh?"

"Chips!" she says, and giggles because *chips* is a funny word, especially when you say it like Simone does when she's stoned.

"No, what did you say before?"

She shoves some of the chips into her mouth. "Skissors!"

"No, not that."

"Suh-gar!"

"That was me."

"She-mata! Like the comic book."

"It's *Schemata*," I tell her automatically, pronouncing it correctly, but at the same time, I'm trying to think ten million things at once. How does Simone know about *Schemata*? How does she know anything at all? Did I tell her? I don't *think* I did. I don't think I ever mentioned it to her.

Simone isn't paying any attention to me—she wanders off with her bag of chips, leaving me in the kitchen by myself. I feel like the world's spinning around me and like my brain is spinning, too, but in the opposite direction, and it makes me all dizzy and crazy. *Did* I tell her about *Schemata*? What did I tell her? *When* did I tell her?

Holy crap. How could I tell her about something like *that* and not remember it? Am I totally losing my mind?

And goddammit, now I don't feel stoned anymore. I'm totally straight now, totally sober, totally pissed, and I wish Jecca was here in the kitchen, because I need someone to kiss me, someone to kiss me and not to talk, never to talk.

27

Dear Neil,

So, here I am, back home, writing to you for the first time from somewhere other than the hospital.

In case you're interested, my first day back home sucked bigtime.

I had a fight with my dad, which is nothing new, but still. It's never fun. And I went to a party and got high and made out with someone, which confuses me every time it happens. And then someone said something that really just . . . It just didn't make any sense.

I'm babbling. Wow, babbling with a keyboard! Babbling with a keyboard in a letter to Neil Gaiman!

Then again, it's not like the letters I wrote to you in the hospital made much sense, either, I bet. I bet if I looked at them now, I would be like, *What the hell were you talking about, Kyra?* But I wrote them and they're done and I'm not going to look back.

That's my new thing, Neil: Not looking back. I'm going to try to look ahead. Like, I'm going to forgive Fanboy and I'm going to try to be his friend again. That's a good thing. That's what adults call "a step in the right direction."

It's not always easy for me. And I think that's what pisses me off more than anything else. People say, "Behave!" and "Don't do bad things!" and "Be nice!" as if those things are easy, as if they're simple. But they're not, Neil. They just aren't. The world is a really, really shitty place, so doing those good things, those nice things, isn't always easy.

And sometimes you have to be mean. Or angry. Sometimes that's the only way to get something done or explain something to someone. And sometimes it just feels good and right and— more important—*honest*. Isn't honesty important? Doesn't honesty matter?

OK, it's really late and I'm really tired and I think I'm still a little bit stoned, so I'm going to bed now.

NINE

HERE'S A LOUD BEEPING SOUND filling the universe, waking me up. I lie in bed for a minute, wondering what the hell the sound is before I realize it's my alarm clock.

God, how weird. I haven't woken up to an alarm in *forever*. I'm in my own room. Not the hospital. My own room. Strange.

Last night is already fading . . . I have the real world to deal with now.

God, it's November. I can't believe it. I missed the end of my sophomore year and the beginning of my junior year. All because my dad freaked out.

As if he can hear me thinking, Roger taps on my door. I want to yell out, *Eff off, Roger!* (I want to do that a *lot!* All the time!) Instead, I don't say anything. His taps become more insistent and he finally gives up being nice and says, "Kyra, I'm counting to three and then I'm opening the door!"

By the time he comes in, I'm at my closet, picking out my clothes for my big ole triumphant return to South Brook High. Ha.

"Didn't you hear me?" he asks.

"I'm thinking," I tell him.

"What's there to think about? It's all black."

This is true. My closet is like a refugee shelter for black clothes.

"What do you want?" I ask him.

"Your teachers all know what you've been going through," he says. "They'll be sympathetic. Like last time."

I just keep staring at the closet. I want to say, *Eff off, Roger!* Again. Because "last time"—back in middle school, when I tried to kill myself—sucked bigtime. Everyone treated me like a freak when I came back to school. Besides, how can my teachers know what I've been "going through" when *I'm* not even a hundred percent sure?

Here's the thing about parents—about adults in general, really: They think they're In Charge. They think they Rule the World.

But in reality they're just as clueless and effed up as everyone else. The world is just a gigantic effing wave, a *tsunami,* and it washes away all of us—kid, parent, student, teacher—alike.

That's the world. That's a *fact,* OK?

"Did you hear me?" he asks.

I sigh out a "yes" like it's the longest word in the world. "Can I get a shower now?"

The bathroom is another weird place for me. My own bathroom. My own stuff. No one messing with it. No one pounding on the door to come in.

I left the cap open on my hair gel while I was gone, so it all dried out. No spikes for me today.

No hair dye, either. Did I run out before I went away, or did

Roger pitch it while I was gone? Roger probably pitched it. He never liked my black hair.

I don't have many options, so I just take the top and back and tie it into a stub, leaving the long bangs to hang down. Not bad. My bangs are not normal bangs. They're awesome.

Roger sees me on my way out the door and says, "Can't you get that out of your eyes?" He means my Bangs of Doom.

And I think, *Uh, no, dumb-ass. Because then people could see me.*

And he says, "People can't even see you."

Duh.

And he says, "You know, Kyra, the world isn't so bad when you can actually see it."

Gag.

TEN

HATE THE BUS. ANYONE WHO'S SANE should hate the bus. Ugh.

I have no friends on the bus, so I have time to think. I start thinking about Fanboy and that makes me remember Simone last night, talking about *Schemata*. Was that real? Did I just imagine it? I don't do pot a lot—maybe a couple of times a year—so maybe the whole thing was in my imagination. Maybe that's it.

Maybe.

I look at the schedule they sent me. Gross—I have Miss Powell for English. I *hate* Miss Powell. I had her for English freshman year, with Simone. Miss Powell sucks for many, many reasons. I can't believe this.

The bus stops at South Brook High, and for the first time my stomach does a weird little lurchy, hiccupy type thing.

Chill, Kyra. This is no big deal. It's just school.

I go inside and head for the office. That's where I'm supposed to "report" today. To Assistant Principal Roland J. Sperling, known far and wide (especially wide) as the Spermling. One of my favorite adults to eff with.

And once I'm there, I crack my first smile of the day. Because the Spermling isn't alone in his office—he's got Miss Channing, the secretary, there with him. Probably because the last time I was in his office alone with him, I walked out crying and with my shirt untucked so that everyone would think he molested me. Sucker.

The Spermling harrumphs and is nearly strangled by his own fat and tells me where my new homeroom is and how he's aware of my "issues" and how if I have any trouble I should feel free to come see him . . .

"As long as we have a chaperone, right?"

He clears his throat, and his meaty lips clash together in a way that makes me realize that—somewhere under that fat face—he's gnashing his teeth.

"You created this situation, Miss Sellers. We're merely living it."

"Yeah, I control things. Don't you forget it."

"Miss Sellers! We are *trying* to help you. One more comment like that and you'll have the dubious distinction of ending up with detention before you've even gotten to homeroom!"

I think about it for a second. That would be kinda cool, actually. It would really rub the Spermling's nose in it and it would piss off Roger, too.

But no. I have to stay focused. I need to find Fanboy.

Of course, I'm not about to tell the Spermling any of that, so I just sit there with a smirk on my face and glare at him from behind my Bangs of Doom and tap my foot because I'm dying for a cigarette.

He lets me go. I resist the urge to look over my shoulder and say, "Stop looking at my ass!" as I leave.

ELEVEN

I HAVE A FEW MINUTES BEFORE the bell rings, so I go looking for Fanboy. I feel all light and puffy inside, like someone filled me up with a cloud or something. The Spermling doesn't bother me. Roger doesn't bother me. I'm going to find Fanboy and then everything is going to be fine.

No, wait. That's wrong. Everything is going to be *perfect*. Because I'm going to make it that way this time.

I'm halfway down the hall when something catches my eye. It's a poster on the wall, sort of a combination of computer type and artwork . . .

The artwork . . .

Jesus! It's *his*. It's *Fanboy's* artwork. I would know that style anywhere.

The poster says LITERARY PAWS VOL. XX #3 and then COMING BEFORE THANKSGIVING.

And then . . .

Holy shit.

Under that: FEATURING THE NEXT CHAPTER OF *SCHEMATA*!

No. Effing. Way.

TWELVE

I T'S NOT JUST SIMONE. THE WHOLE *world* . . .

The posters are *everywhere. Literary Paws* is the school's literary magazine. No one gives a shit about it. It's like a total joke. It's run by Mr. Tollin, this eight-hundred-foot-tall English teacher who spends all day talking about how he played college basketball and almost made it into the Final Four one year. (Whatever *that* means.) He's a total loser and he only runs the magazine because he's the newest English teacher and they must pass this thing along like it's a pissed-off skunk.

I don't get it. *Schemata* is running in *Literary Paws*? Did the whole world go crazy while I was away?

The bell for homeroom will ring soon, but I can't help myself—I have to see him. I have to find out what's happened.

So I rush to his homeroom, hoping for maybe just a minute before the bell.

And . . .

Yes, the world has definitely gone crazy.

Because there he is, there's Fanboy in all his Fanboy glory, sitting at his desk.

Surrounded.

Surrounded by like half a dozen people. They're all laughing, and here's the thing—they're not laughing *at* him. They're laughing *with* him.

And then his friend—the jock, Cal—starts waving them all away and busts out this fake ghetto shit: "Yo, yo, all y'all gotta back off my dawg here, OK? My man needs *space* to be the *ace!*"

I want to puke. What the hell?

And Fanboy kinda chuckles and starts drawing something. He holds it up and it looks like some caricature of one of the kids standing around him and everybody laughs and . . .

Caricatures?

He's wasting his effing time drawing *caricatures?*

And since when is he *popular?* God, I was the only person he showed *Schemata* to. Now he's . . . he's serializing it? In the effing literary journal?

None of this makes any sense.

I back out of the room before anyone can see me. Dimly, like it's off in the distance somewhere, I hear a sound—the homeroom bell.

And I don't care.

THIRTEEN

'M LATE TO HOMEROOM, BUT MRS. Reed doesn't say anything other than "Welcome back, Kyra," which makes everyone look up at me, which I don't like, but whatever. I plop down in my seat and I stare out the window. I can see the roof of South Brook Elementary, which is across the street and down a hill from here. It makes me think of the playground there, the first place I met Fanboy.

The last place I saw him before I became DCHH.

That's what they called me in the hospital when Roger sent me there six months ago. DCHH. I didn't know what it meant at first, but I found out. Oh, yeah, I found out.

And why were you in the hospital, Kyra? Well, Kyra, because *Fanboy* ratted me out. Told Roger about the bullet, so Roger decided to hustle me off to have my brain scrubbed clean.

Thanks a lot, Fanboy.

What an asshole. I was *right* to be pissed at him. I was right to hate him. Why did I ever think I was wrong? Why did I ever think I owed him an apology?

He talked so big about being an artist, and what does he do? He publishes his "great masterpiece" in *Literary Paws*. God, how lame can you get?

And it wasn't even *done* yet. He still had all this work to do. How could he start publishing it when it still had so far to go? He's compromising his art. I was helping him with it and he just . . . he just goes off and does this, this stupid thing, without thinking about . . . thinking about . . .

God, I'm so pissed I can't even think straight!

He doesn't deserve to succeed. Not if he's willing to settle for *Literary Paws*. Pathetic.

"Kyra?"

I blink and turn away from the window. The room is empty, but some kids are starting to file in from the hall. What the hell?

"Didn't you hear the bell?" Mrs. Reed asks.

I didn't. I was totally off in fantasyland, but I'm not about to tell *her* that. I stare at her instead.

"Kyra? Are you OK?"

Why do people always ask me that?

"I'm fine."

"You look a little . . . spaced out. Maybe you should—"

"I was just *thinking,* OK? God! Get off my back."

"The bell—"

"I don't need a *bell* to tell me how to live my life," I say to her.

She looks over her shoulder at the kids clustered in the doorway, all watching. Great.

Then she looks back at me and holds out a hall pass. "I think you should head down to the office, OK? Maybe talk to a guidance counselor."

I roll my eyes behind the Bangs of Doom.

"Your first day back can be tough," she goes on, and just to shut her up, I take the hall pass. Before she can keep lecturing me, I push my way through the kids coming through the door and head to the office, where I get to hang with the Spermling and Miss Channing again, lucky me.

"This has got to be a record, Miss Sellers," the Spermling wheezes. "Even for you."

For once, I can't think of anything to say. Because it really *is* a record, and I'm kind of distracted by that. So I just sit and stare at him.

"Your father and your therapist assured us that you were doing better. That things would be different this time. What happened?"

I shrug. "She wouldn't leave me alone, is all. I wasn't hurting anyone."

He watches me with his beady little eyes. They look like tiny chocolate chips in a huge bowl of lumpy cookie dough.

"Maybe we should have you speak to the county psychiatrist," the Spermling says.

"Jesus Christ!" I can't help it. "All I did was space out for a minute and you all are acting like I brought a gun to school or something!"

"Given your history—"

"The hell with my history! Just leave me alone and let me do the shit I have to do here and . . ."

I trail off because there's no point in talking anymore. The Spermling's not listening. He's made up his mind already. Hell, he probably made up his mind the minute I walked in here with Mrs. Reed's hall pass. Blowing up in his face just confirmed the decision for him.

I sit in silence as he sighs and picks up the phone. Pretty soon he has Roger on the line and he's saying things like "Maybe it was too soon" and "I'm sure you did" and "Right now, I don't see any other choice."

The Spermling hangs up. "Your father is coming to pick you up. You may wait in the outer office with Miss Channing."

I go into the outer office with Miss Channing, who types away on her keyboard and answers the phone and shit. You'd think after all the times I've come here and sat outside with her that she would, like, talk to me or something, but no. It's like I'm not even here.

Time goes by. Bells ring. Some kids and some teachers come in and out. I ignore their stares. I just glare at them from behind my Bangs of Doom.

Eff all of them.

And eff *him*, too.

Who said he could be happy? Who said he could just forget about me?

Roger arrives.

Great.

Well, at least I don't have to deal with Miss Powell today.

FOURTEEN

THE DRIVE HOME IS FILLED with shit like ". . . made me leave work *again*" and ". . . couldn't behave for one day, could you?" and "Here we go again, Kyra. Here we go again." He sounds like he's tired of saying it all.

I know I'm tired of hearing it all.

"Whatever, Roger." I say it because I know it drives him crazy.

"Goddammit, Kyra!" He slams his hand on the steering wheel and for a second there I imagine what would happen if the air bag suddenly exploded open right in his face.

"I thought this was the end of it, Kyra. You told Dr. Kennedy you wanted to go back to school."

"No. I told him I was *ready* to go back. I never said I wanted to."

I guess the worst part about it is this: I was ready to try. I really was. But then I was betrayed. How am I supposed to be nice to people who stab me in the back? Fanboy shared the thing that had only been between the two of us. And Cal, acting like he had always been there, like he was the best friend, when

I know for a fact that it wasn't *Cal* that Fanboy first showed *Schemata* to—it was *me*. It was *me*, and *I* should have been the one standing there, brushing off the admirers and telling them to give *my* ace some space . . .

"—listening to me?" Dad rants. "I can't even tell if you're *awake* with your hair down over your eyes like that."

Then shut up, I want to say to him, *and let me sleep.*

At home, he tells me that I'm grounded for the day, the night, forever. I can go back to school in the morning and I'd better "shape up." For now, I'm banished to my room and he's going to have to stay home and "keep an eye" on me.

Great. My room. Like the hospital. Roger sends me places—that's what he does. That's all he does.

So I sit in my room and stare at the computer. I think of how I first saw Fanboy, standing in gym class, all noble and un-yielding while this big blond asshole punched him over and over in the shoulder. Took a picture with my cell because I couldn't believe what I was seeing.

Here's the thing about Fanboy: He's really smart and talented and all that, but he's also like really stupid. Naive, I guess. He thinks that not having anyone looking for you is the same thing as hiding.

Wrong!

That's how I found him the first time—an old MySpace page of his that he didn't use anymore, but the account name was XianWalker76 and I figured that he would probably use that for everything . . . and he did. It was his IM name, so it wasn't hard to track to him down.

And you know what?

He couldn't be bothered to do the same. To track me down

when I went away. To even *try*. The whole time I was gone, the whole time I was DCHH—nothing. I came back home and I checked my computer and there was no e-mail from him at all.

I was disappointed, and then I figured . . .

I don't know what I figured. There weren't many e-mails from Simone or Jecca, either, but they knew where I was and they knew I couldn't get e-mail there, so they called me and sent me letters and stuff.

But *him* . . .

He's moved on. Obviously.

He's gone.

And I'm . . .

What?

Dear Neil,

I wish it were easy. I wish life were easy, like one of your comics.

I don't mean that your characters have it easy. That's not what I mean. Because you do some really terrible, really awful things to your characters sometimes. (And I kind of like that, so it's cool.)

What I mean is that I wish life could be simple like the actual page of a comic book. You look at a comic book page and there are rules, rules that make sense. The page is always the same size. There are panel borders and you know that the artwork goes inside the panel borders. Word balloons. Caption boxes. One panel leads to the next, one balloon to the next, and it makes sense, OK? It all fits together and if you tried to look at just part of it, it really wouldn't work. You look at the whole thing, though, and you have a little piece of the story.

It's simple. You can do anything on a comic book page, but at the end of the day, it's all based on these simple ideas, right? It's all lines and blocks and that's good.

Everything makes sense.

So I wish life were like that. That's all.

FIFTEEN

So, Roger has banished me to my room. Like this is supposed to change anything. Please. I can outlast Roger. I've been sent to my room by *professionals,* man.

After writing a letter to Neil, I log on to chat, but no one's available. Which makes sense, because everyone's in school, but I thought maybe Simone might be in the library.

Literary Paws is on the school's website, but I don't think I can bring myself to even look at it. But then I do anyway.

And I see it, but I don't believe it. My brain just won't accept what my eyes are showing it. This can't be. This is impossible. What was he *thinking?* What the hell is he trying to do?

Schemata. There it is.

It's too painful to look at the whole thing. I do notice, though, that Fanboy has made some changes: The main character's—Courteney's—hair is no longer blond like Dina's, but jet black. Her nose is shorter and her eyes are wider. It's still Dina, but only if you know what you're looking for and sort of squint really hard.

I can't bear looking at all of it, though. Every time I try, I get all caught up in a bunch of different emotions and they're all bubbling and gurgling inside me like I swallowed a bunch of seltzer and salsa.

It's not even noon yet. I can hear Roger moving around out there in the rest of the house. I roll up my sleeves to look at the scars on my wrists. They haven't changed much in the years since I put them there.

You and your scars, Fanboy said. That day in his bedroom. That's what he said to me: *You and your scars.* Like they didn't mean anything. Like they didn't matter.

I touch my right wrist. The slight raise-bump there. I remember every second, every *instant* when I did it. When I pulled the box cutter across, it's like all of a sudden my eyes and my mind became completely clear. It's like I could see the sharp lines and edges of the world, where the blade met my flesh, where the blood bubbled over, where the cuff of my shirt lay crisp against the skin. And it was all burned forever into my brain so that I could never ever forget it, even if I wanted to, which I don't.

And he sneered at me. At me and at *it.* At this . . . this *moment* in my life, when for the first and only time *ever* things made perfect, almost holy, sense.

(The blade, sliding . . .)

And he said, *That's just a cry for help. That's just attention. Everybody knows that. Cutting across just gets you to the hospital.*

Remembering it, it's like I'm there again, in his bedroom. How could he *do* that to me? How could he treat me that way? God, I tried to *explain* it to him. Tried to explain women to him. I . . . I showed him myself. Opened myself to him in every way possible. But all he could do was mock me. *A cry for help.*

Everyone knows that.

But everyone doesn't.

I didn't.

That day. That day I made the first cut and received that amazing clarity of vision, I really thought I was killing myself. And I really wanted to die.

But I effed it up.

You didn't really try to kill yourself, Fanboy said to me. *You just wanted attention, but you screwed up.* And then . . . And then the harshest . . .

Try harder next time.

That's what he said to me: *Try harder next time.*

And I left his house that day thinking, *I will.*

MAGIC BULLET

THIS IS WHAT HAPPENED THAT DAY when I came home from his house . . .

I'm surprised I made it home at all—my eyes were all blurry and effed up with tears because Fanboy was such an asshole to me.

But that didn't last long. Because by the time I got home, I was angry, not sad. And the tears went away and I got madder and madder and then I started to think about what he'd said, about how I wasn't *really* trying to kill myself. He thought I was faking. Even if he thought I really wanted to die, he would think I was stupid for effing up. I didn't know which was worse.

But I had something. I had his bullet now. I had stolen it from his hiding place while his mom was yelling at him.

I slid my hand into my pocket and I touched the bullet there and God! *I got it.* I understood. I understood why he carried it with him.

It was power.

I mean, a gun is *useless* without a bullet. Bullets do all the damage. The gun just, just *throws* them.

I couldn't keep my hands off that bullet. I lay in bed that night, rolling it between my fingers. I loved the brassy smell it left on my skin.

And I thought how easy it would be. If I had a gun, it would be *so easy*. One bullet. One shot.

I could show him. I could show him that I *could* get it right.

I actually got out of bed. I went into the kitchen and got the big knife Mom used to cut up chicken and stuff—before she died.

I sat on the floor. The cold kitchen tile made my butt go numb.

This time I wouldn't screw it up. This time I knew how to do it *right*, Fanboy, and this time you wouldn't be able to call me a wannabe.

But I turned my wrist up and my hand was closed and I had to open my fist, I just *had* to, and I saw the bullet lying there, a perfect little dull spot of brass.

Not with the knife, I thought. *Not like that. Been there, done that. Do it with the bullet this time. With* his *bullet. That'll teach him. That'll show him.*

So I put the knife away. I put it away and I stood up and went back to bed. I slept with the bullet clutched in my hand and I thought, *I'll find a gun. I'll find a gun and do it that way and I'll win.*

Sixteen

So, yeah, that's what I thought that night as I drifted off to sleep. Obviously, I didn't do it, because I'm still here, six months later.

I don't know what happened or what changed in my sleep, but by the time I woke up the next day, I wasn't suicidal anymore. Angry, yes. Still, I . . . It was weird. As angry as I was at Fanboy, as much as I hated him, I still cared about *Schemata*. So I called him that night and I told him what was wrong with it, and I thought that was going to be it, but . . .

God! Eff him! Eff him!

I tried to help him. I was his *partner*. I was giving him advice and shit and then I went away and he just forgot about me and went on with his life and now whenever I think about him, my gut feels wrong and my head hurts and my breath doesn't come out right.

It takes a while, but eventually all my hot rage burns out and goes cold. Which is better. When you're hot, you're not thinking clearly. You just sort of lash out and do stupid shit.

But when your anger goes all cold . . . That's when you can think straight. When you can plan and execute.

I've made up my mind. I've decided.

I'm going to destroy him.

Ah. I feel better already.

SEVENTEEN

I TOSS AND TURN ALL NIGHT and wake up with my head pounding from thinking too much and sleeping too little. That's bad enough. But I also want to wear a skirt to school today and that's when I realize that Roger has taken away my razor.

Please.

He's in the kitchen, making coffee. "Roger. I need my razor." I'm standing there in a ratty old bathrobe, and my boobs would be spilling out of the damn thing if I wasn't holding it closed really tight.

He doesn't even look at me. "Sorry."

"'Sorry'? What does that mean?"

"I can't let you have it."

I'm trying to imagine how someone could kill herself with a Schick Silk Effects. You'd leave a nice, smooth corpse.

"I have to shave my legs. And my pits." Ugh. I effing hate having to even *say* it to him! It's none of his business.

"I'm sorry, Kyra."

"What the eff am I supposed to do, Roger? Walk around

like Bigfoot or something?" And this is the worst part of it all—that suddenly I give a flying eff what people think about my appearance. Why can't I wear a skirt without shaving my legs? I mean, why should I care if I have hairy legs or armpits or whatever? But I guess I do. And that bugs the shit out of me.

"Hang on." He disappears into the garage for a second, where we keep all kinds of shit. Then he comes back with a container of Nair. "Here."

I take it and start to walk off. "No thank-you?" he asks.

Bite me, I want to say. Somehow, I restrain myself. "I want a razor."

"I'll get you an electric one, how about that?"

It's better than nothing, I guess. I go off to de-hair myself. The Nair smells and burns. That's it—I'd rather go hairy than use this stuff again.

Before I go out to the bus, Roger stops me. He's at the mirror in the hallway, tying his tie.

"Are you going to behave today?"

"Sure. Why not? Might be interesting."

"If you can get through to Thanksgiving break without getting kicked out again, maybe we can take you to get your driver's license."

Oh, damn. Here we go. Roger likes to hold that over me. He has no idea how much driving I actually do. Or did. I haven't been behind the wheel since before I went away.

"OK." I keep it short and to the point.

And then he does something really disgusting: He brushes my Bangs of Doom out of the way and plants a kiss right on my forehead. Gross. I'm gonna get zits there now.

"I want you to think before you do or say anything, OK?

Just try to behave. I know it's tough, Kyra. I swear, I know that. I know you don't think I do, but I do. OK?"

Yeah, right, whatever. I nod my Bangs of Doom back into place. God, do I love my Bangs of Doom.

PHASE ONE

SCHOOL. MIRACLE OF MIRACLES, I'VE MADE it to third period—
Miss Powell, ugh—without any trouble or incidents. Mostly,
people leave me alone. My teachers don't seem to want to
talk to me. I was tutored in the hospital a little bit, so I'm
not *too* far behind, and they just pretend I've always been sitting there.

I tune everything out. *Especially* Miss Powell, who's talking
about "metaphor" the way people on TV talk about personal lu-
bricant.

There was some preliminary "Hey, Kyra!" stuff from, like,
the ten people I can stand at this place and that's it. Basically,
I've spent the day doodling in my notebook, thinking of ways to
destroy Fanboy.

Because he totally deserves it.

Best part of it is this: We don't have any classes together. We
don't hang in the same circles. He doesn't even know I'm back,
and if I keep my head down, he *won't* know.

Until it's too late.

My plan is pretty simple. Fanboy has a big ole hard-on for Dina Jurgens, right? Dina's gone now, off to college somewhere, but her sister, Michelle, is still around. They're what my mom used to call "Irish twins"—there's only, like, eleven months between them. So Michelle's a senior now.

I wonder how she would feel knowing that Fanboy based the main character in his comic book on her big sister? Especially with all those scenes of Courteney in her lingerie and shit. All those fantasies. All the sex stuff that's coming up.

I *know* what's coming up because I read most of the script and saw a whole crapload of the artwork. Stuff that hasn't been serialized in *Literary Paws* yet.

If I had a sister, I would be pretty grossed out that some guy was fantasizing all kinds of sex stuff about her. And even if that didn't gross me out, I would definitely be grossed out that he was writing it all down and drawing it all and then publishing it for the world to see.

And even if Michelle doesn't care about *that*, here's the thing: It's a secret. Fanboy was really embarrassed when I pointed out that Courteney looked like Dina. I mean, *obviously* he was embarrassed—he changed the way she looks! So if he was all embarrassed by *me* knowing, he'll be embarrassed to death when Michelle knows. And tells Dina. And the rest of the world.

So at lunch, I skip the cafeteria. I asked around a little bit in homeroom and found out that Michelle's involved in the senior play. Which means she'll be spending lunch in the auditorium, working on sets or something.

There's a bunch of drama nerds and some popular kids like Michelle in there. The senior play is where people who wouldn't normally hang out together end up hanging out, I guess, because they're all talking and joking.

God, I hate Michelle Jurgens. I hate her sister, too. I hate effing blond bimbos who flaunt their giant boobs. I mean, yeah, I'm well endowed in the boob department, but I have the decency to keep them under wraps, all praise the minimizer. Michelle just lets them jut out there for everyone to see. I hate it.

But I swallow the hatred. I make myself smile and I walk right up to her. She's wearing a sweater that hugs her boobs and has a v-neck, so you can see, like, an effing Grand Canyon of Cleavage. And tight jeans and boots and her hair up in a ponytail because she's supposedly, you know, Hard at Work.

I wait. I linger for a few seconds until the people around her start to turn away, and then I say, "Hey, Michelle?"

She turns around and smiles at me like we're old friends, and God I hate that phony shit. She doesn't know me. Why is she smiling at me like that?

"What's up?" she asks. "You with the stage crew?"

"Uh, no. I wanted to talk to you for a second."

Not even a flicker in the smile or in her eyes. You'd think she was genuinely happy to see me.

"I need to show you something."

"OK." And she says it like the word can *bounce*. Ugh.

We go off into a corner of the auditorium and I pull out the page of *Schemata* that I printed from the website. It shows Courteney getting up in the morning, basically, and she's all disheveled and—I guess—sexy. I hold the page out to her.

And now the smile falters, just a little. She looks at the page. "Yeah?"

I wave it at her, urging her to take it. She takes a step

back like I'm a strange dog or something. "Look, I don't know what you're—"

"Look at it!" I tell her. "Look at *her!*"

"I don't know what you're after. I mean, I guess I've seen this in the lit mag, but it's just a—"

"Don't you see it? Can't you tell?"

Michelle's smile goes all nervous. She's trying to be polite, but she wants to get the hell away from me, I can tell. "I don't know what you want me to say," she says at last.

Shit. Goddammit.

He changed Courteney too much. The art. The resemblance. She doesn't recognize her own sister. It's obvious to *me* because I know. Because I saw the original art. And it's no good if I tell her. She needs to notice it on her own. It's more shocking that way. And when she's shocked, when she sees how Fanboy lusts after her sister, she'll spread the word and Fanboy will be a laughingstock.

At least, that's the plan.

"Never mind," I tell her, lowering my head so that I can only partly see her through the Bangs of Doom.

Shit.

THE LAST TIME I SAW HER

the room the room the room is rosevomit because
roger left roses and
mom threw up before i came in
perfect timing

EIGHTEEN

Simone and I blow off study hall, which, like, isn't even a *challenge* anymore. We go hang out in the teachers' bathroom on the second floor near the English department. The plumbing's been busted for months, Sim says, so it's supposed to be locked up and off-limits, but I figured out how to pick the lock. I'm good like that.

So we just kick back and light up and chill.

She hands me a fresh pack, the cellophane still intact. "Here. I know your dad's making it tough for you to get cigs."

"Thanks." I go to put it in my messenger bag, moving things around to hide the pack in case anyone decides to look inside for some reason.

Simone grabs my wrist, stopping me. "Hey, what's that?"

With her free hand, she plucks the *Schemata* page out of my bag. "I didn't know you were so into this. I shoulda guessed. You like that comic book stuff."

"I don't really like it." I snatch the page back from her and feel guilty even for saying it, because it's not just that it's a lie.

Lies are fine. I tell lies all the time and don't feel guilty about them in the slightest. What bothers me now is that I'm telling a lie about something important. About *Schemata*. About art.

"Then why are you carrying it around?"

"I used to hang out with the guy who does it." I blurt out the truth before I can think of a lie.

Simone's eyes go wide. "Are you serious? You know him?"

"Used to," I clarify.

"How do you know him?" It kills me that she even cares. A few months ago, no one knew who Fanboy was, and if they *did* know they sure as hell didn't care that they knew. Now he's some kind of high school celebrity or some shit like that.

"I was friends with him for a little while," I tell her.

"He's kinda cute," Simone says. "In a geeky way."

And that's when it hits me. I know exactly what to do. Exactly how to get to him.

"He's gay," I tell her. "I was in his bedroom alone with him and he didn't make a move."

Simone arches an eyebrow and snorts smoke through her nose. She thinks it makes her look sophisticated. And it sort of does. (Not that I'd ever tell her that.)

"Really?" She doesn't believe me. "Just because he didn't make a move on you?"

"Yeah, he told me himself."

"No way. Are you making this shit up?"

"Way. He has, like, some boyfriend that he has sex with and everything."

"Wow. Like, oral or anal? Because oral's no big deal. I mean, I do that all the time."

I don't want to hear about Simone's sexual exploits. I love

Simone to the end of time and she's like totally my best friend, but the thing is, I have to be honest: Simone is a Big Freakin' Ho. I wish she weren't, but she is. It was bad enough when she would call me after every milestone or every "event." Eventually, though, it got to the point where she was making out with every guy in sight, so even *she* got bored with calling me all the time.

"It's really not a big deal," she goes on, "having that thing in your mouth."

Oh, God. I wish I could, like, turn off my ears or something. I don't want to hear about this.

"Right."

"But I have to admit, most of the time I'd rather just have sex with them instead. It's much better."

Sexual philosophy courtesy of Simone. Thank you, God. Just what I needed.

"So he didn't make a move at all?"

Good. Back on safe ground. Back to lies.

"Yeah. I mean, he . . ." Hmm. Do I tell her I had my shirt open? And my bra? Or does that make me sound like a slut?

Oh, hell, who am I kidding? This is *Simone* I'm talking to. She's probably gotten laid twice since homeroom.

"I wasn't sure," I tell her, editing reality a little bit, "and I wanted to find out, so I showed him my boobs."

Simone's eyebrows jump. "Yeah?" It's like she's pleased. Like I'm a show dog she's been training and I finally figured out how to jump through the ring of fire. Because, you know, everyone should be as easy as Simone.

"I had my shirt open and my bra off and he didn't do anything." Which is *kinda* true. He actually moved toward me, but I cut him off. Simone doesn't need to know that, though.

All Simone needs to know is this: Fanboy is gay. The new hotshot artist, the school's new hero, is gay. That's all she needs to know.

Because Fanboy's a horny little piece of shit. I know that. And nothing will kill him like everyone thinking he's gay. He'll argue and protest and the more he does, the more people will believe it.

But that's not enough.

I need to do more.

Dear Neil,

An entire day at school without being called down to the Spermling's office. I even went to most of my classes. That's got to be a record or something, right?

But that's not why I'm writing. I want to know: Why does it have to be so complicated when it comes to guys and girls and sex and all of that?

In *A Game of You*, you sort of try to explain the differences between boys and girls, the different ways they think and react. I spent a lot of time reading that particular part of *Sandman*, over and over again.

And I just want to know why it has to be so hard.

Why do people like Simone feel like they have to sleep around in order to get what they want? And why do people give a shit about things like other people's virginity? Simone is always telling me just to go and get laid. Why should she care? Why does it matter to her?

Why does any of it matter to anyone? I mean, I'm going to make people think that Fanboy is gay, and that will be great because it'll embarrass him and make no girls want to go out with him, but, really, why should anyone care in the first place? And am I only wondering that because I'm also wondering what people would think if they knew that Jecca and I had kissed a bunch of times? And why do I even care that other people care?

But people *do* care, so it's like you have to keep all this shit straight . . . This person slept with this person and this person blew this person and this guy tried to screw this girl, but he couldn't get it up or he only lasted five seconds or this girl made out with this guy and her best friend found out and they got in a fight because the best friend liked the guy and on and on and on. God! It's such a pain in the ass! Why do we have to care? Why do we have to keep track? Why does any of it matter?

In a way, I feel sorry for boys. They're weak. You show them boobs or a butt and they just fall apart.

But I feel sorry for girls, too. Because girls get screwed, even when they're not naked with a guy. Everyone hates girls—even other girls. I mean, "girl" is like an *insult,* you know? "That's so girly." "Stop being a girl." "You're like a little girl."

Hey, you know what? I was a little girl once and I *kicked* ass. I was awesome.

But no. It's all . . . It's like this story my dad told me once. There was this football coach and his team was losing the game at halftime and he made his team sit in the locker room and wait and they all sat around and were waiting for him to come in and yell at them, but he didn't show up, so they just sat there and waited and waited and then—at, like, the last minute—the coach just pokes his head into the locker room and says, "Oh, I'm sorry, ladies—I was looking for the Notre Dame football team." And it pissed them off so much, they went out and won the game.

Because, like, the worst effing thing in the world—the worst thing in the *world,* the thing that enrages you and pumps you up—is being called a *girl?*

Really?

And even other girls do it. They get sucked into it. They say they're strong—Miss Powell, my English teacher, does it all the time—but they're not. They go ahead and they watch the stupid movies and TV shows, like the ones where the guy kisses the girl and she resists, but then she gives in. Because, oh, yeah, sure, like if we don't want to kiss you it can't possibly be because we don't want to—it's got to be because we just didn't know how great a kisser you are. Well, if I don't want your tongue down my throat, you're not going to change my mind by trying to put it in there anyway.

Or the ones where these strong career women end up having these miserable, empty lives until they get a husband and a kid because—right—life isn't worth living without them. It's like they're selling this idea to me, like the whole effing world wants me to get married just because . . . I don't know why. I don't know why they care if I get married or if I kiss Jecca or if Fanboy's gay or not. I don't know.

But people care. They keep butting into other people's lives and other people's business. And so much of it is about who's kissing who and why.

Why, Neil? Explain it to me. Explain why it matters at all.

You know all of this. You understand it. I know that's why you made Death a girl. The most powerful force in the universe and you decided that it was a cute, slender, cheerful goth who had dimples when she smiled.

God, I love that.

But even though you get it, you can't explain why the world is the way it is. You understand a lot, but even *you* don't know the answer to this.

ONLINE

simsimsimoaning: *r u sure hes gay*

Promethea387: *Yeah. He told me.*

simsimsimoaning: *becuz lisa says he chex her out*

Promethea387: *Bullshit. He's gay. He's not checking her out. Lisa thinks she's hot shit.*

simsimsimoaning: *u dont even kno her*

Promethea387: *Whatever. Just trust me.*

simsimsimoaning: *i told billy & he totally blieves it*

Promethea387: *Good.*

NINETEEN

ROGER'S NOT HOME YET, SO I wander the house, alone. It doesn't feel like I belong here anymore, if I ever did. I'm like the ghost of someone who's not dead yet, haunting a place where no one wants me.

And when I catch myself in the living room mirror . . .

I see a girl.

I see someone who's tough.

But I *don't* see . . .

I don't see *me*. I don't know how to explain it. I know it's me in the mirror, but sometimes I just don't recognize myself. The mousy brown hair doesn't help.

I have a red stone through my nose and a cute little silver ring at the corner of my mouth. I love my piercings. They make me look like me; they make it easier for me to identify myself. But people like to give me shit about them. My grandparents and my dad, for starters. But even just random people. They see my piercings and they assume that I'm, like, a skank. Or a druggie. Or whatever they don't like.

Roger had such a shit fit when I came home with them a couple of years ago. And even now—even after all this time—he still looks at me like I did something dangerous. Something wrong.

"I guess I should be glad you don't have any tattoos," he said once, like he'd just dodged sniper fire.

And just because he said it, I considered—for, like, the millionth time—getting a tattoo. Simone has a dragon that winds around her left leg, starting near the ankle and ending somewhere around midthigh. Here's the thing, though: I don't have the patience for it. Waiting forever for some guy to finish inking me. I don't think I could stand it.

I've got all this time before Roger gets home, so I hide my cigarettes and scrounge around the house, trying to find my razor and stuff like that. He also took my scissors ("skissors"— heh; it's still funny). He took *everything*. Hell, there's nothing sharper than a butter knife in the kitchen, and even the friggin' *hedge clippers* are missing out in the garage.

He's taking this seriously.

On one of the cabinets in the garage, there's a big padlock that wasn't there before. It doesn't take psychic powers to know that my razor's in there.

I spend some time trying to pick the lock, but it's not happening. Stealing cars is actually easier. For one thing, you can usually find someone who's been stupid enough to leave their car unlocked. Back doors are the best—people are always putting shit in the back seat and then forgetting to lock it. But even if it's locked, there's still a bunch of ways to unlock a car that have nothing to do with picking the lock.

But you can't slim-jim a padlock. You have to get in there and make it happen, you know? I dick around with it for a little while, but then I give up and go look on the Internet for some tips. At least it's not a combination lock. I would have to find Roger's combination or just cut the damn thing off.

The whole time I'm working on the lock, I'm also working on my Fanboy problem. Telling Simone he's gay is fine—by the end of the week, it'll be all over the school. Hell, if Simone just tells the guys she makes out with this week, that'll be half the school right there. I picture it: *Ooh, baby, oh, yes, ooh, baby, yes, hey did you know that kid's gay? Ooh, yeah.* Or something like that. I imagine there's a lot of "ooh" when Simone has sex.

But it's not enough. What I really need is the original artwork. I know he has sketches in his sketchbook and shit like that. Probably original files on his computer. He has to have images of Dina somewhere. I need to get my hands on them and show them to Michelle. I'm not sure exactly what will happen— she might get pissed, she might laugh—but the thing is, he's kept his Dina-worship a secret, so exposing it can only be a good thing for me.

And there's only one way to do that.

I have to be his friend again.

TWENTY

B y the time Roger gets home, I haven't managed to pop the lock—even with the instructions from the 'net—but I'm all sweaty from trying. I get out of the garage when I hear his car in the driveway and I'm sitting innocently at the kitchen table when he comes in.

"What have you been up to?" he asks, all suspicious.

"Nothing, Roger."

He glares at me for a second, giving me Pissed Off because I guess I don't look as innocent as I thought. Pissed Off is OK—it's easier to hate him when he's showing Pissed Off.

It's actually easy to hate him a lot of the time. He's such an effing phony. When he meets people and gives them that big man-handshake and that big shit-eating grin, he always talks about how "Roger means I get it," as in "roger, over, and out" and all that nonsense. What he never says is that "roger" is also an old colonial-era euphemism for the F-word. So when I call him "Roger" it's not because I'm trying to be one of these hip, well-adjusted brats who call their parents by their first names. I'm just telling him to eff off.

"Seriously, Roger. Nothing."

He nods slowly, slipping into Sad, Tired. He hands me a plastic bag from the drugstore. There's a Lady Remington inside, along with batteries.

"Thanks, Dad."

Oops. I called him "Dad." He shifts to maybe halfway between Sad, Tired and Blissed Out. He sits down at the table with me, like we're a big happy family or something.

"We need to talk a little bit, OK? About what happened right before you, you know, went away."

And *eff him!* Any sympathy I just felt because of Sad, Tired is now *gone.* Because I didn't "go away." I was *sent* away. By *him.* Made DCHH.

"That boy who called me at work. The one who gave you a bullet. I need to know his name."

Fat chance. They tried to get that out of me in the hospital, too. But I'm no narc. I have my own ways of getting revenge.

"Kyra, talk to me. Please. I don't want you being mixed up with someone like that. You've had a tough enough time without someone else making it worse for you."

God, what an idiot! He doesn't get it. Being with Fanboy didn't make things *worse.* It made things *better.* I could talk to him like I couldn't talk to anyone else, not even Simone or Jecca. I could . . .

Shit. Now I'm leaking tears.

Roger sees 'em. He tries to take my hand, but I pull it away. Goddammit. Why am I doing this? Fanboy *betrayed* me. He sold me out to my dad, and I could have forgiven that, I *did* forgive that, but then he moved on without me and sold out his art. And those things I *cannot* forgive. Those things I *will not* forgive.

"Leave me alone, Roger." I mean to say it angry and loud, but the tears do something to my breathing and it barely comes out at all. He gets up and comes around the table to put his arms around me and there's a second—just a second, but it's there, I have to admit it—where I just want to let the tears go and fall into his arms and wail like a baby and call him Daddy and let him make everything better.

But he can't. He can't make everything better. I know that. I know it because he's screwed up too much.

So I just get up and I can barely see through the tears, but this is my house and I know how to get around, so I make it to my room and slam the door and he's calling out to me, but I don't care, don't care, don't care.

TWENTY-ONE

A LITTLE WHILE LATER, HE KNOCKS on my door and says he's coming in no matter what. So I let him in.

"We're *going* to have this conversation, Kyra. Whether you want to or not."

So I sit on my bed with my arms crossed over my chest and stare at a little crack in the paint on my windowsill. Because here's the thing: You need two people to "have this conversation." And if I'm not one of them, I don't know where he's going to get another one.

"Did you really have a bullet? Or was it just a prank call? Because he sounded really worried and really convincing to me. I need to know who it was. The police will want to talk to him, and I want to at least talk to his parents."

The police . . . *There's* a thought. But no—Fanboy would just say I stole the bullet and I could lie and say he gave it to me, but it would be his word against mine and he's a goody-goody, so they would believe him and not me.

"Do you have any idea what I went through? Hanging up

the phone? Rushing out of work, driving home at a hundred miles an hour, thinking you'd be . . . you'd be *dead?*"

Yeah, I know. I know because he told me over and over again when he sent me away, and then he told me again every time he came to visit.

"You owe me an explanation."

No, I don't. I keep staring at the crack. I don't owe him anything. I'm allowed to have my secrets.

Just like Fanboy has his. His "third thing." He told me that there were three things in the world that he wanted more than anything. Three, OK? One, two, three. And then he only told me two of them.

And when I asked about the third, he lied and said he meant there were only two, so I kept at him and he admitted there was a third, but he wouldn't tell me what it was.

The thing he wants more than *anything else in the world.* And he wouldn't tell me. Bastard.

I told him *everything.* Even when I lied, I was telling him something.

"Kyra, goddammit!" Into hard-core Pissed Off. I can always count on Roger.

Staring at the crack. Wondering where it came from. It was just *there* one day, like it had always been there. I don't remember doing something to cause it. It's like the world just decided to break right there, right on my windowsill.

"I don't understand how you can be in the hospital for so long, dealing with all those wackos and doctors, and not understand how goddamn serious this all is!"

"Eff off, Roger!" I spin around to him and he actually takes a step back, which is so. Damn. Cool. "I was in the hospital because *you* put me there. And guess what? *I* was one of the wackos. So get the hell off my back!"

He stares at me. Still Pissed Off. But bleeding back into Sad, Tired. Because the truth hurts, bitch.

"You gave up the right to ask me questions when you locked me up somewhere for *other* people to ask me questions."

Ooh, to the gut! He deflates. He goes all guilty-looking. Easiest thing in the world, making him feel guilty. I'm pretty good at it.

"You can't blame me for that," he says, but there's no strength behind the words. None at all. "You were out of control."

"You got a phone call. A goddamn phone call. And you committed me."

"You have a history—"

"Of slitting my wrists, not blowing my head off."

Now he's fully in Sad, Tired. He's guilty. He's wondering if he's a Bad Dad.

I could go on, but there's no point. Right now, nothing I say—absolutely *nothing*—could be one-tenth as bad as what he's got scrolling through his brain. So I just look back at the crack, staring at it until he leaves.

THE DREAMING

I HAVE A DREAM SOMEONE IS touching me.

Not just, like, touching me on the shoulder or something. I mean *touching* me. Hands from behind, cupping my breasts, and for the first time in my life, I don't mind them. For the first time in my life, I *like* that they're big. The weight of them—the heft—feels good in someone else's hands.

Lips touch the back of my neck. The side of my neck. My collarbone. Oh, God—I'm naked. I just realized it. I'm totally naked. And someone is behind me, arms wrapped around, lips on my skin, hands on my breasts and now moving down, down, and God oh God I didn't know. I didn't know—

It's Jecca. I know her lips. Oh. Jecca. I turn. Turn to see her. To kiss her.

But it's not Jecca.

It's not a *her* at all.

TWENTY-TWO

WAKE UP. NOT A HER. Oh. Shit. Shit and goddamn. What the hell is *wrong* with me?

I lie there in bed, confused, messed up, effed up. My breath is coming too fast. I feel warm but I want to shiver at the same time.

I don't understand. What was I . . . ?

No. Just stop it. Just stop it.

I am *not* going to think about this. It was just a dream. It doesn't mean anything.

I crawl out of bed. I can't shake it, no matter how much I want to. I keep thinking about . . . I keep thinking about the way he looked at me there in his bedroom. When I was open to him.

At first—when I was just unbuttoning my shirt—it was just this shock. He just couldn't believe it was happening. And then, when I opened my bra . . .

God.

He just . . .

Ten million things all warring on his face, in his eyes: Surprise. Disbelief. Want. Need. Concern. Fear. Joy. Lust.

And I made it all happen. I *created* that moment for him, created those thoughts and feelings. Me.

And now . . .

And now, what the hell is he doing to me in return? Why am I dreaming . . . ?

In the Sandman series, there's this bit . . . It's early on. I think it's in *The Doll's House*. Where Morpheus goes into this woman's dream and he's flying with her and she says something about how when you dream about flying, you're really dreaming about sex.

And Morpheus says, "Well, then what are you dreaming about when you're dreaming *about* sex?"

God.

Shit.

There's a full-length mirror on the back of my door and I stand before it, staring at myself in my T-shirt and my sleep-messed hair and my puffy eyes.

And you know what? I'm sort of OK with what I see, minus the brown hair. I don't get these girls who go all schizo over their bodies. I mean, sure, my boobs are just out of control. I get that. But that's why God invented the minimizer bra.

It pisses me off when these bulimic and anorexic chicks go all spastic. Or the girls who, like, cut themselves and shit. I mean, give me an effin' break, OK? If you don't like your body, just fix it. Deal with it.

When you feel like things are out of control, you *take* control.

So, yeah.

I go into the bathroom and look at myself in the *that* mirror. Nothing has changed; no magic in this mirror. My pits are stubbly. My legs are rough. I wield the Lady Remington and glare at myself in the mirror from beneath my Bangs of Doom.

When you feel like things are out of control, you take *control.*

Yeah, that's what you do. Take control.

I thumb on the Lady Remington. She whispers to me in a buzz.

Oh, yeah.

TWENTY-THREE

IT TAKES LONGER THAN I thought it would take. I thought it would be like in the movies—zip, zip, zip and you're done.

But no. My hair's thick and when I try just plowing through it with the razor, the whole thing jams up and stops. So I take, like, five minutes cleaning the thing and getting it to work again.

I stand in the shower with a makeup mirror in one hand and a pair of cuticle scissors in the other. I found the cuticle scissors in the back of the medicine cabinet—it's the one sharp thing Roger forgot to hide. It takes a long time to cut my hair down enough that I can get the Lady Remington to go through it. At one point, Roger gets agitated and knocks on the door. "Kyra? Everything all right in there?"

"I have cramps!" I tell him, which usually shuts him up.

Back to my hair. Between the scissors and the razor, I manage to get most of it off my head. My body isn't so lucky—I'm covered in hair clippings. I look like the floor of a barbershop. This is a little more complicated than just dyeing it, it turns out.

I run the shower to wash it all off of me and the drain starts to clog up. Shit! This is supposed to be *easy*.

I scoop up as much wet hair as I can. The drain starts, y'know, draining again, like it's supposed to. The water feels strange on my semibald head. It's too cold, then too warm, while my skull skin gets used to it. My head's, like, supersensitive. I run the tips of my fingers over it, skipping the patchy, stubbly parts. Maybe this is what babies feel like? All new and just born?

Wow.

New.

Just born.

I wash off all the hair clippings on me, then scrape clear the drain and dump the hair into the trash can. When I'm clean, I turn off the shower and dry my head—the towel's scratchy and coarse against the new skin.

Roger knocks on the door again. "Kyra. I have to get going to work. You're gonna miss the bus."

"I'm almost done!" I tell him. I look at myself in the mirror. Ugh. This didn't work the way I wanted it to: I'm all . . . mangy. I have patches of stubble and patches of longer hair, broken up by swaths of naked head. I look like one of those topographic globes, with hair representing altitude or something.

"You need to get going," he says.

"Jesus Christ! I'm almost ready!" Which is a total lie, but whatever.

I can almost hear the gears turning in his head on the other side of the door. On the one hand, he totally doesn't trust me to get ready and go to school on my own. On the other hand, he's thinking, *Haven't I lost enough time at work already because of her?*

So the other hand beats the one hand and Roger leaves. Excellent.

I scrounge around in his bathroom for his shaving stuff. But Roger now uses an electric razor. Damn! Doesn't he know I could just get a knife or something from Simone or Jecca or someone else at school? What does he really think he's accomplishing here?

So I have to do a little better. I have to think this through.

First of all, I have to get rid of school, so I use my favorite trick: I log on to Roger's e-mail account and send an e-mail to the Spermling:

Roland,
I've decided to keep Kyra home today. We had something of a breakthrough last night and I'll be staying home from work as well to work through it with her. Thanks for your understanding, and I'm sorry again about the incident at school.
Roger

Classic. The Spermling has never even noticed that I set the e-mail to respond to *my* account, not Roger's. So I'm the one who gets the "Roger, no problem, thanks for letting me know, hope everything works out" bullshit that the Spermling always sends back.

So now I'm free for the day. Excellent.

I can do a lot in a day.

First, I need a car.

How I Steal Cars

IT'S ACTUALLY NOT AS TOUGH as you'd think. Most of the time, you can just rely on people's stupidity.

The first time I stole a car, it was a crime of opportunity. I was at the mall, waiting for my dad to pick me up, and I saw a car parked off all by its lonesome. I wandered by and saw that the keys were in the ignition. I figured that the owner must have locked his keys in the car, because who would be so effing stupid that they'd leave their car keys in the ignition and the door unlocked, right?

But for some reason I tried the door. And it opened right up.

And then it was like I couldn't help myself. I couldn't *stop* myself. I didn't even look around. I just slid into the driver's seat like I belonged there and started the car.

And for the first time . . . For the first time in a long time, I felt great.

I felt *in control.*

I drove that car all around the parking lot. I weaved in and out of spots, threading the other cars. Roger had been teaching me to drive with Mom's old car even though I was only fourteen at the time. He claimed he wanted to get me "ready early," but I knew the truth. He was trying to buy my love and my caring and my giving a shit by putting me behind the wheel. Tempting me with the promise of a learner's permit and eventually a license.

So I knew how to drive pretty well and I just hauled ass around that parking lot until it occurred to me that a mall cop might pull me over. I parked the car on the other side of the mall. I left the keys in the ignition, but I locked all the doors before I left.

Some people need to learn the hard way, you know?

The second car I stole was my mom's.

She was dead, but we still had the car and Roger promised me I could have it when I was old enough to drive. So I figured I wasn't really stealing it—I was borrowing it from my future self, which totally ought to be cool, in my book.

Roger was out somewhere, so I opened the garage door and just drove that sucker all over town. And again—*in control.*

After that, it's like the effing universe was just *begging* me to steal cars.

Everywhere I went, it was like I was noticing people leaving their doors unlocked or their keys in the car or both. It happens *a lot.* It's just that most people don't notice it. But it also confirmed something I've always believed, which is this: Most people are idiots.

So, getting into cars is easy. Even if people don't leave a door unlocked, it's pretty easy to slim-jim a lock.

Getting them *started* is tougher. New cars are the worst because they're all protected and shit. Older cars, though, like ones from the eighties, they're pretty easy. You can hotwire them or you can actually rip out the whole ignition and put in your own. That's kind of cool, but it takes a while and it's tough. I've done it a couple of times and I always end up banging my knuckles with the slide hammer. I learned all of these cool tricks from this repo man on the Web.

When I'm really desperate, I sneak onto a used-car lot, find some old eighties piece of crap, and swipe it. I'm always real careful to wipe everything down when I leave, too, so that I don't leave any fingerprints. But here's the thing—I always return the cars. I drop them off in a parking lot or car sales place or something. So it's not like I'm stealing them *forever* or anything. I'm just borrowing them for a while.

That's all.

I guess technically I'm not *supposed* to do it. But if that's the case, then why the hell is it so damn *easy*?

TWENTY-FOUR

I COVER MY HEAD WITH A SCARF because right now if I go out in public the way I look, someone will probably try to cart me right back to the hospital.

I feel conspicuous looking for a car to jack in broad daylight. I can't take Mom's car because Roger caught me with it once and now he checks the odometer. So I have to steal one. There's a little shopping center about a half a mile up Route 54, so I head there. Even this early in the day, there are plenty of cars.

I mosey around the parking lot a little bit, checking out the insides of the cars. I'm looking especially for baby seats in the back. Moms are always freaked out that they're going to lock themselves out of the car with the rugrat trapped inside, so there's a good chance they'll have one of those magnetic key boxes with a spare.

Sure enough, I find a sedan with a car seat and a key box in the driver's side wheel well. I look quickly—no one's around.

This is the toughest moment. You just have to commit at this point. I mean, I could get royally screwed if Mommy suddenly comes out of the store and I'm climbing into her car. But I could be equally screwed if I just stand here waiting to get busted.

I don't get all excited or anything in these moments. It's not like in the books: "Her heart raced!" or whatever. Nah, I get real calm. I figure whatever happens, happens. I just get this peace that flows through me.

And then I unlock the car and climb in and slam the door.

The key slides into the ignition. I bite my lip and turn it. You're only supposed to put special keys in those boxes, keys that only unlock the car and don't work the ignition. This way people like me can't steal your car.

But most people—like the people who own the car I'm in—don't bother getting the special key. They just make a dupe of their regular key. The car starts up on the first try, and I ease it out of the parking space and out of the parking lot, and then I'm gone, and my heart feels warm like it does when Jecca kisses me.

TWENTY-FIVE

THE WOMAN WHO OWNS THIS CAR has shitty taste in music. Her CDs all suck, so I blast the radio instead, which is only a little bit better.

I go to the mall. I park in the most inconvenient place I can find so that it's less likely anyone will be around to see me when I leave. When I get out of the car, I take off my scarf to wipe off the steering wheel, the door handle, the gearshift, and the radio knobs.

I toss her CDs in the trash. Trust me, I'm doing her a favor.

OK, it's officially *weird* to be at the mall during a school day. Because there's no one here worth seeing or talking to. It's all old people. I don't mean parent old. I mean, like, *grandparent* old. Maybe even *great*-grandparent old. Why do old people even *come* to the mall?

I go buy a new razor and some blades. That's only twenty bucks, so I still have money to spend and God knows when I'll get back here. So I should spend it now, right? I should get some clothes to match my new look.

On my way to my usual store (all black, all the time), something in a window catches my eye. It's a display for some new store, and I guess I notice it because the manikins in the window are all bald. They don't have fake hair or anything, so they kind of look like what I'm going to look like as soon as I get home and shave off the rest of this stuff.

Anyway, I stand there for a minute, looking at the display, and then I go in and I try some stuff on and I buy it. It's a totally new look for me. The guy at the counter looks at me a little weird, like, "Why are *you* buying *this?*" but he just rings me up and then I'm done.

I still have about fifteen bucks left, so I go to the music store and poke around in the bargain bin until I find a CD that has a few decent songs. I take it back to "my" car and put it in the CD player. Then I wipe everything down again, lock the car, and put the key back. Too risky to drive this back to where I found it—by now, Mommy has called the cops, I bet.

So I wander the parking lot, looking for another car to swipe so that I can drive home.

TWENTY-SIX

AT HOME, I LAY OUT my new outfit. Weird. How am I going to look in this?

I stare in the mirror as I unwind the scarf from my head. I'm all knobby and gross. It's worse than I remember from just a few hours ago. Gotta take care of that.

I unpack the razor and the blades at the sink in the bathroom. I try not to think of the way the blade felt on my wrists. It was years ago, but I can still *feel* it. It's like it happened yesterday. It's like I could look over my shoulder and *I* would be standing there, the me of then, the me of *ago,* standing right there, smiling up at me while blood ran down her palms and dripped off her fingertips.

I look into the mirror, but there's no one behind me. I'm all alone.

"Are you there, Despair?" I ask the mirror, because in *Sandman,* that's where Despair lives—in a world behind all the mirrors in the world. It should be creepy to think that some pale fat chick who likes to cut herself is living on the other side of the mirror, watching me all the time, but it's actually OK. It's sort of nice not to be alone all the time.

So I snap a blade into the handle and before I can think about it any more, I work on finishing what I started before and pretty soon my head is totally naked and totally smooth and I only nicked myself once just above my left ear.

Wow.

I'm a total chrome-dome.

I look like . . .

Like . . .

Fanboy's voice pops in my head for some reason: "Professor X."

Ugh.

No. Not some stupid comic book character. It reminds me of—

Bendis.

Looking in the mirror, imagining him, it's like a few months ago, when I saw him at the comic book convention, where he rejected Fanboy and I taught him a lesson. My eyes are all wide and surprised by myself, surprised the way *Bendis* was when I flashed him and scared him and made him run away.

Great. Bendis. What the eff. I'm obsessing about him, just like Fanboy does.

Stop it, Kyra. Stop thinking about it. About him. About them. Just stop it.

This is why I tried to . . . This is why I tried to go away. Why I tried to make it all end. Because I couldn't stop *thinking*, no matter how much I wanted to. No matter how much I tried I couldn't stop thinking about

The Last Time I Saw Her

the room the room the room is rosevomit because
roger left roses and
mom threw up before i came in
perfect timing

("Honey?" she said
In that clouded, confused way.)

cancer had eaten a path to her brain
yum—yum cancer loves brains
like zombies
eat her memory
she has trouble remembering   me
remembering   the year

(When I was eight years old, I
Had the stomach flu
And threw up in the kitchen
And then in the hallway
And then twice in the bathroom
—Only hitting the sink once)

i should understand
but I can't
fluvomit does not equal rosevomit

Twenty-Seven

SHAKE MY HEAD AT MYSELF. I imagine Despair laughing at me through the mirror. Well, no. Not this time, bitch. I'm not giving into you or to little-*d* despair.

So I try on my new outfit and look at myself in the mirror and it's totally unreal. It's like I'm another person. With my white makeup on, it's like I'm already dead. It's like I really *am* a ghost now.

See, the outfit I bought is totally, purely *white*.

It's the complete opposite of everything I normally wear. The shirt is this high-necked thing with a little collar and the sleeves have buttons halfway to the elbow. I love it. It comes all the way to my chin, practically, and there's no chance in hell of any cleavage ever showing. And with the sleeves buttoned all the way, my scars will never show, either.

Just to be safe, though, I put on a whole bunch of white rubber bracelets.

The pants are white jeans. They're a little tight, but they fit fine. I even have white sneaks and socks that I dug up from my closet. It's all awesome. I look like some kind of pissed-off angel or something. Final touch is my reverse-smiley button. It's the only bit of color anywhere—the black background and yellow eyes and mouth. But I have to wear it. I *always* wear it.

I walk around the house, checking myself out in every mirror. The only thing that doesn't work is my black lipstick, so I wipe it off and use the only other color I have: a deep blood red.

God. That's *it*. That's *perfect*.

I've lost the Bangs of Doom, but it was a sacrifice worth making. Because, I mean, I honest-to-God only know it's me in the mirror because I *know* it's me. But it's like looking at another person entirely. The shirt doesn't hide my boobs as well, but it's like for the first time ever, I don't care. Because it's not *me* in the mirror. It's someone else.

For some reason, that makes me really, really happy.

Twenty-eight

ROGER COMES HOME A LITTLE WHILE later and walks into the kitchen, where I'm getting something to drink.

"Kyra, are you—"

I turn around. He's staring at me, whatever he was going to say forgotten. Now that I'm facing him completely, he just stands there, his jaw working, no sound coming out.

Thud.

His briefcase, dropped. It lies there on its side next to him. He just keeps staring.

It's pretty cool. He's totally spazzing.

"Kyra, what the . . . What the *hell?*"

"What the hell *what?*" Like there's nothing new.

"What did you *do?*"

"This? You're the one always saying I should wear more than just black."

"Not that! Your head! Your goddamn head!" He's shaking.

"Oh. That." I touch it. It feels slippery—I rubbed some moisturizer on it before. "Do you like it?"

His jaw works again—open, close, open, close. His eyes bug.

"Go to your room."

What? Did he really say that?

"Go to your room," he says again.

"Bite me. I can shave my head if—"

"Go to your room!" he screams, and spit flies from his mouth and his face is all red and veiny. "Go! Now! Go to your goddamn room this *instant!*"

What the *hell?*

Fine.

Like I care.

I was going back there anyway.

I take my soda and I go to my room and I slam the door *super* hard, just to make my point. Eff him. Eff him up his stupid ass. I can shave my head. It's *my* head. He can't make me do what he wants me to do. He doesn't *own* me. He can't *control* me. Eff him. I hate him. God, I hate him.

I'm *glad* I hate him. It feels good.

So why am I crying all of a sudden? I don't get it.

ONLINE

simsimsimoaning: *were were u 2day*

Promethea387: *Home. I needed a mental health day.*

simsimsimoaning: *lol u go grl*

Promethea387: *Did I miss anything? (Yeah, right.)*

simsimsimoaning: *no*

simsimsimoaning: *bio was boring, english sucked, math = teh worst*

simsimsimoaning: *u back 2morrw?*

Promethea387: *Probably. I want to get out of here. I need a mental health day from THIS place now.*

simsimsimoaning: *roflmao!*

simsimsimoaning: *want 2 com her e2night?*

Promethea387: *Better not. The Pirate is pissed.*

simsimsimoaning: *arr matey*

simsimsimoaning: *jolly roger is ANGRY*

Promethea387: *Screw him.*

simsimsimoaning: *yuk no ur dad is NOT hot*

simsimsimoaning: *lol*

simsimsimoaning: *:)*

xXxjeccatheGIRLxXx is joining the chat

xXxjeccatheGIRLxXx: *do u think brad likes me?*

Promethea387: *Hello to you, too.*

simsimsimoaning: *totally*

xXxjeccatheGIRLxXx: *he ignored me 2day n bio*

simsimsimoaning: *hes totally nto u*

xXxjeccatheGIRLxXx: *yeah?*

simsimsimoaning: *yeah right k?*

Promethea387: *Whatever. What are you talking about?*

xXxjeccatheGIRLxXx: *come on kyra!!!!!!!!!!!!!!!!!!!!!!!!!!!!!!!!1!!! brad lewis.*
from the summer

Promethea387: *I don't know. I never pay attention to Brad Lewis.*

simsimsimoaning: *what?!?!?!?!?!*

xXxjeccatheGIRLxXx: *hes only teh HOTTEST junior @ sb!!!!*

Promethea387: *Why do you care if he's into you or not?*

xXxjeccatheGIRLxXx: *duh hottness ^^*

Promethea387: *So what?*

simsimsimoaning: *prometheas a VIRGIN*

xXxjeccatheGIRLxXx: *she can stil thik a guys hot*

Promethea387: *Get off my case.*

simsimsimoaning: *get it overwith*

simsimsimoaning: *its no boig deal*

xXxjeccatheGIRLxXx: *leav hera lone*

simsimsimoaning: *just havin fun*

simsimsimoaning: *i dont mean anything*

simsimsimoaning: *does promethea still love me?*

simsimsimoaning: *:-)*

Promethea387: *Yes, you dumb bitch.*

xXxjeccatheGIRLxXx: *lol*

simsimsimoaning: *i knew it :) :) :) :)*

xXxjeccatheGIRLxXx: *how can i make brad lik me?*

Promethea387: *LICK you?*

simsimsimoaning: *LOL!!!!!!!*

xXxjeccatheGIRLxXx: *LIKE me!*

xXxjeccatheGIRLxXx: *shit*

xXxjeccatheGIRLxXx: *help me out*

simsimsimoaning: *jecca needs to get her groove back lol*

xXxjeccatheGIRLxXx: *dont make fun - i really LIKE him*

simsimsimoaning: *u need new clothes*

simsimsimoaning: *god i know he cheks out shari cause she wears that designr slut shit*

simsimsimoaning: *fea rnot slutgoth is here!!!!!*

xXxjeccatheGIRLxXx: *is kyura stil on???*

Promethea387: *Yeah.*

simsimsimoaning: *shes no help w/this stuff*

simsimsimoaning: *hav u talked 2 him since last week?*

xXxjeccatheGIRLxXx: *no :(hes ignoring me ALL MONTH!!!!*

simsimsimoaning: *we hafta chang that!*

xXxjeccatheGIRLxXx: *ill do whatev u say sim*

xXxjeccatheGIRLxXx: *so hell like me AND lick me lol*

simsimsimoaning: *thats my girl :)*

xXxjeccatheGIRLxXx: *dont want 2 go another month*

Promethea387: *I have to go.*

Promethea387: *Jolly Roger is knocking.*

simsimsimoaning: *avast!*

xXxjeccatheGIRLxXx: *walk the plank*

Promethea387: *See you tomorrow.*

TWENTY-NINE

LOG OFF TO THE SOUND of Roger pounding on the door.

"Now, Kyra! Or I knock it down."

I think about letting him do that. That would be cool, actually, just to see if he *could*. Would it be like in the movies? Would the door go flying into pieces, Roger coming through it like some monster or something? Or would it just drop off the hinges and fall in one big slab to the floor?

But he won't knock it down. He'll just go get a screwdriver and pop the lock. And that's boring.

So I unlock the door and throw myself on my bed as he comes in.

"We need to talk." He's got Pissed Off going, but he's moving into Sad, Tired.

Whenever Roger says "We need to talk," what he really means is that *he* needs to talk and I'm supposed to listen. Ideally, I'm supposed to pay attention and something he says is supposed to magically make me all better (as if there's something *wrong* with me) and I turn into this ideal, perfect daughter.

But he keeps saying the same thing every time. And it's never worked before, so what the hell does he expect?

When I was in the hospital—when I was DCHH—Dr. Kennedy said to me, "Do you know the definition of insanity, Kyra? It's doing the same thing over and over and expecting a different result each time."

By that definition, Roger is a total effing lunatic.

"Why did you do this?" he asks, his voice very, very hoarse.

"You always bitch that I only wear black, and now I'm—"

"Not that. Not *that*." His face is all tight and angry and hurt. "That." He points to my naked dome. "Your *hair*."

"What the hell do you care? You hated the black dye and the spikes anyway."

"You look . . ." He sinks into my desk chair and puts his face in his hands and takes a deep breath. I think if I push it just a little bit more, he might actually start crying.

"Jesus, Kyra! Why are you doing this? Why?"

I've never made my dad cry before. I always figured it would feel pretty good to nail him like that, but now that I'm right there, I just feel cold instead. I start shivering. It's just gross and weird and wrong somehow to think of him sitting there bawling his eyes out like a little boy.

"You look like *her*." He looks up at me. "Christ, you look *just. Like. Her.*"

And now I'm not shivering anymore because I'm totally paralyzed. Just frozen on the bed.

"After all the chemo. And the radiation? Jesus Christ . . ."

I close my eyes, which is a mistake, because when I do that, I can do more than remember—I can *see*. I see her. All skinny and smooth-headed.

"Why?" he whispers. "Why would you *do* that to me?"

I clench my jaw. I wasn't doing anything *to* him. I was doing something *for* me. I wasn't even *thinking* about Mom.

"Why are you punishing me, Kyra? Why? I just want to help you. I just want you to let me in. I just want—"

"Oh, yeah, Roger? Well I don't effing care what you want! I hate you and I want you out of my life forever!"

He jerks like I punched him and he goes *instantly* to Pissed Off, rising from the chair.

"You think I don't know that? Do you think I don't know that, Kyra? Huh? I would bring her back in a second, in *less* than a second, if I could. But I can't. I can't! So I'm what you're stuck with, OK? I'm sorry you got such a shitty deal, but that's how it is. That's how it is!"

Before I can say anything, he storms out of my room, slamming the door so hard that the whole room vibrates and my mirror falls off the door and the *Sandman* posters on the wall slip.

Wow.

OK, wow.

THE LAST TIME I SAW HER

the room the room the room is rosevomit because
roger left roses and
mom threw up before i came in
perfect timing

("Honey?" she said
In that clouded, confused way.)

cancer had eaten a path to her brain
yum—yum cancer loves brains
like zombies
eat her memory
she has trouble remembering me
remembering the year

(When I was eight years old, I
Had the stomach flu
And threw up in the kitchen
And then in the hallway
And then twice in the bathroom
—Only hitting the sink once)

i should understand
but I can't
fluvomit does not equal rosevomit

dead already, to me
dead and gone
seventeen months of slow death
of hospitals and
hospices and
doctors and
radiation and
chemotherapy (latin for "poison")

("Honey, come close and let me see you.")

smell of death above the rosevomit
twelve and i had never smelled death before—
—but i knew
        (I knew)
I know

this is what death smells like

THIRTY

So NOW I'M, LIKE, SERIOUSLY messed up.

I mean, I can't think. I can't focus. I just sit in my room for a while, staring at myself in the mirror.

Like her.

Yeah. I look like her.

I really do.

I don't know how to feel about that. I don't know how to feel about . . .

Dear Neil,

OK, I have to admit it: I miss my mom.

My shrink says I hate my mom because she died, but that's stupid because I hated her before she died, too.

When I was a little girl, we got along great. I mean, we were like best friends.

And then . . . I don't know. It all changed. *She* changed. Or maybe . . . maybe it was me. That's all.

Or maybe it was both of us.

But, see, it's like everything went wrong when I stopped being a girl and started growing up—cramps, boobs, etc.

I got my first period the same week—the same *day*—that Mom got really sick.

It's like, she wasn't feeling well. And *I* wasn't feeling well. My stomach was all cramped up, like when you have really bad diarrhea, but it wasn't diarrhea and it wasn't in my stomach—it was lower. I didn't understand.

Mom had prepared me. She sat me down one day when I was nine and she told me all about The Vagina and The Penis and The Uterus and Your Period. She warned me that it would hurt—"like a tummyache," she said.

But this wasn't a tummyache. This was . . . something clenching its fist inside me, over and over again. This *couldn't* be what she was talking about, right? It was *too bad*. It was *too much*. There was just no way—no way in *hell*—that I could tolerate this *every month* until I was an old lady.

She wasn't feeling well and *I* wasn't feeling well and I was eleven, so of course I went to her and said "I don't feel well" and she just blew me off—my own mother!—so I was on my own, curled up on my bed in a fetal position for hours at a time.

I had tried to be tough because Mom was coughing all the time and losing weight and didn't know why.

And then on that day, everything *happened*.

I was watching TV, curled up on the sofa, and it was like I suddenly thought, *Oh, God! I just peed in my pants!*

But that wasn't it. I went to the bathroom and closed the door and bang, there you go.

And here's the thing—the pain was so bad that I couldn't imagine that *this* is what Mom had been talking about when she told me about getting my period. A *tummyache*, she had said! A tummyache! This was no tummyache. There was something massively wrong with me. I thought I was bleeding to death.

Simone had already had her first period a couple of months earlier. So had a couple of other girls we knew. And it was nothing like this, according to them. It wasn't anything like this at all.

I screamed, "Mom!" Sitting there on the toilet, panicking. Screamed it again. And again.

Nothing.

I padded my underwear with toilet paper and went out into

the house looking for her. I didn't even bother putting my pants back on—I just went out there with my underwear on, now all bulky and lumpy with toilet paper.

I found her in her own bathroom, leaning over the sink. "Mom! Didn't you hear me? God, Mom, I'm—"

She looked over at me. Her face was gray. It was actually gray. Mom had this dirty blond hair and it was tied back in a ponytail and her eyebrows practically glowed against that gray skin.

"Kyra." Her voice was weak. "Not now."

"Mom, I'm bleeding. And my stomach feels like—"

She swallowed. I remember that part—it was like it took forever for her throat to make the motion. Like she had sharp rocks caught in there.

"Not now. OK? Put a Band-Aid on it."

A Band-Aid? "But, Mom!"

Then she seemed to realize what I was talking about. I guess she noticed the state of my underwear.

"Oh, for God's sake . . ." And then she started to cough. Really hard. The kind of cough I'd been getting used to hearing for a little while now. A bad chest cold, she'd been saying. The flu, she'd been saying.

"Mom! I'm—"

"Jesus!" She rasped it out, strings of saliva webbing between her lips. "It's just your period, Kyra. Every other woman on the planet has had to deal with it, OK? Use the pads like I showed you and get some Advil and lie down, OK?"

"But—"

And she coughed again.

Only this time it was different.

This time, blood came out.

I don't know why I'm telling you all this, Neil. Maybe because in your comics, you do such a good job writing about women. It's like you get it, sort of. So maybe you understand. Maybe you can understand how it all went to hell that day. Next thing you know, I've got these gigantic boobs and I'm suddenly having trouble in school and I'm tired all the time and pissed off and once a month I feel like someone has dropped a load of concrete in my Fallopian tubes.

And oh, yeah—my mom is dying, too.

Then that part ended and the pain got manageable all of a sudden.

But on that day, there we were, the Sellers women, in the bathroom together, both of us bleeding and not understanding why.

THIRTY-ONE

LIE ON MY BED FOR A while, trying not to think about *it*, about *her*, about anything.

I try to think about anything other than my effed-up family and my effed-up life, and that makes me think of Fanboy. God, I've been so freaking worked up about shaving my head and pissing off Roger that I totally forgot about Fanboy.

I go to turn off my computer after writing the letter to Neil and there's an IM from Jecca waiting for me:

xXxjeccatheGIRLxXx: *kyra u there?????*

I sit with my fingers over the keyboard and I think about kissing her and I think about *Brad* and I think *Eff her* and I turn off the computer.

Back to the mirror. You in there, Despair? You don't have your hook in me yet. See, I figured out how to avoid you a while ago. It's pretty easy, actually. I didn't tell Dr. Kennedy, but I learned how to get around you.

It's all about anger, see?

When you're angry, you can't despair.

Hell, you don't even feel like killing yourself when you're angry. Because there's so much to *do* to people when you're angry.

Like I'm angry at Jecca. And I hardly know why because it's not like we're in *love* or anything and it's not like I'm a *lesbian* or anything, but why does she have to talk about Brad to *me*? So she's in love with some guy. Or in lust. So what? Don't rub it in *my* face. It's like she has this convenient amnesia or something. And I can't figure out what any of it means, mainly because she won't even talk to me about it. Like, this one time? This one time we had been making out and I said to her, "Why are you doing this with me?" and she was all like "Shut up" and tried to stick her tongue down my throat again and I didn't let her but then I did.

Anyway.

I don't want to think of that.

So I won't.

That's my ability: I can totally make myself *not* think about things.

I think about Fanboy instead. I forgot about him for a little while today because I was so caught up in other stuff, but I'm ten times as pissed at him as I am at anyone else. Even *Roger*. Why? Oh, so *many* reasons!

THE MANY SINS OF FANBOY

1. He reads really shitty comic books about super-jerks.
2. He kissed Dina Jurgens.
3. He saw me cry.
4. I was in the hospital for *six effing months* and how many e-mails or phone calls or letters or IMs or texts did I get from him? None, none, none, none, and none.
5. He based his main character on Dina Jurgens. (I don't care that he went back and changed it—I know the truth.)
6. He's got this great graphic novel, but he's publishing it in *Literary Paws.*
7. He kissed Dina Jurgens . . . and then *told me about it.*
8. He thinks I don't know how to kill myself.
9. He told me I'm a suicide wannabe.
10. He told me to *try harder next time.*
11. He wanted to kiss me.
12. He didn't kiss me.
13. He never told me his third thing.

There.
For all of those sins, he deserves pain.

THIRTY-TWO

I GET DRESSED IN BLACK AGAIN and sneak out of the house. It's late. Roger's dead to the world.

It's friggin' *freezing* outside. It feels like someone just dumped a bucket of ice water over my newly naked head. I wrap my scarf around it and then put on a hat, but it's like I can still feel the cold. Maybe this wasn't such a bright idea. Oh, well. Too late now.

I need another car, but this one's easy. This late at night, I can always—and I mean *always*—rely on Mrs. Yingling, who lives up the street. She left her car out on the curb one time, with the keys still in the ignition. It was like that all night! It's like she was begging me to take it, like she'd left a note on it: *Dear Kyra, Please steal my car for me. I have left the keys for you, with the door unlocked and a full tank of gas. Thanks! Mrs. Yingling.*

So not only did I take it that one time—I also had a copy of the key made. So now when I need to get away, I swipe her car and it's easy. I don't do it *all* the time because she would start to notice, and the more you do it the better the chances that she'll wake up at three in the morning with a craving for Ben & Jerry's or something and decide to go to 7-Eleven and oops, where's my car?

But for now, I risk it. I slide right into the driver's seat like I belong there—and I do, I really do—and I start up the engine.

This is the most dangerous time. I always figure someone will hear the car starting deep in the ass-end of the night/morning and bang! Busted. But no one has ever come running out of the house screaming, "What the hell are you doing?"

And no one does tonight, either.

My heartbeat goes back to normal. I pull away from the curb and out of the neighborhood.

WHY I STEAL CARS

BECAUSE I CAN.
Duh.

THIRTY-THREE

WHEN I DRIVE, I DON'T THINK. It's nice.

It's good. Because I don't want to think about Roger or Mom or Jecca or any of it.

I find myself driving somewhere without thinking about where I'm going. Before I realize it, I'm in Fanboy's neighborhood.

I park a couple of houses away and kill the engine and the lights.

That bastard.

That little *bastard!*

I helped him with *Schemata*! I helped him make it better, and does he even *thank* me? Does he put a little blurb in the effing magazine that says, "Special thanks to Kyra Sellers" or something like that?

No.

Nothing.

I sit here and I stew and I get angrier and angrier, and I think of something my mother told me once, which is that you get angriest at the ones you love. And thinking *that* just makes me even angrier! She told me that when she was dying. It was early on and the doctors were still all like, "We caught this late, but not too late," and "With the new treatments, you have decent odds, Mrs. Sellers," and shit like that.

(They were wrong. They were all, literally, *dead* wrong. Assholes.)

And I was angry at her all the time because . . . Because . . . Because . . .

Because she deserved it.

Right?

She must have.

God, I can't believe I'm sitting here in a freezing car in the middle of the night, thinking about this shit! She must have deserved it, otherwise I wouldn't have been angry at her, right? And anyway, I don't love Fanboy. That's just . . . That's stupid, OK? Love is stupid. It doesn't solve anything. It makes things worse.

Like, in *Sandman,* Morpheus falls in love with Thessaly, who's this total bad-ass witch. And she leaves him and he's all depressed, and because he's the Lord of Dreams, the whole world gets bad dreams.

Who needs that?

And then, later, there's this bit with Nuala, the little faerie girl who's in love with Morpheus. And Morpheus is in trouble because the Kindly Ones are coming to kill him and Nuala sort of blurts out to her brother, "Morpheus is in dire need and he doesn't love me!" And her brother is all like, "Well, would it be better if he was in dire need and *did* love you?" That's just great. That's one of my favorite panels in the whole comic because it's so true. It's like, have some perspective, you know? Whether or not Morpheus loved you, he's still going to die. Love doesn't stop the world. Love doesn't change the world.

Love just makes you think that the world can *get* better or *be* better.

My phone beeps at me. I flip it open and there's a text from Jecca: *want 2 come over?*

I close my eyes for a second. Just a second. Sometimes I wonder what it would be like. With Jecca. To go farther. To be naked with her, maybe. What would it be like to feel her skin? Her skin against mine? What would that be like? To let her— maybe to . . . to let her go down on me. What would that be like?

I shiver. It's effing freezing in this car!

I know what Jecca wants. I'm not going. Not after all of that crap about *Brad* before.

I'm all cold and shivery, but I'm also burning up because I'm pissed. I'm twice as pissed as I was before. I'm mad at all of them—Jecca, Roger, Mom . . . but Fanboy especially. Oh, yeah.

Mrs. Yingling has a little notebook and a pen in one of her cupholders. I tear out a sheet of paper and write something quickly. Then, before I can change my mind, I hop out of the car and walk to Fanboy's house.

The wind picks up and my head feels like a dome-shaped ice cube, even under the scarf and hat.

There are no lights on at Fanboy's house. Three cars in the driveway. That's new. One of them is new to me—an old junker from, like, the nineties. That must be Fanboy's. He turned six-teen while I was away. Someone got him a car.

How sweet.

Maybe I should forget about the note and just key the hell out of his car instead . . .

Nah. He wouldn't even be able to tell. And I want him to know. I want him to know someone was here.

I look at the note again:

"I know what you did!—D.J."

D.J. Dina Jurgens.

That ought to mess with his head.

Unless . . .

What if Dina found out about him using her in *Schemata* . . . and didn't care? I mean, if someone had based a character on *me* and then drew that character in lingerie and having sex with her husband and did all kinds of stuff exploring sexuality and fantasy . . . I would be *pissed*. But what if Dina thought it was *flattering*?

Oh my God. Is that even *possible*?

No. No way. What are you thinking, Kyra? Dina is hot and popular. When you're hot and popular, you're not flattered by geeks who lust after you. You're *disgusted* by it. I see how the hot girls look at the non-hot boys—like they're rats or mice or cockroaches or other gross things.

I tuck the note under his windshield wiper and then run like hell back to my temporary car.

This isn't going to do it, though. Leaving him a note from Dina will mess with his head, yeah, but it won't punish him.

I don't have any choice. If I really want to hurt him, I *have* to become his friend again.

THIRTY-FOUR

CLIMB INTO BED AND FALL ASLEEP and five seconds later my alarm goes off and I have to be up for school.

I dress in my new white clothes and leave my head exposed. Roger says nothing to me when we bump into each other in the kitchen. He's nicked himself a couple of times shaving and he looks like he barely slept at all last night. It's a whole new expression: beyond Sad, Tired and all the way to Exhausted and Crushed.

Since he's not saying anything to me, I don't say anything to him, either. I just eat some toast—with napkins all over me so that I don't get anything on the white clothes (wearing white is hard!)—and then get out of the house.

On the bus, I get all kinds of stares. It's like I've gone back in time or something, back to when I first started the whole dyed-hair/bleached-face/black clothes thing. I remember the looks I got *then*, too. Looks and little whispered comments, like right now.

I don't care.

When I was a little kid, I always thought that people who made themselves look different, who stood out, were freaks. The navel rings and the pink hair and the tattoos and the nose rings and the buzzcuts and the strange eyeshadow. Why would anyone want to stand out? I was shy—I just wanted to be left alone.

Then Mom died . . .

I realized something one day, pretty much by accident. I realized this:

Standing out . . . sometimes it makes people stay away. They might laugh or gossip, but they stay away and that's what I wanted.

That's what I've always wanted.

Like right now. People are talking, but they're staying away. They're not asking questions. And that's good.

It lasts pretty much until I get to school and connect with Simone in our usual spot near the lunchroom.

"Whoa! Kyra! What the hell?"

Simone is decked out in her typical "no, really, I'm a goth" outfit—black pleated skirt, torn fishnets, chunky boots, and a halter top that would totally get her sent home to change clothes if she weren't also wearing a denim jacket over it. (Simone loves to play layer games at school, peeling stuff off for as long as she can, then covering up when a teacher bitches.)

"What the hell! Check you out," she says. She doesn't even ask for permission—she just reaches out and rubs my head. "Smooth."

"Yeah, I know." I duck away from her hand. "It's still kinda sensitive."

"Sorry. So, like, *why?* What the hell were you *thinking?*"

It's like she's my dad. Wish I had an answer to that one. I do a lot of stuff without really thinking about it ahead of time. "I just felt like making a change."

She takes a step back and tilts her head to one side. "Damn. You look *bih*-zarre, Kyra, with a capital 'Bih.' Doesn't she, Jecca?"

Jecca comes around from behind me, her eyes wide. "Holy shit, Kyra!"

I can't help it—I'm kinda psyched to get a rise out of her, after all the Brad talk.

"What the hell?" Like Simone, she goes for the head rub, but I'm ready for it and I duck. I don't want her touching me.

"It's a little sensitive," Simone says, as wise as the world.

"What is *with* you? This is really different," Jecca says. She can't stop staring at me. "Hey, have you ever worn that shade before?"

Who calls white a "shade"? And then I realize she means my lipstick—I'm wearing the really deep red. It's called Vital Vermeil.

"Yeah, a few times."

"Your boobs look bigger," Simone says, eyeing my chest like she's at the meat counter.

"Great. Just what I needed." I sort of slump forward and hold my books over my chest.

"Kyra, when you've got 'em, you gotta use 'em." Simone throws her shoulders back and Jecca does the same and a boy walking by almost trips and collides with the guy he's walking with. Simone and Jecca laugh.

"I didn't realize the white wouldn't hide things as much," I tell them. "I need to get the next size up next time."

Simone's eyes light up. "Hey, I'll drive us to the mall after school. You can get something there."

126

Jecca checks her watch. "We have time for a smoke before the bell."

"Yeah, I gotta go, though—I have something I have to do." She looks sort of disappointed, which makes me happy because of *Brad*.

And then I'm off, looking for Fanboy.

THIRTY-FIVE

PEOPLE I DON'T KNOW AND PEOPLE I do know suddenly have something in common—they all stare at my bald head as I thread through the halls. A bunch of people reach out to touch it, like they're in a horror movie and my head's some alien egg they found somewhere. *Hands off, assholes!* I don't just *think* it.

I find Fanboy at his locker. It's total luck on my part—I'm headed for his homeroom and I happen to see him.

I feel all sorts of shit welling up inside me. I'm angry at him. Pissed that he never tried to get in touch with me while I was away.

But there's something else, too. I can't help it—my heart kind of does a little flippy-floppy thing, and I don't know what to do with that.

I should say something, but my mouth doesn't work. So I just stand still and watch him. He's gotten a little bit taller, which just stretches him out and makes him ganglier. But it's cool because there's something *new,* too. I don't know what it is. His shoulders aren't slumped as much. It's like he's growing up.

He shuts his locker, spins the combo lock, and looks over at me. There's absolutely *nothing* in his eyes except for that quick assessment guys do, that fast little dart up and down. I still have my books over my chest, so he's getting nothing there.

"Uh, hi," he says, and flashes me a little grin before turning and starting to walk away. He has no idea who I am.

"Hi yourself," I tell his back.

He stops dead in his tracks. Turns to me.

"Holy . . ." His eyes get real wide, searching me all over, like he's looking for me in fog. *"Kyra? Kyra?"*

"Who the hell else did you think it was, Fanboy?"

"Oh, my God! You look . . . you look *amazing!*"

I grin at him and his face splits in a huge smile as he rushes to me. I figure he's going to try to manhandle my dome, like everyone else, but instead he throws out his arms to hug me. There's a second when I'm ready to let him do it, too, when I'm ready to let him put his arms around me and hug me and—who knows?—maybe make me feel as comfortable and as safe as I do with Jecca.

But I can't let that happen. I step back.

"Hey, watch it. Who said you get to touch?"

"Oh. Oh." He catches himself and stands there for a funny moment, his arms still out, before dropping them to his sides. "I'm sorry. I just . . . I just . . . Wow. You look . . . Well, you look *awesome*, Kyra. Different. But amazing."

"Don't sling the bullshit my way, Fanboy. I look like a freak."

"No. Uh-uh." He shakes his head like a spaz. "You look *awesome*. Seriously."

"It's OK. I *like* looking like a freak."

He gives up. "When did you come back to school?"

"A couple of days ago."

His smile goes away. He looks like a puppy that's just been kicked. "But . . . why didn't you call me? Or text me? Or come see me?"

I force myself to keep grinning. I want to grab him by the shoulders and throw him against the lockers and shout, "Shut the eff up, you asshole! Why didn't *I* call *you*? I was gone for *months* and you didn't send me so much as a single effing e-mail!"

But instead I remind myself of my mission: Get close to him. Destroy him. "Been busy. Getting back into shit. Catching up."

"Oh. Sure. Yeah. I get it. I've been busy, too."

Before I can say anything, he flashes me a smile. It's totally . . . disarming. I didn't expect it. Not from *him*. He was always sort of cute in a shy, geeky way, but now it's like he doesn't hate himself or something. It's like he's not afraid to smile at someone, and that just totally *smashes* my brain.

"I'm really glad to see you!" He practically shouts it, and I can tell by the way he's twitching that he wants to hug me so bad. And I have to admit—I want him to. It really sort of surprises me, how bad I want it.

It's a great moment. It really is. He wants me and I want him to want me, and that's terrific and liberating, so of course—of *course*—I go and ruin it, because that's what I do.

"So, still got three things you want more than anything?" I ask him with a sneer. (I know I'm sneering because my lip ring always bumps my cheek when I sneer.)

It stops him cold. "Well, gosh, Kyra . . ."

"'Gosh, Kyra . . .' Shut the eff up."

He doesn't react the way he's supposed to. He doesn't go all quiet and timid and Fanboy-y. Instead, he just . . . grins. He *grins* at me.

"'Eff'?" he says. "What the hell. Are you afraid to say—"

"Shut up! I don't say that word!"

And we stare at each other. How the hell did this happen? How did *he* end up questioning *me*? How did I end up on the defensive?

He shrugs. "OK. Cool. That's fine."

He's way too relaxed. What happened to him in the last six months? I have to chill out. I'm supposed to be his friend again.

"Sorry," I say, and it takes every last ounce of strength I have in me to say it.

"It's OK," he says. "I'm just glad you're back from . . . you know."

Yeah. Yeah, I know.

The hospital.

Where I was DCHH.

DCHH

STARTED OUT IN THERAPY TWICE a week when I was in the hospital. Three times, really, if you count Group. But in the beginning I saw Dr. Kennedy twice a week—Mondays and Thursdays. Group was on Wednesdays, so Thursdays were usually just a chance for me to bitch about Group. Because the people in Group were this crew of burnouts and idiots who let their boyfriends beat them up and shit like that. Why was I in with that crowd?

"Because you can learn from them," Kennedy told me every week. And for some reason—even though it was total bullshit—I believed him when he said it and I didn't hate him for saying it and I wanted it to be true even though it wasn't.

I didn't hate Kennedy. That was pretty weird in and of itself, because I basically hated everyone in the hospital: the effed-up patients, the retarded orderlies, the clueless asshats who ran Group, and the nurses.

Especially the nurses.

I hate how on TV shows and shit they always make the

nurses like these effing angels of mercy. It's all bull. The nurses treated me like crap. Like I was something they saw on the hood of their car when they came out of the house in the morning and they just didn't have time to deal with it.

"What's D-C-double-II?" I asked Kennedy one day.

For the first time since I'd met him, he flinched. He looked like I'd jabbed him with a hot fork. I felt good about that for, like, half a second, and then I felt really bad about feeling good because it was Kennedy, not some useless douchebag.

"Where did you hear that?" he asked, but he asked it in that weird way people have when they already know the answer. Like he was stalling for time because he didn't want to answer.

"From the nurses." The more honest answer would have been *Where* didn't *I hear it?* Because I'd heard the orderlies murmur it, too, but it was mostly the goddamn nurses. Mumbling it at night when they came in to check my vitals and to make sure I hadn't killed myself by leaping off my bed or something. Snickering it to each other in the hall outside my room, when they thought I couldn't hear it, or maybe they didn't know or care if I could hear it. I don't know.

Kennedy leaned back in his chair. He was a tall, rangy guy. That's the word: *rangy*. I looked it up to be sure.

"I'm sorry you heard that," he said, and then—before I could snark something at him—he leaned forward real quick and said, "No, no, strike that. I'm not sorry you heard it. I'm sorry they said it. I'm sorry they *thought* it."

I just sat there and gave him nothing. I liked Kennedy, but I wasn't going to help him with this.

He fidgeted some more and then took a deep breath. "I told you from the beginning that I would never lie to you,

Kyra. I'm not going to lie now. DCHH is an acronym that some of the staff here uses. I don't like it. It's mean-spirited. They do it as a way of blowing off steam, but that doesn't excuse it.

"It means 'Daddy Couldn't Handle Her.'"

THIRTY-SIX

AND HERE'S THE THING: IT WAS true.

I couldn't even get mad. Because it was true. Roger *couldn't* handle me. So he sent me away. And now I totally understood the contempt that the people working here had for me. They were seeing burnouts and drug addicts and abused women and then along comes this girl with a rich daddy and they probably figured I should just take my Wellbutrin and my Effexor like a good little girl and let myself be drugged so hard that I can't think anymore and maybe stop dyeing my hair and powdering my face white and take out the piercings and wear some colors and just be *normal* because that's all it is, right, I'm just *acting out,* I'm just being a little bitch, I'm just trying to get attention from Daddy and eff all of you anyway because none of you knows, none of you understands.

Whew.

I started to giggle.

Kennedy just watched me. Not what he was expecting, I guess.

It felt good, though. I understood them now. I knew where I stood.

And that's the problem with Fanboy: I'm still getting a handle on where I stand with him. (Other than, you know, between two rows of lockers.)

A bell rings and saves me. "I have to go to homeroom," he says.

"Sure you do. Can't be late. Gotta follow the rules."

He laughs, which is *not* cool! He's supposed to feel all wussy and ashamed because I basically just called him a goody-two-shoes.

"Yeah," he says. "I guess so. Hey, what period do you have lunch?"

"Fourth."

"Me, too! Cool. Can we eat together? You know, and, like, catch up?"

I hear myself saying "Sure" before my brain has finished processing all of this. Then he runs off to homeroom and I'm left standing there like an idiot, trying to figure out what just happened.

THIRTY-SEVEN

See, it used to be simple: I was in charge. Fanboy was my friend, but it wasn't an equal relationship. He was clueless; I clued him in. Simple.

And now . . .

I don't know what the hell to think now.

I make it to homeroom just as the second bell rings. Look at me: respectable and everything today!

Mrs. Reed acts like the other day never happened—she just looks at me brightly during roll call and says, "A new look, Kyra?" which is, like, the stupidest thing in the *world* to say. Because, duh.

So I look at her with my best, most innocent look, and I say, "What do you mean?"

She keeps smiling. "Well. You look." Just like that. Stops dead in the middle of a thought.

I tilt my head and look at her like I'm wondering what she's getting at, when what I'm *really* wondering is how she hears anything at all with the wind and echoes in her head.

She shakes her head and moves on without another word. I roll my eyes and get some chuckles from people around me.

I go to my first class, which is algebra, which I hate. On the way, I get lots of looks, but people also stay away, totally in keeping with my Theory of the Freak Look.

My phone buzzes when I sit down in algebra. I'm not supposed to have it on in class. I look at it real quick:

r u pissd @ me?

It's from Jecca. Because I didn't text her back last night and then sort of blew her off this morning.

How do you text back *It's complicated. I don't know how I feel. I like guys and I think about guys and sex, but I also like you and when I kiss you, I feel like nothing can hurt me in this world. But then I learned that something can hurt me—you can. You did. You do. When you talk about Brad. You fall for some guy over the summer while I'm gone and you don't have the guts to tell me until I come back. And then you throw some bull my way about how you told me all of this in e-mails over the summer, but I read your e-mails (the few you bothered to send) and you never mentioned Brad. Not once. So you lied about that and then you spring it on me in a chat of all places. And I don't know if maybe the Brad stuff is just so that Simone won't think you're gay. And I don't know if you are gay. And I don't know if I'm gay, because like I said: I like boys. If you didn't kiss me, I don't know if I would ever kiss another girl again. So it's like I'm jealous of Brad, but I don't get it. I don't get any of it and I don't want to get it. I just want to kiss you and not worry about it, and maybe someday kiss . . . a boy. And maybe then I can compare and see which one I like more. But in the meantime, please shut the ever-loving eff up about Brad, because every time you mention his name I want to rip your eyes out.*

But I don't know how to text that, so I just turn off my phone.

THE THIRD THING

'M SUPPOSED TO BE PAYING ATTENTION, but when in my life will I ever need to know how to add $x-y^2$ and $x+2y$? (Who adds *letters*, anyway?)

So, here are the possibilities for Fanboy's third thing:

1. Sex. (Duh.)
2. For his parents to get back together. (He doesn't seem that clueless, though. Especially since his mom is having this other guy's baby.)
3. To be Dina's boyfriend.
4. To have his graphic novel published. (Which I guess he's sort of achieved now, but *Literary Paws* is a lame way to go.)
5. To be popular.
6. To be some big, muscled, buff-looking idiot because he thinks that's all girls care about.
7. To live with his dad.
8. To fall in love.

9. Seriously, sex. Maybe something really kinky or gross.
10. Me.

Ha. Just kidding about that last one. LOL and all that . . .

Thirty-Eight

No one calls on me in any of my classes. Which is par for the course because a) I never raise my hand, and b) they're terrified of what I might say.

I have English with Jecca right before lunch. She comes into the room, scans it. She sees me sitting on the opposite side of the room and she waves her cell phone to get my attention and stares at me like she's trying to push a thought into my brain.

Translation: *Why didn't you answer my text?*

I give her the Innocent Look. Translation: *I have no idea what you're talking about.*

She waves the phone again. *My text, you dummy!*

I widen my eyes like I'm just getting it and shake my head. *My phone isn't on.*

"Put the phone away, Jessica," says Miss Powell.

Jecca slides into her seat and I pretend I'm really busy with my book, even though I haven't read it, so I have no idea what Miss Powell is talking about when she starts yammering about *metaphor* and *analogy* and shit like that.

Again: Am I ever going to need any of this?

I tune out. I really, *really* hate Miss Powell. She's a hypocrite, and I've known that since I had her for freshman English.

She always talks about Feminism and Female Empowerment and the Marginalization of Women in Our Society, but she's also hot (for an adult) and she always wears these tight shirts with the top button unbuttoned and skirts with slits so that when she sits sideways on her desk to read something to us, you can see halfway up to her ass.

At first, I didn't hate her for this. At first, I totally didn't make any kind of connection, OK? I just noticed that all of the guys in class kind of got this stoned look and some of them would make those quick crotch adjustments that guys—for some reason—think no one ever notices. (How can we *not* notice? You're adjusting your *dick*. How can anyone *miss* that?)

I thought it was sort of funny that she had all the guys yoked by their hormones and drooling on themselves, and that's always entertaining, even though it's sad. (If there are going to be sad things in the world, it helps if you can also laugh at them.)

Then one day I was in the bathroom with Simone. We were sneaking a smoke between classes because we were cool, even as freshmen.

"Do you think I should get breast implants?" Simone asked.

I was pretty sure I hadn't heard her right. "What?"

"Implants. Come on."

"We're fourteen."

She shrugged. "Yeah, not *now*. But, like, when I'm sixteen. I saw on TV where this girl got them for her sixteenth birthday."

Simone's boobs are smaller than mine. (Most are.) But she

actually shows them off, with thin, skimpy tops and push-up bras and all that crap.

"You're fine the way you are."

She grabbed them and pushed them up and together, creating a chasm of cleavage. She stared down into it. "I can't pull off the look I want."

"What do you mean?" Simone's "look" was endless variations on slutty goth, and she pulled it off just fine.

"Miss Powell was wearing this outfit yesterday with a blue shirt, but I could make it work in black, but my boobs aren't big enough."

"What?"

Simone dropped her handfuls of boob and leaned forward, all excited. "I went to the mall yesterday and found the same shirt, in black. Same material. Same everything. I tried it on, but it just didn't look the same, you know?"

That's when the bell rang and we had to flush our smokes and haul ass to class.

Even though that happened two years ago, I never forgot it. I watched Miss Powell the rest of freshman year, watched as she *posed* herself on the desk, tossing back her hair, pushing her tits out for everyone to see . . . like we could avoid the damn things.

Gross.

Just . . .

Gross!

I had already starting hiding my own boobs by then, but I had been thinking just about *me* and *my* body. But then I started paying attention to the bodies *around* me, and how the girls all dressed up and the boys just didn't give a shit how they dressed, in baggy pants and gigantic-ass shirts ten sizes too big. And the girls spent a million years and a million dollars on *just* the right outfit.

And then it got even worse. Because I realized that girls were being told one thing with words but something else entirely with pictures and actions.

It's like, Miss Powell loved to say shit like, "Be strong, girls!" Any time we were reading something and the female character would do or say something stupid or old, she would shake her head and say, "That's the old way. Be strong, girls!"

And any time the female character would do or say something awesome, she would clap her hands and say, "That's what we like to see, right? Be strong, girls!"

But then she would drift over to the desk and clear her throat to make sure everyone was looking and then effing drape herself over the desk like she was a supermodel or something.

And when a male teacher or the principal or someone would come in, she would totally do all the slutty, flirty shit they talk about in magazines—touching her hair, toying with her necklace, touching them on the arm. Shit like that.

Simone thought it was awesome. She saw the same things I saw, but she didn't see the problem.

"It's power," she told me. "Guys are stronger, but we have sex appeal. It's our biceps and our lats and stuff. We use sex as our strength."

By that time—midway through freshman year—Simone had already slept with three guys and blown like half a dozen, and I don't even *know* how many handjobs she'd given.

"How is it power to let a guy come in your mouth?" I asked her.

She pulled a face. (I guess it could have been from my ques-

144

tion, but I like to think it was from the memory of the last time she'd swallowed some guy.)

"You just don't *get* it, Kyra."

"Yeah, I don't get how doing something gross makes you powerful."

"Jeez, Kyra! It's all about . . . It's all about *control*, OK? When you're, y'know, going *down* on a guy, you're in control, OK? Like, if he's close, you can pull back and make him wait, you know? Or you can speed up and get him there. And it's totally up to you. You're in control of him."

"If you're so in control, then how come Billy Odenkirk doesn't talk to you?" Billy was a junior that Simone hooked up with at a party two weeks earlier. She went out back of the house and under the deck with him and gave him a blowjob. He didn't return the favor, but he was "really nice" according to Simone, "and even said thanks" when she was done.

Yeah. "Really nice." He hadn't even *looked* at her since then.

I knew I was hitting her where it hurt—she really liked Billy—but she deserved it.

"You're a bitch, you know that, Kyra?"

"You're a slut."

"*Virgin*." That was the worst curse in Simone's vocabulary.

But even though we argued about shit like that *all the time*, I was still glad she was my friend. For one thing, we had a lot of fun together. We'd known each other for*ever*, and that means something.

For another thing, though, she was this great example of what *not* to be and what *not* to do. Because I've been watching Simone fall for the same shit over and over.

Holding her hand *four separate times* while she cried in a

bathroom somewhere, waiting to see if the pregnancy test would turn blue or not. (It never did, proof positive that there are people in this world who are just immune to consequences.)

Cheering her up when yet *another* guy didn't call her back after promising he would.

Riding a bus into the city with her so that she could go to a clinic to get an STD test without her parents finding out because the guy lied and didn't put on a condom.

All of these things made me realize that while I liked Simone there was no way in hell I was going to be anything like her. I wasn't going to turn my life into an endless pursuit of A Guy.

And it went further than actually *doing* shit with a guy. Because I realized that every time we bat our eyelashes or let a guy bump our boob accidently-on-purpose or bend or twist just right so that a guy gets a glimpse of something special . . . Every time we do these things, we are—metaphorically (how do you like that, Miss Powell?)—sucking a dick. Because we're doing what *they* want. We might think we're "empowered" or "using our sexuality," but the fact of the matter is this: Just like Billy Odenkirk coming in Simone's mouth (in her *mouth!*) and then saying "Thanks" and nothing more—ever, ever—once a guy gets (or *sees*) what he wants, he's done. It's over. He walks away, and if you think he's thinking about you at all after that, you're nuts.

It's a weakness. It's a weakness we have as girls. We've convinced ourselves that it's a strength . . .

No, wait. No. That's not right. We've *been convinced* that it's a strength. By women who've been there before us, who've used their bodies and now call it "strong" so that they don't feel weak or slutty. By men who, let's face it, have everything to gain from it.

I won't let myself be used or manipulated like Simone. I won't let myself be a hypocrite like Miss Powell.

I am for *me*.

I am not weak.

For anyone.

THIRTY-NINE

AFTER ALL THAT THINKING, I have no idea what Miss Powell talked about during English. But I did learn that she's wearing bright orange underwear today, so that's nice.

Jecca grabs me on the way out the door. "I sent you a text."

"My phone's off."

"Are you pissed at me?"

Jecca's a little bit taller than I am. You don't notice it when you're lying down together, but it's just enough that I would have to stretch a tiny bit to kiss her right now. What would she do if I did that? If I just leaned over and up and kissed her right on the lips? Not even with tongue or anything, but just a kiss? What would she do?

It hits me—the momentary weakness. It's no good. I won't be weak.

"Kyra?"

"I have to get to lunch," I tell her. She has a later lunch period, so I've dodged this yet again.

Simone's at the goth table when I get to the lunchroom. I

don't see Fanboy anywhere, so I go stand by her for a minute. Everyone reaches out to grab my head, like it's covered in diamonds, and I smack them all away.

So they appraise me from a safe distance, with lots of "What the *hell?*" I think it's the all-white as opposed to the lack of hair, but regardless: When the goths are saying "What the hell?" you can be pretty sure you've struck a nerve somewhere, which is cool.

"Why aren't you sitting down?" Simone asks.

That's when I see Fanboy heading to an empty table with his tray. "I promised him I'd eat with him." I point.

Lauri, this girl I barely know, whistles. "Score. He's cute."

Simone, bless her, jumps in with authority: "He's gay."

Lauri snorts. "Figures."

I go to Fanboy's table and sit down. He goes all grinny. "This is cool, Kyra."

"You use that word way too much."

"What? Kyra?"

"No, asswipe: *cool.*"

He laughs. "I know. I was just messing with you."

"Hey, look, Fanboy. There's a serious division of labor here: *I* am the messer. *You* are the messee."

"Still with the 'Fanboy' stuff?" But he says it like it doesn't really bother him.

"Yeah. Not only that, but I've decided something. I've decided you're now Fanboy with a *capital F.*"

"Um, OK. I thought that's what I was before."

"No. Before, it was a lowercase *f.* Because it was just describing you. But now I've decided it's your *name.*"

I figure that should bug him, but he just shrugs while he

munches on a french fry. "Whatever. I hate my real name anyway, so that's cool I guess."

He is just *way* too relaxed these days. It sort of pisses me off,
but it'll make it that much sweeter when I nail him.

"Aren't you going to eat?" he asks.

"School food's gross."

"You could bring something."

"Not hungry."

"OK."

And then there's silence for a little while, "a little while" being equal to the amount of time it takes for him to eat half a
hamburger and drink most of his milk.

And all I can think is this:

It's strange to sit and talk to a boy who's seen your boobs.

BOOBS

BREASTS. MAMMARIES. GAZONGAS. MELONS. SWEATER KITTIES. Knockers. Hooters. Jugs.

Tits.

I'm sort of tired of them. I saw a movie on TV once—I think it was on Lifetime; it was probably Lifetime—about this woman who had breast cancer and they just chopped 'em off. "Modified radical double mastectomy," they called it. And the whole movie was about this chick boo-hooing how she didn't have boobs anymore and learning how to still be a woman without them and all that shit.

And I remember thinking, *Who the eff cares? Take mine! Just take 'em!*

Because things would be a lot easier, you know? Those things—*these* things—are just like effing eyeball magnets and I hate that. It's bad enough when the boys at school look (and then probably go home and jerk off—ewww). But it really creeps me out when *men* look. Don't they have better shit to do than fantasize about being an effing pedophile? I'm sixteen! And I've been carrying these goddamn things around for*ever* and I hate them.

I know I'm supposed to say, "Oh, they're the center of my womanhood!" and all that shit, but that's just stupid. I've got a uterus and I pee sitting down—I don't need much more woman-hood than that. If I woke up tomorrow and they were gone, I wouldn't miss them at all. At least then every time I talked to a boy, I wouldn't have to watch his eyes drift down. And at least if someone liked me, I would know they like *me*, not the couple pounds of boob fat stuffed into my bra.

But here's the thing. I have to admit this:

Boobs = power.

Don't blame me. I didn't come up with this. And it's very twisted and convoluted, because it's not a simple kind of power. It's like in those stories where people make a deal with the devil and get screwed in the end. That's what boob power is like. Be-cause you can use that power, but it turns around and attacks you. Because using that power will get you what you want, but at the same time it's giving guys what *they* want . . . which is your boobs. And that's giving up a piece of your soul.

If boobs are power, then big, young ones are a *lot* of power. But that power is kind of like money. Once you use it, it's gone. Like, have you ever noticed that once an actress takes off her top in *Playboy* or something, she usually becomes *less* popular? It's just like how guys slaver over these girls and then once they get them into bed, they lose interest. This happens to Simone all the time, and she doesn't get it and it drives me *crazy* that she doesn't get it. She lusts after some guy and she gets him into bed, and maybe she gets him into bed a couple more times after that ("Because I'm gooooood," she says all the time, practically purring), but then it happens: The guy loses interest and Simone mopes around until she finds another guy that'll screw her.

So she got what she wanted—she used her power—but she lost it right away. It's complicated.

When you're a woman, your body is this mystery. It's this secret. And the tighter you hold on to that, the more badly people want a piece of it. And you can use that to your advantage or you can throw it away, but you can't do both. Not really. You can be Miss Powell and try to have it both ways, but guys will only go for that for so long. Eventually they'll get tired of waiting to see the goodies and decide you're a tease, and then they just totally dismiss you and file you away.

Now, when I flashed Bendis (oh, the Great and Powerful Brian Michael Bendis, Lord of Superhero Geeks!) at that comic book convention . . . I was showing him my power. I was completely in control of that moment. Everyone within eyesight of my chest was completely under my spell. I *owned* them. I gave them something they wanted, and it was totally within my power to take it away, too.

And I felt sort of ashamed later. Like a hypocrite. But I have to admit . . . for the first time ever, I sort of understood Simone because—wow—it was an effing rush!

It's like everyone spazzes out and says boobs are, like, taboo or something, but they're not. Because you can see almost everything at the beach or in an underwear ad. What's taboo are *nipples*. And really, only girls' nipples.

And that's just effing *stupid*. I mean, that's just moronic times ten billion! You get all these people getting into trouble and all these dumb boys and men going all gaga over, like, a little circle of skin. That's it. How stupid is that? Who comes up with this shit?

And it's like, you can walk down the street and see chicks without bras and their nipples are practically poking through their shirts, so it's not like the nipples are even taboo. It's just seeing them naked. It's just so stupid! There ought to be a National Nipple Day, when everyone walks around with their nipples hanging out but everything else covered. Like with little slots cut out of our shirts so that just the nipples show. And all sorts of people would lose their shit over it, but they would also have to see how stupid it is, how it's just a little bitty bit of skin, right?

Now, for *me* . . .

For me, it's like this: When my dad noticed my boobs, that's when I knew they had to go away for good.

It's not like he's ever touched me or anything. Because he hasn't. And it's not like he checks me out or anything because, like, *gross,* OK—he's my *dad* and I know there are sick effers out there who like to check out their own daughters and sometimes even do worse shit than that, but that's not my dad, OK?

It's just that he *noticed* them.

I was thirteen. And I had this really awful growth spurt or something I guess and Mom had been dead awhile already and I just sort of never talked to Roger about girl stuff because he's a guy and Mom already told me everything about my period ("Stop complaining . . .") and birth control and sex and all that shit back when I was younger, so it was no big deal.

But one day I put on this shirt and it was too small and that was stupid, but I had to do laundry and I was just hanging around the house, so who cares, right? And I went out into the living room and Roger was watching TV and he kind of looked up at me . . .

And there was this *look*.

I don't know how to . . .

No, wait—I *do* know how to describe it. I do.

It was this look of *Holy shit. My little girl has grown up.*

It was like a combination of *What the hell are* those? along with a shock of recognition and this wave of embarrassment. Like he couldn't figure out what the hell the things on my chest were and then he *did* figure it out and then he wished he hadn't.

And I just wanted to die. I felt like I'd flashed him or something. Like I was some skank who was so effing desperate that she was trying to, like, score with her own *dad*.

I went back to my room and I stared at myself in the mirror and that was when I realized it: As long as these stupid things were hanging off my chest, no boy would ever look me in the eye. No boy would ever talk to me like I was a person. I would just be a pair of tits. If even my own *father* noticed them, then every effing boy on the planet would be staring at them, right?

I had to make them go away.

So I did.

FORTY

"SO, UH . . ." FANBOY SAYS.

I blink and come back to the present. Fanboy's been toying with his food, sort of half eating and half mumbling nonsense while I was spaced out. But now he's cleared his throat like he's ready to take the plunge into an actual, you know, conversation.

It's like that one time we spent together, that really awesome day. (I hate to admit it was awesome . . . but it was.) I took him to my favorite spot, a little dried-out pond hidden back in the woods in my neighborhood. It's my favorite spot because it's quiet and peaceful and it's also a perfect reminder of how stupid people are: They drained this beautiful pond because they were afraid of mosquitoes and, like, West Nile virus or something. And they justified it by saying that they would build a park there, but of course they didn't, so they just ruined this perfect little pond for no good reason.

I took him there one day and we just hung out and I told him how Mom had died and how I tried to kill myself that one time and I think maybe he wanted to kiss me or something and on that day—on *that* day—I think I probably would have let him.

He was all nervous, though, and it was sweet and cute and not annoying at all. And now he seems all nervous again, and it's like I know what he's going to say before he says it:

"What was it like?"

I make him work for it: "What do you mean?"

He waits so long to respond that I figure he's chickened out. "In the, uh, the hospital."

I remind myself not to be angry at him, or not to *show* my anger, at least. He could have written to me or *something*. And even if he was afraid of running into Roger or getting his name picked off an envelope, he could have at least sent me a lousy e-mail!

"It was fine. No big deal. I can be in the hospital all day and all night. It's nothing." I grin at him because he likes the grin, but inside I'm seething. I wouldn't have *been* in the hospital if not for him. It's all *his* fault. He's the one who called Roger and told him I had the bullet. And that set Roger off on a paranoia trip and *that* made Roger realize that Daddy Couldn't Handle Her, so he just shipped me off.

"But I bet . . . I bet . . ." he stammers, ". . . it was probably a little bit scary. Right?"

I don't say anything. He's right. It was scary. But I'm not about to tell him that.

Simone and Jecca were cool about me being away, being in the hospital. But they didn't really get it. They didn't get how freaked out I was. They just thought it sucked and it was a bummer, and it *did* suck and it *was* a bummer, but it was more than just that. It was also terrifying. Being so powerless. Knowing that all it takes is Roger picking up the phone and calling a judge and there I am—locked up. Powerless. DCHH and there's nothing I can do.

"I was worried about you," he goes on. "I mean, no one knew anything. And I thought about you all summer, and . . ." He shakes his head. "Anyway, then the new school year started and you *still* weren't here and—"

"Whatever, Fanboy." I wave it off, but my stomach's gone tight. I don't want to think about it. About being away. "Somehow you managed to survive without me. Good for you."

"Well, I had to. You weren't talking to me. You were pretty pissed at me. You sent me that picture on your cell . . ."

Flipping him off. Yeah, I remember.

"And then," he goes on, "I just didn't hear from you . . ."

"It's done with. Over. Move on. New topic. I'm bored."

"Oh. OK. Well, uh . . . uh, I'm still working on *Schemata* . . ."

"I noticed."

He brightens and smiles. "Yeah, it's pretty cool, isn't it?"

I'm trying to be nice to him, but if I'm *too* nice, he'll get suspicious. "Sure, if you've totally given up."

His eyes narrow. "What do you mean?"

"You know what I mean. You had all these dreams. You were going to show it to Bendis. You were going to get Marvel to publish it or something. And instead you decided to publish it in *Literary Paws*. You were supposed to be worshiped by the world, but you settled for being worshiped by effing *Brookdale*. Hell, not even Brookdale—just South Brook."

He thinks about that for all of half a second. "I *did* show it to Bendis, but . . . Look, Kyra, it's more complicated than that."

"Sure it is."

"I still want to get it published as one big graphic novel. But—"

"You're going about it all wrong, then."

"Wait, just . . . hang on. Look. It was Cal's idea . . ."

Of course it was. Effing *Cal.* The super-black superstud. More powerful than a stereotype. Leaps tall clichés in a single bound.

"He looked at what I had and he thought it was really cool and he had this idea to put it in *Literary Paws* so that I could, you know, get feedback, right? And then I could make it even *better* so that I could send it to Image or maybe Top Shelf—"

And I start laughing. "Top Shelf? What the hell do you know about Top Shelf, Fanboy?"

He stops for a second. And then he does something that really pisses me off—he keeps talking.

"I know plenty. I did my research. I'm not an *idiot,* Kyra."

He's not supposed to talk back! I shoot him down; he shuts up. That's how it works.

"I did all kinds of research. Cal and Mr. Tollin and Mrs. Grant helped me. Image and Top Shelf and maybe even . . ."

I kinda tune him out. I can't believe this. He just went on without me. He just kept working on it. With *Cal.* After everything I told him about women and stuff. He just moved on.

". . . and since it's been in the magazine, I've been getting great feedback—"

"Feedback? From these jackasses? Why do you care what they think? They're not your audience."

"But they're *an* audience. It's like having a bunch of editors working on it for free. They've already found all kinds of things. Stuff I never thought of before. Like, you remember the scene where Courteney goes to her student's house? The thing with the mom?"

I remember Courteney looking like a certain senior hottie, I want to tell him. But I just nod. "Yeah, I remember it."

"Well, someone pointed out to me that it would make more sense if the mom was afraid of the same thing as the daughter—the father dying in Iraq. Because then you would have these overlapping visions, right? And it would be this cool contrast between these two women, both afraid of the same thing, but in different ways. It works *much* better now than it did before."

"OK."

"I'm serious, Kyra. It really does."

"I said OK! Sheesh!"

He grins. "This is great. This is really cool. I'm so glad you're back."

The bell rings for next period. Damn! I didn't accomplish anything I wanted to accomplish. I need to get my hands on those original pages so that I can show them to Michelle Jurgens.

He gets up with his tray, but just as he turns to go, he stops and answers my prayers: "Hey, Kyra? Want to come over to my house after school? I can show you some of the new stuff."

Sweet.

FORTY-ONE

I CATCH UP TO SIMONE BETWEEN CLASSES. "Hey, I can't go to the mall with you after school. I have to do something else."

Fortunately, she doesn't ask me what, because I don't feel like explaining.

Jecca has history with me at the end of the day. She kicks it old school and passes me a note: "Why won't you talk to me?"

I pass it back: "I talked to you this morning!" All innocent-like.

She passes it back: "So you're not pissed at me?"

I want to pass it back to her, but Mr. Bachman has stopped writing on the board and is looking at the class now, so I can't. I just shove it in my purse and then stuff my purse back into my messenger bag. Jecca keeps stealing looks at me, though, and I feel bad, so I shake my head at her.

When school's over, I meet Fanboy by the lunchroom doors that lead outside. He saunters up to me like he's a stud or something, his backpack over one shoulder, jingling a key ring. "You ready? You want to follow me?"

I stare for a second. Oh, shit—he thinks I have a car. I try to remember what I told him about my cars, but it was months ago and it all kind of bleeds together with shit from the hospital.

"I'll ride with you," I tell him.

"OK." He doesn't seem surprised. Did he figure out I was stealing cars?

When we get to his car, satisfaction and guilt hit me at the same time: I was right about which car was his. I put the fake Dina note on the right car. So why do I feel bad about leaving the note in the first place?

We get in. "This is weird," he says. He hands me something from the center console. It's the note. I pretend to study it like it's the first time as he starts the car and pulls out. "That was under my wiper this morning. Isn't that strange?"

I pretend to be an idiot. "D.J.? Who's D.J.? And what did you do to him?" I say "him" on purpose.

"I don't think it's a guy. The handwriting looks like a girl's. Don't you think?"

I printed it pretty carefully, but, yeah, I guess it does look sort of girly.

"I guess." I'm getting a little nervous here. What if he knows? What if he's messing with me? I get out my cigarettes and lighter.

"Hey, no smoking. Sorry. My mom would spaz."

I make a big deal out of putting away my stuff and then I totally change the topic from the note: "Are you sure it's OK for me to come home with you?" I remember his mom was like a total psycho about that stuff.

"Yeah, it's OK. It's weird—once the baby came, Mom got kinda mellow." He grins at me and I can't stand it—he's so cute

162

when he does that, I almost forget that I hate him. "I gotta take advantage of it while I can."

I turn away to look out the window. Anything to avoid looking at him. "So, she had the baby, huh?" Ugh. Stupid, Kyra. Of *course* she had the baby! She was, like, a million months pregnant when I met her, and that was six months ago.

"Yeah. And she decided not to go back to work and it's like all of a sudden she's much calmer, even though Betta keeps her up a lot."

"Betta?" What kind of a name is *that*?

"Well, her name's Elizabeth, but somehow we just ended up calling her Betta. I think Tony started it. Here."

He fishes around for his wallet. I can't believe he's actually taking a hand off the wheel—he's been driving so carefully that I could fall asleep. It's like the driving equivalent of that stuff in turkey that makes you sleepy.

He flips open his wallet and holds it out to me. I take it. There's a little wallet-size picture of a baby there.

"See, that's her. My sister. Well, half sister, technically."

It's a pudgy little baby-thing. Why do people think babies are cute? They're sort of ugly, actually. They're all out of proportion, with these gigantic heads that flop around and these little bodies with sunken chests and beer guts. I don't get the attraction.

I never want to have kids. For one thing, I can't imagine having to deal with that big of a pain in the ass. For another thing, it hurts like *hell*. And for *another* thing, like, the *last* thing I need in this world is for my boobs to get even *bigger*. I'm not spending my life as a cow for some bawling ball of snot and stuff.

"She's cute," I lie, and hand it back to him.

"Yeah, she is."

He pulls up into his driveway. The truck is gone, but his mom's car is there.

It's weird, being here again. About to go inside. Last time I was in his house with him . . . The last time, things didn't work out so well.

God, am I *scared?* Is that what's going on?

"You coming?" he asks. He's already out of the car.

"Chill out, Fanboy. You're acting like you're gonna get some."

It's like I slapped him. Good.

"Just . . . whatever. Come on, Kyra."

At the door, he says, "We need to be quiet when go in, in case they're asleep."

"OK."

But they're not. As soon as we go in, I hear his mom, saying, "Ooga-googa-goo? Umma-wummy-boo!"

Well, not really. But it's that singsong crap people say to babies.

"Hi, Mom!" Fanboy calls up the stairs. "I brought Kyra home to show her some *Schemata* stuff, OK?"

She appears at the top of the stairs, carrying the baby. "Oh. Hi." She looks surprised to see me. I don't blame her. I ran out of here in a fury last time. *I* would be pretty damn surprised to see me, too. "Hi. Good to, uh, see you again."

Ha. Like we had a big, in-depth conversation last time.

"You, uh, look a bit different," she says. And I remember: White clothes. Shaved head. It's only been a day, but I'm already so comfortable with it that I forget.

I run a hand over my dome. "Like it?"

"Well, as long as *you* like it."

Fanboy goes up a few stairs and tickles the baby's cheek. "Hey, Betta. Hey, Betta." He looks down at me. "Want to hold her?"

Gross.

Before I can say anything, though, Momma saves the day: "I need to change her. Maybe later."

"OK, Mom."

I just stand there and try not to throw up. I'm allergic to domestic bliss. I'm also dying for a cigarette, but I bet Momma would dive down the stairs and claw my eyes out if I even thought hard about one.

Before he can come down the stairs, she leans over and whispers something to him. He rolls his eyes, but only I can see it. "I *know*, Mom."

Mom goes away. And then it's me and it's Fanboy and he leads me down to the basement once more.

FORTY-TWO

His ROOM IS EXACTLY THE WAY I remember it.

His room is completely different.

Last time I was here, it was like some weird kind of archeological dig—the unearthing of the Tomb of the New Millennium Geek Boy. It's still a geek's paradise, but now you get the impression that there's *work* going on here. Serious work.

It used to be that *Schemata* was relegated to his desk. Now it's *everywhere*. There are pages and sketches and stuff scattered all over. I guess maybe there's a method to it all, but I can't see it. It just looks random to me. He even has pages pinned up on the walls, like he ran out of surfaces and just started tacking things up. The piles of comic books and graphic novels that were on the floor have been stacked neatly on top of a bookcase, out of the way.

He still has the same old crappy computer, though. Nice to see *some* things don't change.

"Uh, let me see," he says, and clears off his chair, spinning it from the desk and wheeling it into the middle of the room. He gestures for me to sit.

Last time I was here, I sat on the bed.

"What did your mom tell you?"

"What?"

"She whispered to you. Just now."

"Oh." He shakes his head. "Oh. Yeah. She said, 'Door open, remember?' Like I'm an idiot or something."

Door open. That didn't stop me last time . . .

"Kyra? Hey, Kyra?"

I blink. "What?"

"You OK? You were kinda spaced out—"

"I was just overwhelmed by the toxic levels of geekitude in this place. You're lucky the EPA doesn't shut you down."

He laughs. Goddamn! Six months ago, he would have started apologizing or tried to change the subject.

"Yeah, Cal calls it Geek Central. Sit down."

He's been holding the chair for me the whole time. I sit down.

"So, let me show you some of the new stuff . . ." He starts rummaging around, thrusts a pile of pages into my hands. How do I get the *old* stuff? I need the pages where Courteney looks like Dina.

Before I can do or say anything, though, he says, "Shit!" which surprises me because he's usually pretty clean-mouthed.

"I left the latest pages upstairs. I'll be right back."

He darts out the door and I hear him on the stairs.

I look around. Where would the old pages be? On his computer? Probably. Could I find them and e-mail them to myself before he gets back?

Probably not. Especially with his shitty dial-up Internet.

Damn.

God, it's weird to be here. I get up and sit on the bed. That feels a little bit better.

There's still that old hard drive case sitting on his desk. His secret bullet hiding place. Is it still in there? Should I steal it again, just to mess with him?

I can't help it—the idea makes me giggle.

I move to the spot on the floor where I once planted my feet and unbuttoned my shirt and took off my bra. It's like it was yesterday, not six months ago. It's like it was five minutes ago.

It's like it's happening *right now*.

How would he react? What would he do if he came back down here and I was standing in that same spot, my brand-spanking-new white shirt off, my same-old, same-old minimizer bra unfastened?

Or what if I took off everything? What if I stood there naked for him? Or naked on the bed?

Could I even *do* that? Could I even show myself to him like that? To anyone? I've never done that. Not even with Jecca— we've always kept our clothes on.

Could I take my clothes off for him? Why is my heart pounding? Why does my head feel weird? Why . . . Ugh. Why do my boobs . . . Why are my . . .

Stop it! Stop it!

I have to get out of here. I have to leave. This is insane. I'm losing my effing mind.

Not gonna do it. I'm not getting *naked* for him. What the hell was I thinking? Showing myself like that . . . It was one thing to flash my boobs. To hold my power over him. But naked? That's weak. That's vulnerable. And flashing him again . . . No. The only reason it was OK the first time is because I knew I would never do it again. Because I showed him something he couldn't have and then never again.

If you *keep* doing it, you're no better than Simone. Or Miss Powell.

So, no.

I sit on the bed. Better.

His footsteps on the stairs again. And then he's standing in the doorway. He freezes for a second at the sight of me sitting on the bed. I feel like I should say something, some kind of comforting lie: *It's more comfortable here. I don't like that chair.* Something.

But I've got nothing. So I just start flipping through the pages like it's no big deal.

"Uh," he says after a little while. I've been flipping through pages, but I haven't *seen* a single one. I'm all mixed up inside.

"Uh," he says again, and walks over to me. "These are the newest pages."

"Yeah, yeah, whatever." I try to say it like I'm brushing him off, but I'm having trouble getting the words out. I'm still not seeing anything on the pages in front of me.

"So you're looking at next week's installment," he says. "It's the scene in the cancer ward. You saw it before, but it was later in the book then. I decided to move it up because it's really dramatic and I wanted something dramatic earlier on."

"Right." God, will he just shut up and let me think? Let me focus. For just a second.

He sits down next to me on the bed, and that's it. My brain's fried.

I want him to kiss me. I realize it and it's so hard and fast that it hurts.

That's all I want in the world. I want him to lean over and kiss me. It wouldn't be like it is with Jecca, I know. He's a boy.

He's probably never put moisturizer on his lips in his life. He's got a little bit of stubble on his upper lip. It wouldn't be soft. It would be a little dry and a little scratchy, but I don't care. I want it. I want to do it. And then pull back and see my red, red lipstick smeared on *his* lips.

"And the pages here," he goes on, so totally a boy, so totally oblivious to my need, "are from the issue that'll come out just before Christmas break."

And that finally distracts me because, in looking down at the pages, I see something I can't believe I'm seeing.

She's naked.

Courteney. Courteney is *naked*.

FORTY-THREE

"**W**HOA. WAIT A SEC."

"Yeah." He grins, like he's so proud that he's shocked me.

It's not that I've never seen nudity before, in a comic or otherwise. (Duh. I have the Internet.) It's just that I can't believe *he* did this. He drew this with his own little hands.

For *Literary Paws*.

"This is, like, the season finale for *Schemata*," he says. "That's something Cal and I came up with. Seasons, like on TV, with a break for Christmas."

Cal. Again. Goddammit.

"I moved some stuff around," he goes on, "to end on a cliffhanger right before break. And it's gonna be pretty controversial, keep people talking about it over break."

I want to yell. And scream. I want to yell and scream that he shouldn't be listening to Cal, that he should be listening to *me*, that he's just doing porn now, just for shock value, just to get people talking. I want to tell him that he's *better* than this, better than just dropping *tits* into his book to get people to sit up and take notice. I know—from experience. I showed my boobs to Fanboy and I showed them to Bendis, and it wasn't worth it either time.

But I'm too shocked to say anything. I can't stop staring at Courteney, who no longer looks *exactly* like Dina Jurgens, but man—if she *did!* If she did . . . and if I could find the original pages, with the original art, and show them to Michelle . . .

Now my heart starts pumping fast for all-new reasons. Show Michelle the original pages. Then she sees the nudes. And she realizes that Fanboy is going to draw her *sister* naked. Draw her naked and then publish it for the whole world to see.

And maybe Michelle gets pissed and brings the Wrath of the Popular, Beautiful People down on him. Or maybe she just thinks it's pathetic and that's fine, too. He'll be embarrassed. He'll never want to show his face at school again. He'll sure as *hell* stop being the popular kid. He'll just be the sad geek who gets his rocks off drawing girls he knows naked in his comic book.

Oh, yes.

". . . and it's not like it's for show or controversy," he's babbling. "You have to *read* it. It's *artistic,* you know? I know *you* know. But I showed it to Mr. Tollin and he's OK with it. He says it's artistic and he'll defend me to Dr. Goethe and the Spermling if he has to."

There's a blank moment of total silence. I'm still staring at Courteney. I have to admit—he did a good job. It's not like he traced a porn star or a Playmate or something. She looks like a *real* woman, just naked. I mean, a gorgeous and incredibly in shape woman, but still. She's not posed like a model or anything. Real. Not fake.

"So, uh," he stammers into the quiet, "I still have a week before I have to turn it in. Do you want to look at it?"

I grit my teeth. God, I just want to tear his head off. And throw him down on the bed. Both things. I don't get it.

I hear myself say, "Sure." Just like that.

And then: "So, hey, Fanboy . . ." Trying to sound casual. "Where's the stuff I saw before?"

He snaps his fingers. "Right! God, I'm an idiot . . ." He jumps up and rummages in a pile of papers in the corner between the desk and the bookcase. I find myself watching his every move. What the hell is wrong with me?

"Here," he says, coming back to me with a stack of *Literary Paws*. "These are all the chapters you, uh, missed. While you were, you know."

I snatch the mags from him. They're not what I want or need. "In the *hospital*, Fanboy. The loony bin. The Maryland Mental Health Unit."

He flinches, which is nice, but not as nice as getting those original pages.

Or kissing him.

OK, I'm officially insane.

I sit there and I flip through one of the magazines and try to come up with a way to ask him for the *original* art pages. It gets too quiet. He's hovering over me and I can tell he wants me to say something about *Schemata*, because he's needy like that. But it's all blurring together for me—I can barely focus on the pages or the panels.

So I say the first thing that comes to my mind: "It's stupid to put it out like this, Fanboy." (When in doubt, when uncomfortable, I've learned it's always best to fall back on the easy stuff—insults.) "A chapter at a time. It's stupid. Was that another one of *Cal's* ideas? It's supposed to be a graphic novel."

"But—"

"*Novel,* Fanboy. *Novel.* Like, a complete book. Something you sit down and read all at once, you know?"

"Dickens serialized *his* novels, and he was—"

"You think I effing care about Charles effing Dickens? He wasn't doing comics, Fanboy."

He snorts at me, another indicator that he's forgotten who's in charge here. "Oh, please. Gaiman did *Sandman* in issues, you know." When I don't say anything, he repeats it and says, "You *did* know that, right? That *Sandman* originally came out monthly, in single issues? It took them *years* to collect the whole thing into graphic novels."

Yeah. I knew. I forgot, but I knew.

Dear Neil,

I read your greatest work pretty much by accident.

I didn't even know the whole *Sandman* series existed at first. I wasn't into comic books at all. I was a kid and Mom had just died and Roger had taken me to the library. I can't remember why. He did a lot of shit back then that was just, like, flying by the seat of his pants, trying to fill up the days with stuff until it was time for both of us to go to bed. He was trying to numb his entire life, and mine, too.

The thing is, though, that I wanted to feel. Roger thought that the way to deal with his grief was to feel nothing. I knew the truth, though. I knew that the only way to deal with it was to feel *too much*.

So there I was at the library, wandering around, waiting for Roger, because even back then I wasn't hugely into reading. I was in the teen section and I walked past this display.

And there it was.

This graphic novel I'd never seen before (not that I'd been looking), with a dark cover and the word DEATH on it. DEATH. It was huge.

I thought it would freak Roger out, so I picked it up. It was *Death: The High Cost of Living*. And I remember spending a lot of time just thinking about the title. It was so profound. It's like, it wasn't just a title—it was a *statement*. It was a *philosophy*.

I didn't know who you were. I didn't know that you were this bigshot, award-winning writer. I didn't know that this was just a side story to the larger *Sandman* story. I just knew that it was dark and it said DEATH and the title alone made me think.

So I checked it out and brought it home and read it in, like, five seconds.

And oh my God.

It was like nothing else I'd ever seen. It was dark and moody, but also funny and clever. It could have been just relentless and sad, and, yeah, it had some of that, but there was more to it.

It's like, I *got* it. Didi was . . . Didi was nothing like me, but that didn't matter. She had it *together*. She was mysterious. She understood things that no one else understood. She said cool shit that made sense after you thought about it.

And she wore all black and was all gothy, which I instantly loved.

I loved it *all*. I loved that Sexton called his mom Sylvia, just like I called my dad Roger. I loved the crazy British lady, Mad Hettie, who was looking for her heart. I loved the whole idea that death was a person, a comforting presence. Somehow, it made what happened to my mom make a little more sense. Somehow. I liked the idea that there was a person there to tell her, "OK, that's it" at the end.

So I totally devoured it and then I read it again and then I went and looked you up on the Internet and learned all kinds of stuff about you. I found a picture of you and you looked *totally* hot in your sunglasses and someone online said that you never, ever took them off, but then I found pictures of you without them on and that was cool, too. And even though I was only twelve, that night I *totally* had a sex dream about you and I can't believe I'm admitting that.

I made Roger take me back to the library the next day. I checked out the second *Death* book, *The Time of Your Life*, and read it like I was thirsty for it. It was even better than the first one. And I hadn't read any of *Sandman* yet, so I didn't get some of the references to the stuff from *Preludes and Nocturnes* or *A Game of You*, and I gotta be honest—it was my first time reading about lesbians, and that sort of surprised me. Oh, and I also thought, at the end, that maybe you should have reversed the titles of the two stories. Because if you think about it, the first one is *really* about "the time of your life"—Didi's life, Sexton's life— and the *second* one is really about "the high cost of living," when Bruno sacrifices himself so that Foxglove and Hazel and Alvin could live.

But anyway. I finished that and then I went back and I checked out as many of the *Sandman* books as they had. And I spent all of my time just absorbing this amazing, amazing world you'd created. I read your novels, too, but it was the *Sandman* stuff that I couldn't get out of my head. I loved the way Death talked to Dream, the way she didn't let him get away with shit, the way she always told him the truth. I wanted that. I wanted to go around to people and smack them in the head and make them see the truth.

I wanted to dress in all black and be cool and mysterious. Like Death.

FORTY-FOUR

"I REREAD IT," FANBOY SAYS. "*SANDMAN*. Over the summer. I was, well, I was thinking about you and I decided to read the whole thing."

What does he want me to say to that? He's looking at me with this weird combination of Eager and Shy. I don't know what the hell to say to that.

"It was . . . I read it, like, a few years ago. In middle school."

Around the same time *I* read it. Weird.

"So I reread it over the summer, and it was . . . I mean, I liked it the first time, but it was even better the second time. Probably because I *got* more of it, you know? That's what I'm hoping for with *Schemata*. That people will reread it and get more out of it each time."

There was nudity in *Sandman*. So why is the nudity in *Schemata* bothering me? Because it's Courteney, who used to be Dina? Because it's Fanboy? Both?

"They didn't have the whole series at the library, so I borrowed Cal's. He has the originals, when it first came out in monthly comics, you know? And that's when the two of us started talk-ing about how some really great stuff has been serialized first, and he came up with the idea of doing that with *Schemata*. So that's how I reread *Sandman*. It was cool. Because, like, there were the letter columns, you know? They used to have letter columns in comics—"

"God, I know that, Fanboy! I'm not an idiot!"

"OK, OK! Jeez!" He holds up his hands like I was about to hit him or something.

"Look, I'm not like you, OK? I'm into comics, but I don't *live* for them."

"OK, whatever. But I read the comics and the letters in them. It was cool, to see how people were reacting when it came out. And I learned stuff, too. Like, for example, did you know that the series was supposed to be like half as long?"

"What?" God, would he just shut up for half a second and let me think?

"Oh, yeah," he goes on. "There's a letter early on where someone asks if the series is going to end or just go on forever and Gaiman actually answers the letter himself, instead of having his editor do it. And he says that the story will end around issue fifty. But it actually ended up going on to issue seventy-five."

What? My head's spinning. I've got too much going on all at once: the artwork, Dina, Fanboy, and he's babbling about is-sue numbers, when I never even thought about *Sandman* in is-sue numbers.

"So I wonder," he says, "if he added more stories or if he just ended up taking more *time* with the ones he'd already planned out. Like 'Ramadan,' for example. I mean, if he planned out the whole series in the eighties, he couldn't have planned 'Ramadan,' because the Gulf War hadn't happened yet. You know?"

He looks at me with these shining eyes. I want to punch him. Or kiss him. Either will do.

"You know?" he says again. "The ending depends on the Gulf War happening, but that issue came out five years after the start of the series. So how was it *supposed* to end? Was there a different ending? Or did he insert that story into his plan at some point? How much was planned out and how much of it was flying by the seat of his pants?"

He stops, and this time it's pretty obvious that he's going to wait until I say something.

"I have no idea," I manage.

He laughs like I said something witty. "God, I *love* thinking about stuff like this."

Yeah. Yeah, he does.

He loves it.

And me?

What do I love?

Who do I love?

LOVE

*L*OVE MAKES YOU WEAK. THIS I know for sure.

Mom loved Roger. Roger loved Mom. And look what happened there. She died. She thought her love made her strong. She kept telling me—after she was diagnosed—she kept telling me, "I'm going to beat this, Kyra. I'm going to come out of it. I love you and I love your father and that love is my strength. You're my strength."

And sometimes she would go on and on about it: "I want to see you graduate from high school. And college. I want to see you get married. I want to hold my grandchildren." She would get teary. I would get teary. There's a word for it—I learned it in Miss Powell's class, the only thing worth learning: lachrymose. That's the word. Mom was lachrymose. I was lachrymose.

"I'm strong thanks to you, Kyra. You're my strength."

And who the hell was she to put that burden on me? I was her strength? Then what did that mean as the cancer ate her from the inside out? What did that mean as she got weaker and weaker and weaker? When the cancer migrated to her brain and made her forget things and space out randomly?

You can't rely on other people to be your strength.

You have to be your own strength.

You can't rely on love. Love will let you down every time. Every. Single. Time.

I don't love Jecca. I don't love Fanboy.

But . . .

God, the *buts* in life will kill you absolutely every time, won't they?

I don't *love*. But I *need*. I can admit that to myself, I guess. When Jecca pretends like nothing happens between us, I get angry. I don't know why; I just do. And then I ignore her. Punish her.

And the whole time I was gone, the whole time I was DCHH, I missed Fanboy. I missed him, OK? I don't like admitting it; I don't like thinking it. But there it is.

My first week in the hospital was sheer hell. The doc who did my intake didn't listen to anything I said. He looked at my history and he just went ahead and put me on all kinds of meds. I did a pretty good job of pretending to take them, but the nurses were sly and they caught me a few times, so I had to take the meds sometimes. And those things just totally messed with my head. The first time I saw Dr. Kennedy, he took me off the meds and my brain straightened itself out.

But that first week, I was a mess. I would lie in bed and dream, only I was still awake while I was dreaming. It's so stupid. It's so dumb. I would . . . I would think of *him*. I would dream of him. Little things. Meaningless things. I would imagine cold.

Cold.

Freezing outside.

And I'm sitting with Fanboy and he's wearing a hoodie and

he takes it off and gives it to me and puts his arm around me to keep me warm.

And then bigger, even stupider things.

At night, after my psycho roommate whined and rocked herself into something like sleep, I would lie there, my head pushed and pulled and generally turned into taffy by the meds, and I would think, *Please, God, get me out of this place. Don't make me stay here forever. Don't leave me here. Don't leave me here, drugged up and left here and gone forever. Get me out of here. Please, God.*

And then I would start to cry—quietly, though, because I didn't want to wake up the psycho and have to put up with her shit—and I would go to my worst place, my most shameful place. Lying there in bed, curled up like a baby in the womb, I would cry, and my tears felt *numb*. They were numb because of the drugs. I don't know how else to explain it. I cried my numb tears and at my absolute worst, I dreamed of *him,* dreamed of him saving me, rescuing me from that place, coming to me in a cape and tights and a giant *F* on his chest, my knight, my love, my hero, my superhero.

In the light of morning, the tear tracks dried on my cheeks, I would fake taking the morning meds (the morning nurse was an idiot—the night nurse was savvy) and my head would clear a little and I would hate myself for my weakness, for wanting to be rescued.

And I would hate him for not rescuing me.

FORTY-FIVE

HIS MOM CALLS HIS NAME from upstairs. "Dinner soon! Is Kyra staying?"

He looks the question at me. I can't believe it. I must look totally normal. It feels like everything going on in my head should be so *obvious*. It should be plastered all over me. But it's not.

I blame/thank the bald dome and the clothes. He doesn't know how to read me anymore.

"I don't think I can," I hear myself say.

I've totally botched this. All I have for my troubles is a stack of *Literary Paws*, naked artwork, and a lecture on *Sandman*. Nothing useful.

"OK, well, I guess I better take you back to school, then."

I've accomplished nothing. I just stare at the naked Courteney.

"It's all because of you, you know," he says.

"Huh?" I look up at him.

"This whole scene." He gestures to the pages in my hands.

"The whole 'season finale' thing. It's all thanks to you. Remember how you told me she shouldn't just get all pissed off when she sees her husband's fantasies toward the end of the book? She should, like, realize she has her own, too? That's what I'm setting up here. It's foreshadowing. So, you know, thanks."

I just stare at him. He listened to me.

He actually listened to me.

And changed his book because of me.

"In fact . . ." He gets all shy and bumbling all of a sudden. It's like six months ago all over again, when he had no idea how to react or talk to me. Only I'm not doing any talking, so he's on his own. "I was gonna . . . I wanted it to be a surprise . . . But since you're . . . Oh, what the hell, right?"

He grabs another sheet of paper. This one is larger. He holds it up to me. It's the opening splash page for his "season finale," the exact same image that I'm holding—shrunken to regular paper size—in my hands already. Only *this* version is lettered, with a title and everything:

SCHEMATA: SEASON ONE FINALE
DREAMING WHILE I'M AWAKE

And then, at the bottom of the page, the credit box, with "Writer/Artist" and his name, followed by:

Editor/Letterer: Cal Willingham
Advisor: Craig Tollin
For *Literary Paws:* Gina Horowitz

But then, under *that*, in bold letters that even a blind person could see . . .

Extra-special thanks to <u>Kyra</u> <u>Sellers</u>, who made it possible.

FORTY-SIX

STARE AT IT.

Why did he have to go and do something nice? Why couldn't he just keep being a dick so I could keep hating him?

He's grinning at me like he's just given me the world's greatest Christmas present. My brain splits in two.

The first part snorts and says, "Thanks a lot, Fanboy," hitting just the right tone of voice. He's used to it. He'll think I'm secretly happy.

The second part . . .

I smile at him. "No, seriously, thanks. It's too much."

He believes me. God, am I good or what?

"Well, you deserve it. You made this all possible."

I point to the page. "So I've read."

"Ha! OK, let's go."

We go out to the car. I pile up all of the *Schemata* stuff on my lap and soon we're out of the driveway and heading back to school. It's weird, having him drive. He does the speed limit and he's really, really careful.

I have to make a decision. He's taking me back to school because he thinks I have a car there. And he thinks this because I always lied to him and told him I had a car, even though I was stealing them.

So, do I let him take me back to school and then walk home? Or do I tell him the truth?

It's cold out. My head is vulnerable. I sigh.

"Hey, Fanboy." I go All Tough with him. My tone will brook no shit. That's a great expression my dad uses sometimes, though he says "crap" instead of "shit."

"Yeah?"

"I took the bus today, so I need you to take me home."

"Oh, yeah?"

He sounds way too smug.

"Nothing wrong with taking the bus, Fanboy. Except for the assholes."

"What happened? Couldn't find a car?"

I've been watching him the whole time, but as he says this, he turns quickly to look at me and I have to look away. I *have* to. It's like magnets, when you put two of them together with the wrong ends facing and they force each other apart. I turn away. It's like my neck muscles have locked into place and if my life depended on it, I couldn't turn to the left to look at him. My cheeks flame and burn. Hell, I think my *scalp* is blushing.

"I figured it out," he tells me. "Eventually. You really had me going for a while there, with all that crap about your mom's car and your sister's car and your sister's boyfriend's car . . ."

My sister. God, that's right. Katherine. I used Katherine and I told him I had a sister. Man, I really laid the lies on thick, didn't I?

Busted.

"But then I realized," he goes on, "that none of it made sense. And once your dad told me you didn't *have* a sister, I figured out that, uh, you know, you must have been, like, stealing those cars."

"Big effing deal, Sherlock. You think you're Batman or something 'cause you figured that out?" Inside, I'm curled up in shame. Outside, I have to be tough. That's how it works.

"No. No. I guess not. I just . . ."

"Just *what?*" Stop it, Kyra! Stop goading him! Just get home and get the hell out of the car.

He sighs. "I'm just really glad you're back, is all. I hope . . . I hope it helped. Being—you know . . . being *away*. Like that."

If I weren't all tense and freaked out, it would be funny, listening to him stumble over the words and the phrases and even the goddamn syllables. But I am, so it's not.

"Whatever, Fanboy."

"I just . . . I was really worried about you, so I hope you got the help you needed and that you're doing better."

God. What an effing *baby*.

Here's the thing. Here's the thing I hate: His concern is like a really warm drink when your body is cold, and you feel it go all the way down your throat and then into your stomach, where it pools and spreads out.

But the problem is that cold is *good*. Cold is *numb*. And when you're numb, you can't feel pain. You can't feel pain until some stupid warm drink makes you not numb anymore and then you can feel again.

I'm not weak. I'm *not*. And he can't change that.

"I'm fine," I tell him, and I've lost the edge in my voice, the "get off my back" edge that keeps people away. Where the hell did it go? What did he do to it? Why is he making me all weak and needy? And *how?*

"Well, that's good. I'm glad. Heh. I'm saying 'I'm glad' a lot, aren't I?"

He pulls into my driveway, so I don't have to answer. I just get out of the car, my messenger bag over one shoulder, my copies of the *Schemata* stuff under my arm.

"So, uh, take a look at everything and let me know what you think," he says, all eager. "Some stuff has changed from what you saw before."

And then it hits me. It hits me so hard and so fast that I don't even think it—I just say it.

"Sure. Hey, Fanboy, look, since things have changed . . . it would be cool if I could see the old pages. You know, the originals. So I can compare the changes and everything."

I figure there's no way in hell he'll buy it. Why would he? But he's so happy to have me back, so happy to have me involved again, that he just nods like an idiot. "Oh, yeah, sure. I get it. OK. I'll print that stuff out and bring it to school tomorrow."

And then he backs out, honking the horn as he pulls away. I raise my hand and wave to him before I even realize what I'm doing. It's the same hand I'll use to stab him in the back.

FORTY-SEVEN

THAT WAS ALL THE FIRST PART of my brain. The part that feels out of sorts. Like, I've won and it was easy because he likes me and he trusts me. I don't know how to feel about that . . .

But the second part is off and scheming. I have to do this now. I'll get the original Dina art and with the new art I can do a sort of exposé, showing them side by side. I'll do *more* than just take it all to Michelle. Hell, I'll make *posters* and put them up all over school. I'll make a website about it. I'll show the *world*.

That will mortally embarrass Fanboy beyond belief. I'll destroy him.

I should feel triumphant. I'm going to win.

Instead, I just feel like crap.

Maybe I shouldn't do this. Maybe I should just . . .

Maybe I should just *ask* him. *Hey, Fanboy! What the hell? Why didn't you e-mail me—at least—while I was away?*

Yeah, right. Puh-lease. This is *Fanboy*. He'll just lie. He'll say he *did* e-mail and the e-mails must have gotten lost or caught in a spam filter or something. That's what he does—he makes things up for fun. Why the hell should I trust him?

I stand out in the cold until Fanboy's car turns at the main road and disappears, then I go inside. Roger isn't home yet.

I throw all of my stuff on my bed. My phone goes off—it's a text from Simone: *get ready!*

What?

And then I get like six pictures in a row, all snapped from Simone's cell—it's her and Jecca at the mall, in the Victoria's Secret changing room, dressed up all slutty and shit, pretending to be like the models on TV. They won't actually buy anything—they're just messing around.

Final text: *wish u wr hr.*

Yeah, whatever. I'm done playing those stupid games.

I look at myself in the mirror. It's still a shock—the blood red lips, the shiny head. I thought my ears might look huge and Obama-y without my hair, but they're actually sort of cute and small. Score one for me.

All that white . . . I see what Roger was talking about. I *do* sort of look like Mom, toward the end. If I'm gonna pull off this white thing, though, I need more clothes and *looser* clothes, because my boobs look like they could take over a small third world country right now.

The garage door rumbles. Roger's home.

I meet him in the kitchen. He looks tired, but that's nothing new.

"Hey, Dad?"

He tosses his keys on the counter. "What do you want, Kyra?"

"What makes you think I want something?"

"You only call me Dad when you're about to ask for something."

Oh. He noticed.

"Uh, well, I was wondering if you could drive me to the mall?"

He stares at me like I'm some alien child who's beamed down from the mother ship.

"I need to buy some more clothes."

"You want me to take you to the mall."

I resist the urge to say *Duh*. I just nod.

"After all the crap you've put me through the past few days? After all the crap you've said to me? After you did *this*"—he gestures up and down my body—"to yourself?"

I bite the inside of my cheek to keep from snapping at him. I learned that in drama class last year. School's good for *something*. If I snap at him, he'll *never* take me to the mall.

"I was good in school today," I tell him.

"What, so you want a reward for doing what you're supposed to do? Jesus, Kyra."

I bite the other cheek.

"Well?" He doesn't give up. "Is that it? You go to school for one day and you think you deserve a reward?"

"No. I just need clothes, that's all." I tilt my head to make my bangs fall over my eyes so that he can't see them, but nothing happens because I shaved off my hair. Shit! Alas, poor Bangs of Doom . . .

"God, Kyra. I thought it would be nice to come home and have one day, maybe, without the drama and the bull, you know? Just one night where I could actually re*lax* for once—"

"Then take me! Take me to the mall and leave me there for a couple hours and just chill out, Dad. Seriously."

He thinks about it like he's trying to figure out the angle, but I can tell that he doesn't really care what the angle is. He just wants to give in. So he does.

He drops me off at the mall, tells me, "I'll be right back at this very spot in three hours and if you're *not* here, I'm not waiting. I'm calling the police, got it?"

Which is *so* Roger: He can't be bothered to figure me out. He'd just rather call in the reinforcements. DCHH.

I don't know if Simone and Jecca are still here or not. I don't really want to see them. I just want to get done what I need to get done. I don't feel like being around other people right now, which is why the mall is perfect—no one at the mall is a *real* person. They're just like these background zombies from *Dawn of the Dead*. People just wander, all hypnotized by the lights and the stores and shit.

I have three hours, which is like two and half hours more than I actually need, so I kill some time in the food court first, just sipping a smoothie and watching the people. People walking by keep staring at me because it's like they've never seen a girl with no hair before, so I randomly flip them off, which is fun.

Brookdale Mall isn't really much of a mall. It's one story, for one thing. There's maybe twenty stores and a crappy food court and a movie theater and that's it. The movie theater isn't even digital.

This is where Fanboy and I had our first . . . meal. It wasn't a date. Not really. I've never been on a date before. I'm sixteen and I've never been on a date, not that I care. Dates are useless— if you like someone, why do you need to go on a date with them? And if you *don't* like them, they why would you go on a date with them in the first place? Simone goes on dates sometimes and they always end the same because Simone has never met a dick she wouldn't debase herself for.

Anyway, we just came here and ate and he told me about *Schemata*.

God. When he told me about *Schemata* . . . it was like someone set off fireworks in my brain. It sounded *so cool*. I couldn't
believe that *he* came up with it. I mean, he's from *Brookdale*. No
one from Brookdale does anything cool. No one. It's like this
whole town has a coolness-reducing force field over it.

Plus, he's a *guy*. I think that's what killed me, too. He's a *boy*
trying to write about a *woman*. Not even a girl. I would have still
been impressed if *Schemata* was about a teenage girl, but he decided to make it about an adult. He's at an age and sex disadvantage. A *serious* disadvantage, because Fanboy really doesn't
understand girls at all.

But I read it, and it wasn't bad. It needed some work, but
I was basically blown away by it, OK? Blown away by the way
this skinny little shy, geeky guy from effing Brookdale somehow had some sort of understanding of women and the world.
Who knew?

And now . . .

Now I'm going to wreck it.

Right?

That's what I'm going to do.

Right.

And why?

Because . . .

Because I remember this song. My parents loved this one al-
bum that came out a while back, and they used to listen to it all
the time, and one of the lyrics went like this: *A little revenge and
this, too, shall pass.*

It was this sort of mellow rock song and that line just
seemed out of place in a way, but I didn't really listen to the
whole song, so maybe it fit. I don't know. I just know that I've always remembered that line. And I think it means that when

you're all mixed up inside because someone has effed with you, you have to go and get your revenge before you'll feel better about it. *A little revenge and this, too, shall pass.* See?

I finish my smoothie and wander around the mall. I'm here for clothes, but I scope out some of the makeup counters, too, just to see if maybe I want to try something different to go with my new look. Most of the women working the makeup counters sort of avoid me because I guess I don't look like they'll earn any commissions from me, but at this one place this really fat chick with totally awesome makeup (I'm serious—she looks amazing) comes right up to me and starts chattering away, and it's weird, but for once I don't find a stranger totally annoying.

"So was this a choice or a necessity?" she asks, pointing to my head. She's kinda cute and nice and I want to tell her to go lose some weight.

"Choice."

"Oh, nice. Cool. How long have you had it like that?"

"Just a day or so."

She nods. "Are you going to keep it?"

"I think so."

"OK, then . . ." She goes and rummages around in one of the cases, then comes up with two little bottles. "Look, if you get scalp irritation, you're going to want to take some of this— this is lavender oil, OK?—and mix it with some of *this* oil. And it'll help with ingrown hairs, too."

Wow. I never thought of any of that. "OK. Thanks. How, uh . . ." I can't help looking at *her* hair, which is so perfect that I figure maybe it's a wig. Damn. Perfect hair, perfect makeup. If she would lose, like, a thousand pounds, she'd be awesome. "How do you know this stuff?"

"Oh." Her smile shakes a little. "Well, my sister shaved her head. Chemo, you know?"

Shit.

"She had breast cancer and she was going to lose her hair anyway, so . . ."

"Yeah."

"Anyway . . . is that going to be it?"

"Sure." I want to ask her if her sister made it or not, but I don't know how to ask. I want to tell her about Mom, but I don't know how to do that, either. So I just say nothing as she turns to the register to ring me up.

"Hey, do you want to see something?" she asks, and without waiting grabs something from a little stand on the counter. "Check this out. Pretty girl like you, I think you could pull it off."

She hands me a lipstick. It's called ElecTrick Sex.

"Oh, ignore the name," she says.

I twist off the cap. The lipstick is this deep electric blue. It's like someone caught the night sky when a lightning bolt hit and shoved it into this tube of lipstick.

I immediately imagine it: My white clothes. My powdered white face. With my lips surging, blue and sparkling.

And then . . . Blue blurs on Jecca's lips. Blue smudges on Fanboy . . .

Whoa! OK! Back to earth, Kyra!

The makeup lady is still grinning at me. "What do you think?"

"Sure," I tell her.

She rings me up and gives me my bag and says, "You have a great day, OK?"

I stumble out of the store, sort of in shock. I feel like I've been reverse mugged. This person came out of nowhere and was really nice to me and did all sorts of nice things.

I feel bad all of a sudden. Why did I even *think* about her weight? Like, does it really matter? She was really nice and really pretty and happy and good at her job. And she treated me like a person when no one else even looked at me. So does it really matter that she's fat? Who the eff cares? Why the eff does everyone have to be like a magazine cover?

That keeps whipping and whirling through my head the whole time I'm at Minus, which is the only place in Brookdale to buy clothes that are even remotely cool. I find three more white outfits, which ought to hold me for now. I can mix and match these with some other stuff from home and I should be good for a little while. But even as I'm changing and checking myself out in the mirrors, I can't stop thinking about the makeup lady.

So it's strange, because I finish shopping and I still have some time before Roger picks me up, so I think I'm gonna go back into the store and go apologize to the makeup lady for thinking she's fat and then I'm gonna tell her that she's really cool and beautiful and shit like that.

Yeah. That's what I'm—

"Hey, bitch!"

I look over—it's Simone, standing by the wishing fountain. She changed her outfit from school, of course, because she can be much, much sluttier at the mall than in school. She's wearing a thin little black halter that stops just below her boobs so that the world can see her belly ring. She's got on the tiny black skirt she loves, the one that's so tight and short that if she moves one inch in the wrong direction, you can practically see her uterus. Her dragon tattoo winds up from her ankle, disappearing under the skirt. She's all made up with bright red lipstick and so much eye shadow that her eyes look like endless pools. Every guy within a hundred feet can't help looking at her, even the old ones. Especially the old ones.

"You made it!" she says as I come over to her.

"Yeah. I don't have long, though." I steal a look at my watch. "Roger's gonna give birth if I'm not outside in, like, fifteen minutes."

"What did you buy?" Nod to my bag.

"Just some shit. What about you?" She's got a bag from Minus sitting at her feet.

"I'll wear it tomorrow. You'll see."

"OK."

Jecca pops up then, bagless, from the hallway that goes to the bathrooms. "You found Kyra," she tells Simone.

"Duh."

"You didn't buy anything?" I ask her.

"Nah. Everything I tried on made my ass look *gigantic*." She pouts. "I've got major ghetto booty. I need like, ass lipo or something." She twists around to look at her own butt. "Do they do just ass lipo? Can they do that? I want Brad to notice my ass, but not because it's huge."

Simone rolls her eyes. "Enough. We get it. Fifty thousand e-mails over the summer weren't enough. You love Brad. OK."

Fifty thousand e-mails about Brad . . . and none of them to me.

Jecca is always complaining about her ass and her hips. Usually I just let it go, but tonight when she says it I can't help thinking about the makeup lady, and combined with the never-ending Brad worship, it pisses me off.

"Shut up about your ass, Jecca. Your ass is fine. You're sixteen, for God's sake. Why the eff are you thinking about lipo? Be happy with your body."

Simone whistles. "Check out Grrl Power Kyra!"

"Shut up, Simone."

"'Be happy with your body,'" Simone goes on. "Yeah, right. How much boobage did you strap down tonight?"

"Leave her alone," Jecca says. "She's not, like, judging our bodies. That's cool."

Yeah, maybe *I'm* not judging, but everyone else is. All the guys streaming around us are checking us out. Well, they're checking out Jecca and Simone—me, they skip over. The bald chick who's standing sort of slumped over with her bag clutched to her chest so that no one can look at her boobs. Simone keeps moving and positioning herself so that guys can get a better look, and Jecca is standing with her hips cocked in a way that she knows is sexy. It's like it's automatic for them. I don't think they even think about it.

Why do we do this? Why do we care? I don't care what anyone thinks about my body. I want them *not* to think about it at all.

"I gotta go," I tell them. "Roger's gonna be here."

"Text me!" Jecca says, but I pretend I'm already too far away to hear.

FORTY-EIGHT

OUTSIDE, I WAIT MAYBE FIVE MINUTES before Roger pulls up. He looks a little surprised to see me.

"See?" I tell him as I get into the car. "See? Three hours. I can follow directions."

"That's good to know." He sounds a little more relaxed. I guess that's what a few hours away from me will do for him. He must have been *totally* relaxed when I was DCHH.

"What did you buy?" he asks as we pull out of the mall parking lot.

"Just clothes. Oh, and lipstick."

"Something normal, I hope?"

I grit my teeth. Before I can say anything, though, he says, "Never mind. Never mind. I'm sorry. Truce, OK?"

"Sure. OK."

We're silent for a little while.

"I miss her a lot," he says, very quietly, while we're stopped at a light.

Well, no shit, Sherlock.

"I miss her and maybe I'm taking that out on you. I don't

know, honey. I'm drowning here, Kyra. I swear to God, I'm drowning. Your mother was good at the parenting stuff. Your mother knew how to talk to you. You were her everything. Her world, and it killed her to . . ." He stops. Because of what he just said. Because we both know what *really* killed her.

"She hated having to focus on herself," he says. "Right up to the end, she hated it. She wanted to be with you, to think of you. And I kept telling her, 'There'll be plenty of time for that. Plenty of time. Once you're better.' That's what I told her, Kyra. I told her she was going to have years with you."

He has to stop to catch his breath. He can barely talk.

"And I'm not an idiot. I listened to the doctors. I knew I was lying to her. But I thought that if I gave her some hope, maybe she would . . . you know. Mind over matter. A 'positive mental attitude,' like that one nurse used to say. Remember her? Remember that? I thought that if I lied and told her she was going to get better, then maybe she'd believe it and maybe she *would* get better."

Tears gunk up my eyes, but I won't let them fall. I won't.

"The light's changed, Roger." I keep my voice steady and I stare straight ahead as he sniffles really loud and drives us home.

ONLINE

XianWalker76: *hey!*

Promethea387: *Uh, hi.*

simsimsimoaning is online

XianWalker76: *it was really cool 2 see u today!*

Promethea387: *Yeah.*

XianWalker76: *got a sec?*

Promethea387: *I guess. Why are you typing like that?*

XianWalker76: *what do u mean*

Promethea387: *In chat-speak.*

XianWalker76: *it's just faster, is all*

Promethea387: *I hate that shit.*

XianWalker76: *it's just faster*

XianWalker76: *i forgot to give u something today*

Promethea387: *What?*

XianWalker76: *it's a surprise— tomorrow @ school*

simsimsimoaning: *hey bitch*

Promethea387: *Hi.*

simsimsimoaning: *what w the new look?*

Promethea387: *Just trying something new.*

simsimsimoaning: *u still a goth?*

Promethea387: *Deep down.*

simsimsimoaning: *its not bad but u went 2 far*

simsimsimoaning: *u could be sexy baby ;)*

Promethea387: *That's not really the idea.*

simsimsimoaning: *it should b*

simsimsimoaning: *u could get a guy easy if u tried*

Promethea387: I don't want a surprise.

XianWalker76: it's a good 1 trust me

Promethea387: Fine.

XianWalker76: and thanks again for ur help w schemata

XianWalker76: really appreciate it

Promethea387: OK.

XianWalker76: seriously. i want ppl to know you helped.

Promethea387: That's not necessary.

XianWalker76: no i want that. ppl shd know. ppl shd pay attention 2 u.

Promethea387: I don't want people to pay attention to me. I don't want them to look at me.

Promethea387: I don't want a surprise.

simsimsimoaning: ?

Promethea387: I don't want to get a guy.

Promethea387: Get off my back about that.

Promethea387: I need your help.

simsimsimoaning: cool

simsimsimoaning: what

Promethea387: I need to screw over a guy

simsimsimoaning: not screw him? lolol

Promethea387: Jesus.

simsimsimoaning: sry

xXxjeccatheGIRLxXx is online

XianWalker76: lol

Promethea387: What?

XianWalker76: then y do u fLASH ppl?

Promethea387: Shut up.

XianWalker76: but u do. u showed me in my basement.

simsimsimoaning: y?

Promethea387: None of your business. Just help me out.

simsimsimoaning: did sum1 hurt my kyra???!?!?!?!

simsimsimoaning: cus ill kill that mf! 1!!!!!!!!!!!!!!!!!!!!!!!!!

xXxjeccatheGIRLxXx: r u pissed @ me?

Promethea387: No.

xXxjeccatheGIRLxXx: ok

Promethea387: Stop thinking I'm pissed at you all the time.

xXxjeccatheGIRLxXx: u just wernt tlking 2 me 2day

XianWalker76: *u showed BENDIS*

Promethea387: *Shut up. Seriously.*

XianWalker76: *just messing w u*

Promethea387: *Well, stop it.*

XianWalker76: *im sry*

XianWalker76: *really*

XianWalker76: *im sad now* ☹

XianWalker76: *hello?*

XianWalker76: *u still there?*

XianWalker76: *u pissed at me now?*

Promethea387: *No. I'm here.*

Promethea387: *I have to go now.*

Promethea387: *I'll see you tomorrow.*

XianWalker76: *ok!*

XianWalker76: *goodnight*

Promethea387: *Just let me handle this. I need to screw him up bigtime.*

simsimsimoaning: *tell every 1 his DICK is really small*

Promethea387: *Sigh.*

Promethea387: *No.*

Promethea387: *Try again.*

simsimsimoaning: *really really small like tiny like miscoscopiic*

Promethea387: *No.*

simsimsimoaning: *its a good 1 y not?*

Promethea387: *Because then people will think I slept with him.*

simsimsimoaning: *so?*

Promethea387: *I didn't.*

simsimsimoaning: *so?*

Promethea387: *And he's gay anyway.*

xXxjeccatheGIRLxXx: *much*

Promethea387: *I talked to you.*

xXxjeccatheGIRLxXx: *much*

xXxjeccatheGIRLxXx: *tnks 4 saying my ass lks ok*

xXxjeccatheGIRLxXx: *lol*

xXxjeccatheGIRLxXx: ☺

Promethea387: *I just hate when you do that shit.*

xXxjeccatheGIRLxXx: *yeah*

xXxjeccatheGIRLxXx: *hey u shd come 2 the party fri*

XianWalker76 is offline

simsimsimoaning: *thats perfect!!!*

simsimsimoaning: *say u tried to sleep w/ him & he wuldnt but u saw his DICK anyway*

simsimsimoaning: *& it was TINY*

simsimsimoaning: *(shjoulnt be in ALL CAPS lol!!!!!)*

Promethea387: *You're not helping.*

simsimsimoaning: *ill call u*

Promethea387: *What party?*

xXxjeccatheGIRLxXx: *ves*

Promethea387: *I hate Pete Vesentine.*

xXxjeccatheGIRLxXx: *so?*

xXxjeccatheGIRLxXx: *no one likes him*

xXxjeccatheGIRLxXx: *they just go 2 the parties*

Promethea387: *I don't know. Maybe.*

simsimsimoaning is offline

xXxjeccatheGIRLxXx: *pleeeeeeeeeeese!*

xXxjeccatheGIRLxXx: *please*

xXxjeccatheGIRLxXx: *lol*

Promethea387: *I have to go.*

xXxjeccatheGIRLxXx: *ok*

FORTY-NINE

$\mathcal{M}$Y CELL RINGS AS I sign off with Jecca. It's Simone.

"Hey."

"Hey. So, who's the guy?"

I sigh. "Why does it matter? I just need you to fire up your bitchiest bitch parts and help me out."

"If I know who he is and what he did, I can, like, do a better job. Like, poetic justice and all that. *Irony.*"

"Right."

"Did you like that? How I busted out *irony* like that? Totally from English today."

I wasn't paying much attention in English today. Or most days. "Nice, Simone."

"Do you think Miss Powell has slept with any of the guys in our class?"

"What?"

"I'm just wondering. I heard a rumor that she gave a senior a blowjob her first year."

"Where did you hear that?"

"You know. Around."

I can't help it—I start thinking about it. Slutty Miss Powell. I wouldn't be surprised if she's slept with the half of the school Sim hasn't gotten to. "Maybe she effed Josh Mendel."

Simone laughs so hard, she starts coughing. "Oh my God! Crazy J, yeah. Maybe it's like something all the new teachers have to do, you know?"

We laugh a little bit and then she says, "I would *totally* do Crazy J. I don't care how insane he is. That boy is *hot*." She sighs. "He could do, like, whatever he wanted to me."

"I bet he's a real perv. After what he went through? I bet he's only into really kinky, sick shit."

"Don't care. He's that hot."

"You're too young for him. He only screws adults."

"Yeah." She sounds depressed. I guess she really *was* thinking about having sex with him. God, Simone.

"Anyway," she says, "who are we trying to screw over?"

I give in. I tell her.

"Really?" she sounds surprised. "God, I *love* that *Schemata*. We won't mess that up, will we?"

Probably. "Nah," I lie.

"Aren't you friends with him? He's kinda cute. Geek cute."

"I told you before what's happening there. I want to destroy him, OK? And I have one way, but I need to be sure, so I want more ideas."

"What are you going to do to him?"

I look over at my desk, where the stack of *Literary Paws* and *Schemata* pages sit. Tomorrow . . . tomorrow, I'll have the original pages, the Dina pages. But just in case, just in case it's not as obvious as I remember, I want to be ready.

"You'll see when it happens. Come on, Sim. Help me out here."

"Are you sure he's gay?"

"Yeah. He's gay for that black kid he hangs out with. The jock. I'm the only one who knows." By saying that, I've just guaranteed that by lunchtime tomorrow, everyone at school will know that Fanboy has the hots for Cal.

"OK, well, in *that* case, you should *totally* have sex with Cal," Simone says, like she's telling me to go buy a lottery ticket.

"What?"

"Yeah, if you want to piss him off, you should totally have sex with the guy he's crushing on."

"Forget it. I'm not doing that."

I hear her light a cigarette. My lungs cry out in lust. If I smoke in the house, Roger will smell it and bring down the Wrath of Roger. "Kyra, you just need to get laid. You need to get over all this virginity shit. Trust me. I'm your friend and I'm telling you—you're making this a much bigger deal than it really is."

Not *this* again. Simone's been harping on me about losing my virginity for*ever.*

But maybe she's right. Maybe that's what I need. It can't be tough, right? Guys are easy. I could get one easy. I know I could. I saw the way Fanboy's eyes popped out of his skull when I showed him my boobs. He would have done anything I wanted. And there's this kid, this sophomore guy—Greg Titus—who's been staring at me in the cafeteria and during computer class. He's only a sophomore, but he's not bad-looking, and I bet if I went up to him, he'd be all over me in half a second.

Easy.

Guys are easy.

Some girls are, too.

But I don't want to be.

"I'm not losing my virginity just to mess with someone's head," I tell her.

"It's not a big deal," she says. "You're making this into something . . . Like, I was gonna wait, once. I figured I would wait for some guy who loved me or something, or something special. But honestly, the thing is, you just jump in and *do* it and then it's over with and then you can really enjoy it, you know?"

"Simone. Enough." God, I want a cigarette!

"It really didn't hurt that much my first time. I was just sort of sore, is all."

"That's not it. It's not the pain."

"Then what? Are you afraid of getting pregnant? Or getting some disease?"

I think of all those times watching the pregnancy test with her. Of the bus rides to the clinic. Nah. It's not those things. I'm not a total moron—I know how to protect myself.

I think it's . . .

I don't know what it is.

No, wait. That's a lie. I do know. I know what it is.

"It's really good," Simone says, dragging on her cigarette. I want to tell her that I'd have sex with *her* if she would just magically teleport me to that cigarette right now. "Most of the time, it's good, I guess. And when it's good, it's like you totally lose control of yourself. You just can't stop yourself and you do and you say things without thinking. Like this one time—"

"Simone . . ."

No thank you. I don't want that. I don't want to lose control like that. To lose myself like that would . . .

Ugh.

No.

Just . . . no.

"No, Simone."

She waits. "When it's happening, you know the guy likes you."

And now I'm *pissed* at her. "That's stupid. That's *stupid*, Simone. He only likes you because you're having *sex* with him. Once you stop, he doesn't like you anymore."

I hear her blow some smoke. "So? That's when you get another guy. Someone will *always* like you."

God. "Look, it's a moot point because I'm not sleeping with Cal, OK?"

"Fine. Fine." We sit in silence for a little while. I lie back on my bed and stare up at the ceiling. My pillow still feels weird against my shaved head. "Just blow him, then."

"No! Get off the sex shit!"

"OK . . ."

We wait forever, just silence on the phone, until . . .

"Hey," Sim says, "do that thing that happened to Andi Donnelly last year."

"What are you talking about?"

"Oh, right. You were in the hospital when it happened. Someone put up these naked posters of Andi Donnelly all over the school and all over town with shit like 'I love to have sex' on them and her phone number."

"How did they get naked pictures?"

"I don't know."

"I don't have naked pictures of him." And this is weird, but it's a good idea because it would totally embarrass the hell out of him, but for some weird reason, the idea of showing other people what he looks like naked makes me feel bad.

"We could fake something," she says. "Something with a really tiny dick."

For God's sake! "Simone, stop it! You've got tiny dicks on the brain. And don't even *say* whatever it is you're thinking right now!" Because I know she would say something gross about dicks and brains or dicks being on something other than her brain. Eew.

The other end goes silent again, except for the occasional soft, wet pucker of Simone's lips giving up her cigarette. I lick my lips. I can practically taste the smoke.

"I've got it," Simone says after forever.

"Really?"

"Yeah, totally. I saw this once. In *Mean Girls*. I tried it, too. On a guy. It totally works."

And then she tells me, and God, it's perfect.

FIFTY

AFTER I HANG UP WITH SIMONE, I just lie in bed for a while, thinking about cigarettes, thinking about Fanboy, thinking about Jecca, thinking about the fat makeup lady. I think about all of it, sometimes all at once, sometimes one thing at a time.

Then I go to my computer and mess around. I have a message that says that Simone has updated her MySpace page, so I go check it out. (Yeah, Simone's still on MySpace. Please. It's all grownups now, trying to sell things to kids.)

So she has new pictures in her gallery. It's the cell phone pics of her and Jecca in the Victoria's Secret changing room, but there are more of them, including one where they're standing boob to boob. I feel like I *should* feel jealous, but I don't. Instead, I'm just pissed. Like, why are girls always showing slutty pictures of themselves on the Internet? You don't see guys showing their dicks online (unless they're child molesters), but you can always count on a picture of a girl showing her boobs or her butt.

There are comments under some of the pictures:

this is my fav pic of you not only do you look gorgeous but tose
tits look AWSUM and u r the so fierce!!! i love! grls
rulez!!!!!!!!
sigh I wish my boobies loked like that
i wuld totaly hit that
i want 2 hit both of thm
hi will you make a ME sandwich? lol j/k (mabbe)
dam grl!
holy shit so hot
pops wood !!!!booiiinnggg!!!!

And some of those are from other girls! And a couple are from people I don't recognize—total strangers or adults.

I don't get it. Is it just me? It's like everyone else acts this way and I'm the oddball, so maybe I'm just wrong. Maybe Simone's right. Maybe I should just give up and dive in and lose it.

I shut down the computer and lie back on my bed again. Yeah, just go ahead and lose it and get it done and over with. Maybe that'll fix all of my problems.

But I don't know who to go to. I mean, do I go to Jecca and tell her, "Hey, I want to go all the way with you. I want to do it all"? Or do I go to someone else? Do I go to a boy?

I don't know what I am. I don't think I can be heterosexual because I like what I do with Jecca too much. And I'm not gay because I think about boys, too. So maybe I'm bisexual, but I don't know, because why does it have to be defined? Maybe I'm none of those things. Maybe I'm just *sexual,* period.

That makes me start laughing out loud because I picture

myself saying it to Simone, and she would say, "Uh, Kyra, *I'm* sexual. You're *a*sexual, like those things in biology that only re-produce with themselves. You're like a geranium."

And that's it—I'm a sexual flower. I have sex geranium-style, with myself only.

BLUE

ⵑN THE MORNING, MY HEAD is still nice and smooth. I just go over it quickly in the shower and rub in some of Makeup Lady's oil, just in case. I don't want gross ingrown hairs making my head all zitty.

I put on one of my new white outfits. I like this one—it's basically one of my old black outfits, only in white (with a slightly larger top, to hide the goodies better).

Check myself in the mirror. All that white makes my teeth kind of yellow, but I can deal. Maybe I'll get that special toothpaste or those white strip things. Or maybe I'll just say eff it and leave my teeth yellow.

Looking at myself, I feel like there's something missing. I pin on my reverse smiley. Here's the thing: On the other side, there's a little picture of my mom that I cut out, like, a million years ago. That's why I always wear it.

Something's still missing. Lipstick. Black or red?

Oh, I forgot. I grab up ElecTrick Sex and open it. Why not?

After I put it on, I take a step back and look at myself in the mirror again. It's a shock. Maybe that's the "ElecTrick" part.

The missing hair, the white clothes . . . that made me look different enough. But now, with the lipstick, it's like I'm a completely different person. My lips look full and fierce. They shine and sparkle like they could shoot a lightning bolt up your ass. I pucker up like I'm going to kiss someone and imagine electricity shooting out of me. It's like I'm a superhero, but not a lame one.

It's totally different, but it's still me. In fact, it's closer to the real me than anything I've ever seen before. I never knew. I never could have imagined. I stand here and I almost start to cry because for the first time I'm looking in the mirror and holy shit *I recognize the person looking back at me.*

Thank you, Makeup Lady. Thank you, thank you, thank you. I think I'm totally in love with you.

FIFTY-ONE

WHEN I EMERGE INTO THE KITCHEN, Roger is drinking his first of many coffees of the day. He looks up at me and then down at his newspaper and then totally looks up at me again.

"Good morning," I say, like nothing's happening.

"Morning," he says, and keeps staring. I go into the fridge for a yogurt, my shoulders all bunched and tight, ready for the arrow to go right between my shoulder blades.

"Kyra . . ."

"Yeah, what?"

"I can't believe I'm saying this . . ."

I pry off the foil on top of the yogurt. It splits in two. Why does it always do that?

"You look nice," Roger says.

I keep staring down at my yogurt. It's half uncovered. Lemon custard pie yogurt. My favorite. What did he just say?

"I don't know what it is . . . I mean, the whole white thing and the hair thing really freaked me out, but . . . I don't know. You look nice today."

Magic lipstick. Magic new outfit. I have powers.

I look at him. He looks just as surprised as I am by what he's said.

"Thanks," I say while I shovel a spoonful of yogurt into my mouth. I don't know if he could hear me or understand me. Then I go out to the bus.

On the bus, people notice me. Well, they noticed me yesterday, too, but this time it's like they're really paying attention. I hate it and I like it at the same time. On the one hand, it's like, "Stop looking at me, you dickheads." And on the other hand, it's like, "Damn right you should look at me. This is what KICK-ASS looks like, you punks."

Is *that* why Simone dresses like a slut? I mean, beyond the fact that it totally advertises her availability. Does she love and hate the attention at the same time?

I pretend I'm reading my English book and that I'm totally unaware of everyone looking at me, and by the time we get to school, I've succeeded at ignoring them.

I head to the spot near the lunchroom where Simone will, hopefully, be waiting to join me in a morning cigarette so that I can give my lungs that sweet, sweet punishment they need before first bell rings.

But when I round the corner, I stop dead in my tracks.

Simone's waiting for me.

Jecca's with her.

And they . . .

They're both wearing *white*.

Dear Neil,

Are you tired of the whole goth thing? You must be. I mean, people must think you're obsessed with it or something, so I imagine you get tired of it sometimes. It's like that scene in *Brief Lives,* where Delirium goes to a nightclub and thinks she sees her sister. And she goes to talk to her, but it turns out that the girl isn't Death; it's just some random goth chick who *looks* like Death. Was that your way of commenting on the whole goth trend? Were you trying to tell people that enough's enough and they should be themselves instead of trying to ape your character?

People think I'm a goth. But I'm not. I'm post-goth. I hang out with goths and they think they get me, but they really don't. But they're the closest thing I've got to people who *do* get me, so I stick with them.

See, goth was originally all about rebelling and being different. You'd be lucky to see two or three goths together at once. Now they're everywhere. There are, like, stores and stuff that cater to them. There's a website I found once that even does date matching for goths. Bakeries that make cakes with black icing . . .

It's all mainstream.

That's what I hate about this world: It takes everything unique and cool and interesting and makes it mainstream. There's an effing TV channel for everything. A website for everything. A section of the bookstore for everything.

I want to yell. I want to scream to the world: THIS IS NOT SOMETHING FOR YOU TO MARKET! THIS IS NOT SOMETHING FOR YOU TO SELL! THIS IS MY *LIFE!* THIS IS HOW I *FEEL!*

There's no room left to be an individual. Everyone's part of a group. And it sucks.

So I invented post-goth. I made it up on my own and I didn't really tell anyone about it. I just did it and I knew—deep down—that I was different from the rest of the kids with their black clothes and their eyeshadow and their pale, pale faces. People thought I was the same, but I knew the truth.

That's all I wanted. To be myself. To be an individual. And to be left the hell alone.

FIFTY-TWO

"WHAT DO YOU THINK?" SIMONE ASKS, her voice bright and shiny. She and Jecca both pose like fashion models for me.

Simone's wearing white jeans that are so tight, I figure she can't possibly have room for underwear in there, but as she poses, her shirt lifts up and I can see the loop of a bright yellow thong encompassing her hip. She's got on short white boots and her shirt is so sheer that you can see every detail of her yellow bra right through it. She didn't go all the way—she still has her long black hair, but for the first time *ever* it's slicked back and tied in a ponytail and she's streaked it blond.

Jecca went about halfway. She's got on white sneaks and then black pants and then a top that's striped diagonally white and black. She went with white lipstick, though, so points for commitment there.

Simone holds out a pack of cigarettes. I'm frozen between taking one and staying, and freaking the hell out on them both.

My lungs win out—I take the cigarette and join them.

"Come on, what do you think?" Simone asks again, and Jecca nods and bobs next to her like a faithful puppy.

I think you're an effing bitch is what I think! I want to say. *I think you've never had an original thought in your effing life and you just have to take what's mine, take my ideas, and then slut them up.*

"The teachers are gonna bust you for being able to see through that shirt," I tell her instead.

She blows smoke. "Yeah, I know. I brought a jacket. It's white, too."

"Of course."

"We thought we would surprise you today," Jecca says.

I get a quick and intense flash of kissing her, our ElecTrick and white lips mashing together, leaving wet sky blue smudges on each other's faces.

God. Stop it.

Surprise me.

Hell.

"Well, it's a surprise."

They both grin. I can't stay angry at them.

Good thing I have someone else to be angry at.

FIFTY-THREE

$\mathcal{S}$IMONE DOESN'T EVEN MAKE IT to homeroom before a teacher yanks her out of the hallway and into a room and gives her a bunch of crap for her see-through shirt and look-at-my-tits yellow bra. She acts all innocent and shit and puts on her white jacket, which is actually really cute, so I kinda hate her for that.

After homeroom, I run into Fanboy in the hall. His eyes light up and for a second there I forget that I'm supposed to be pissed at him, but don't worry—I remember right away.

"Hey, I brought that stuff you wanted," he says. He goes digging in his backpack and comes out with a big envelope. He hands it over. "Just, uh, don't let anyone see that stuff, OK? I mean, it's the old pages, you know?"

Just then someone walks by and slaps Fanboy on the shoulder. "Hey, man!"

"Hey" Fanboy tosses back over his shoulder. Holy shit. An actual living human being just said hi to Fanboy. I can't believe it. We truly live in an age of wonder.

"You're a popular guy," I tell him.

He shrugs. "People like *Schemata*." We're both holding the envelope. I want to pull it from his hands and go running down the halls until I can find Michelle Jurgens. I picture myself running down the hall like a madwoman, a white and ElecTrick Sex blur, screaming, "I have naked drawings of Dina Jurgens! I have naked drawings of Dina Jurgens!"

"Anyway . . ." He releases the envelope. "Like I said, don't let anyone see this stuff. It's old and I don't want people to see, like, the work in progress, you know?"

"Oh, totally," I lie.

"Cool. Hey, you got a second?"

We're like five steps from my first-period class. "Sure."

He goes back into his backpack. "I meant to give you this yesterday, you know, at my house, but we got all distracted and stuff. So I brought it today. I bought it over the summer. I was at the store and I saw it and the guy told me about it and I thought of you and . . ."

Just when I think he's going to keep talking forever, he stops himself and pulls his hand out of his backpack. He holds out a comic book in a Mylar sleeve. It looks incredibly stupid— a superjerk is at the bottom, holding up some big block of stone that's crumbling all around him, which is, like, Superjerk Pose #108 or something. It has the mind-numbingly idiotic title *Captain Atom*. Right.

"You thought I might like it." Did his brain go on vacation while I was away?

"It's got Death in it. You know, Gaiman's Death. It's like the only time she appears outside of—"

"Right. Whatever."

"No, really, Kyra, I thought . . . I don't know. I just thought you'd like it."

He's still holding it out to me. I think to myself, *I don't care what you thought. And wanna know why? I'll tell you why. Because you didn't care what I thought, that's why. I went away and you didn't call or anything and you didn't wait or anything. You just substituted Cal for me, like you were all, "Well, I don't have a chick, so I'll go for another token. What's the diff?" And then you just kept on with your comic and you didn't care that I was trying to help you, so why the eff should I care about* you?

I already have the envelope. I have everything I need.

I want to yell at him. I want to make him feel all the hurt *I've* been feeling, or at least the chunk of it that *he* caused. How can he be so clueless?

But I need to pretend still. I need to pretend.

So I take the comic.

"Gee, thanks," I say with so much fake sweetness that I can't believe he swallows it, but he does. The bell rings, and as soon as he turns away, I shove the comic book all the way in the bottom of my messenger bag, not caring if it gets wrinkled or torn or whatever.

I go to my first class. I sit there and steam the whole time. I have the original *Schemata* art. I've already won. I can destroy him. I can destroy him so easily . . .

The thought makes my stomach all queasy and churny. Is this what victory feels like? I don't know. I've never really won before.

I think of that stupid comic book buried in my messenger bag. God, what the hell was he thinking? *Captain Atom.* What kind of stupid name is that? Does he know me at all? He deserves what I'm going to do to him. He totally deserves it.

In fact, I can't wait to get these pages home and do all my posters and Web pages and shit like that. I gotta start *now*, and fortunately Simone had that one good piece of advice last night.

I take a detour on the way to English. I don't learn anything in there anyway.

I duck into a bathroom. It's empty. Cool.

I call Fanboy's house on my cell. I know the trick you can use to block Caller ID. Sometimes it's cool to have a dad who works for the phone company.

After three rings, I start to panic. I guess I could just leave a message, but it would be better to actually talk to—

Someone picks up in the middle of the fourth ring. "Hello?"

Score! It's Fanboy's mom.

I clear my throat and try to make it a little deeper and slower, just in case she recognizes it. "Hello. Could I speak to . . ." I pretend I'm looking something up on a list and then say Fanboy's full name.

She hesitates. "He's . . . he's not here right now. Can I, uh, take a message?"

"Oh, I'm sorry. This is confidential. I can't leave a message."

"Confid—"

I cut her off. "But if you could just ask him to call the clinic at Lowe County General Hospital for his test results, I'd appreciate it. Thank you."

Even though I'm tempted to stay on the line long enough to listen to her freak the hell out, I have to pretend I'm some kind of professional with a long list of patients to call, so I just hang up and laugh my ass off.

Simone and her movies rock.

FIFTY-FOUR

MAKE IT INTO ENGLISH CLASS like maybe two minutes after the bell, which—for me—is pretty good. Miss Powell frowns and shakes her head and tells me to get into my seat. Like, duh. What did you *think* I was gonna do? Stand here at the door all day? Idiot.

Simone takes off her jacket, making a big show of it while managing to look totally clueless. Her yellow-bra boobs get pushed up and out as she arches her back, and every single boy in the room watches and drools a gallon of saliva. Yuck. What a showoff.

"Simone, put your jacket back on," Miss Powell says.

"I'm hot." Simone pouts and some guy says "No shit" under his breath and there's an undercurrent of laughter that Miss Powell ends with a sharp "Gentlemen!"

But Simone gets up again and gets her jacket, making a show of bending over to get it so that everyone can see her thong.

And then something really weird happens. Or maybe it's not weird. Maybe it's always been this way and maybe it's just part of life and I've never noticed it before. But this time, I *do* notice.

While Simone puts on her jacket, Miss Powell hoists herself up on her desk, a move that makes her skirt hike up halfway to heaven. At the same time, she lets out a big sigh that gets everyone's attention and then she starts playing with this stone on her necklace so that her hand is right up in her cleavage going back and forth.

Every guy in the room blows a circuit. It's like, nubile little teen slut or hot older woman?

Did she do that on purpose? Did she even know she was doing it?

I guess I should be sort of grossed out that Miss Powell—an adult—is competing with a kid for the attention of a bunch of disgusting horny teenage boys. But I'm not. Instead, I just sit there and watch and think about it. Is this what women are reduced to? Is this how pathetic we are? That we have to compete for who's sexiest, who's hottest, no matter what? Even when you're competing for a bunch of boys who would eff a *dog* if it had boobs?

It makes me proud of myself. Proud that I don't play those bullshit games.

"OK, let's get started," Miss Powell says, but I already feel like I've learned a lot today.

FIFTY-FIVE

WHEN ENGLISH ENDS, I PACK UP my stuff and I'm almost out the door when Miss Powell says, "Kyra, do you have a sec?" all casual-like.

What the hell? I behaved in class today. Can she read my mind now?

"I'm sorry I was late—"

"That's not it." She smiles at me as kids leave all around me. Someone says, "Busted," real quiet, but I hear it. Someone else says, "The freak's in trouble."

Eff you.

I only have lunch after English, so it's not like I'm in a hurry, so I stand there and wait. Miss Powell does some stuff on her computer until everyone's gone, and then she asks me to close the door.

"Have a seat," she says, and points to a chair right in front of her desk.

Oh, shit. If she sits *on* her desk, right in *front* of me, and crosses those legs, I'm gonna scream.

We dodge the scream—she stays behind the desk.

"So, Kyra." She looks up at me and smiles.

"So."

And nothing.

"Uh, I'm really sorry I was late." I'm not, but I'm getting creeped out sitting here and I want to leave.

"That's not the . . . Well, that is a problem. But that's not why I asked you to stay." She heaves out a big sigh. I figure I'm lucky that her cleavage doesn't overwhelm the power of the buttons on her shirt and send them flying. The buttons—heroically—hold.

"Kyra, how are you doing?"

What the *eff*?

"Excuse me?" Believe me—I rarely say *that*.

"I'm a little worried about you," she says. "I know you've been going through a rough time, and then this . . . this *radical* change in your appearance. It's a signal, you know."

It's like she wants me to say something here, but I don't. I just press my ElecTrick Sexy lips together and imagine lightning buzzing there.

"I guess . . ." She sighs again. (This woman should get her lungs examined; I don't think she's breathing right. Maybe she has *lung cancer*. Would that be *ironic?*) "I'm just concerned, Kyra. And I'm thinking that maybe you could use, you know, a friend. Someone to talk to." She tilts her head to one side and smiles at me in what is, I think, supposed to be this way-reassuring manner.

So, I get it. She's one of Them: one of those adults who think kids need an adult who's "just like them" to talk to.

About a million mean, nasty things fly through my brain

and only supreme willpower keeps me from saying all of them. I'm not going to let her get to me.

"I know there's a counselor here and everything," she goes on, "but she's kind of, well, old fashioned, you know? I was thinking maybe, I don't know, maybe just between us girls—"

Barf!

"—we could talk about things that are bothering you and, oh, I don't know, maybe figure out some things. Together."

Please, God, strike me dead right now.

She gets up. "It wasn't all that long ago that I was in your position, you know. I'm not *that* much older than you. I remember what it was like."

Oh, really? You remember your mom coughing up her life in blood? You remember your clueless dad shoving you into an institution a couple of times?

Still keeping my lips pursed. This would be two days in a row I behaved at school. Almost a record for me. Keep it together, Kyra.

She comes around the desk. If she touches me, I'll freak.

"You've been through so much. I totally get it, OK? I totally get it. I just hate to see you doing all these . . . I hate this self-hating, self-destructive behavior."

My hair. She's talking about my hair, for God's sake. Like being bald is dangerous or something. Christ, bitch, that's not self-destructive. That's self-affirming, OK? The scars on my wrists? Now, *those* are self-destructive. Buy an effing clue.

"I see so many girls . . . so many young women, I mean . . . and they're just . . ." She spreads her hands out to the sky, like she's praying for an answer. "They're just *bombarded* with all of these mixed messages from the world, from our society, you know?"

Holy shit. Are you serious? Is she really talking about this? *Her?*

But still I don't talk. I don't say anything. They can't give you shit or get you in trouble if you don't talk.

And then she goes and she does it.

She sits on her desk.

Crosses her legs. I have a front-row seat to her inner thighs for a second. How special for me.

"So, I was thinking," she goes on, "that we could just talk every now and then. If something's bothering you. You know. About life. Or school. Or home." She leans forward and grins at me with this shit-eating grin, like we're conspiring or something. "Or boys."

Don't do it, Kyra. Don't do it, Kyra. Don't do—

Ah, shit. I do it.

"All the boys want to eff you," I say, staring right in her eyes.

Her face freezes with that stupid grin. We're maybe a foot apart. I don't blink. I don't say anything else. I just look at her.

"I'm sorry?" she says. "*What* did you just say?"

And then . . . and then it's like I can't help myself. I can't stop myself. When people are stupid, when they give me shit, I just can't stop myself. It's like I'm watching myself do it, listening to myself. And I just purge everything out of my body. I just puke up all the mean, nasty shit.

"All the boys want to eff you. That's what I said. They all want to eff you. They lust over you in class."

"Uh, Kyra, I—"

"It's really sick to sit here and watch it." I just steamroll right over her. I lean forward a little bit and she finally backs off and gets those tits out of my face. "Every day I'm in here and I watch them check you out like you're not even real, like you're

Internet porn they just downloaded. And the worst part isn't them. The worst part is *you,* because you totally know it. You totally know that all the boys want to eff you because you *make* them want to, don't you? You wear your tight little skirts and your shirts with your boobs falling out and you sit up on your desk and you make sure everyone watches when you cross your legs. Everyone can see right up your skirt. Did you know that? I bet you did. You're wearing blue underwear today. See? I proved it. So you do that every day and all the boys drool and want to eff you and you *love* it, don't you? You love knowing that all the boys want to eff you and you encourage it. So don't tell me about self-hating and self-destructive and all that shit. Don't tell me about girls and society. Don't try to be my friend. I have enough sluts for friends!"

And I get up and grab my messenger bag.

God, it's like I just went to the moon! I feel *light!* I feel like I could fly! Like one of Fanboy's superheroes.

"Kyra!" She clears her throat and I look at her over my shoulder. She's gone all pale and she's off the desk now. "You can*not* talk to me like that!"

"Bite me. I already *have* a shrink, OK? And at least I know what's wrong with me. At least I'm not some Evelyn Sherman wannabe who gets her rocks off making a bunch of *kids* get boners."

And wow—Miss Powell is *ugly* when she's pissed!

"You—I'm trying to *help* you!"

"Don't want it. Don't need it." I open the door.

"Go to the office!"

"Eat me."

I leave and slam her door on my way out.

God. God. God. That felt so good! That felt so so so so so *good*!

I don't go to the office. Eff that shit. I go to lunch.

I sit with the usual crowd. The goth table, usually a sink-hole of black, now has a little salt to go with its pepper. Simone has napkins spread all over herself to keep from getting anything on her copycat white clothes.

"You're going Friday, right?" this kid Troy asks me. He's a tool for the most part, but he does have an awesome horseshoe through his nose. Every time I see it, I think, *I should totally pierce my nose again*. Because I've got the red stone through the left side, but having a horseshoe hanging from the middle would be awesome.

"Where?"

Simone sighs like she thinks there's an Academy Award in it for her. "The *party*. Don't pretend. I *know* Jecca told you about it."

I look around the table like I'm not sure I've chosen the right place to sit. "You all are going to a party at Pete Vesentine's house? He's a jock dickhead."

Lauri says, "So? His parents are gonna be gone and there's gonna be alcohol."

"You *have* to come," Troy says.

Simone saves me from having to answer: "What did Powell want?" she asks.

"She wanted to know where you get your bras and thongs."

Most of the table laughs. Even the people who haven't had Miss Powell for English have heard the stories.

"I'd lend her this one, but her boobs are too big," Simone says, and quickly opens her jacket and arches her back, just in case all the boys missed which specific bra she was talking about. (They double check, just to be sure.)

"What did she really want?" Lauri asks.

So I tell them.

There's some giggling and some horrified looks and some head-shaking.

"What did you say to her?" asks Troy.

So I tell them.

Total silence at the table.

And then they applaud.

"Holy shit!" says Troy. "Holy shit! You're my hero!"

"Whatever."

"That's *awesome*," Simone says. "You really screwed her. That is *so* awesome!"

"I just told the truth. That's all."

For the rest of lunch, I'm the Hero of the Table, the Goddess of the Lunchroom. It's pretty nice.

FIFTY-SIX

ALAS, THERE'S A PRICE TO PAY for such popularity.

As lunch ends, I get paged to come to the office. Troy pretends to check something off on an imaginary clipboard. "Right on schedule," he says.

"The Spermling and your new girlfriend want a disciplinary threesome," Simone cracks.

"Guh-ross."

"Don't worry—the Spermling can't find his dick under all the rolls of fat. Your virtue is intact."

"Nice to know."

I go to the office. Miss Channing barely even looks up at me. "Mr. Sperling," she says (like I don't know), and points to a chair. I flop down. Once again I miss my Bangs of Doom; one of my pleasures in life is sitting in this very chair with the BoD shaken over my eyes, glaring out at the world from under cover.

But I have no Bangs, no hair at all, so instead of slumping down all sullen, I decide to sit up nice and straight—perfect posture. When Miss Channing looks over at me, I smile at her with my ElecTrick Sex lips instead of glowering. It sort of freaks her out. I can tell.

"Are you *on* something?" she says to me in a low voice.

I suppress giggles. "Just high on life," I whisper back.

The Spermling pokes his head out of his office. "Miss Sellers."

I stand up nice and tall and walk proudly into the Spermling's office. He lowers himself into his chair like . . . like . . .

Like something *really* fat being lowered into a chair, OK?

I sit down like I'm the queen of the world. Miss Channing, of course, joins us, standing in the doorway. Because we need a chaperone—otherwise the Spermling will try to have his way with me, ha-ha.

He just sits there and looks at me for a second.

"Well, uh, this is an interesting new look for you, Miss Sellers." I guess the latest gossip hasn't hit the teachers' lounge yet.

"Is that why I'm here? Fashion tips?"

He grimaces. "No. No. Uh." He messes with some papers on his desk. As usual, my disciplinary file is there—it's a massive slab of papers in a folder that has to be held together with big clips.

"I understand you had an, uh, altercation with Miss Powell."

I decide to give him the silent treatment for a little while. I just look at him. Let him do the talking. I'm tired of talking.

"You accused her of, well, of having an inappropriate relationship with her students." It takes him a little while to get the sentence out. I don't blame him. There's a history of this kind of shit in Brookdale. This wacko middle school teacher Evelyn Sherman, she effed Crazy J back when he was in middle school.

It was all over the papers. It was a big deal. "That's a very serious charge, Kyra."

Yeah, whatever. I didn't say she actually effed someone. I said she made all the boys *want* to eff her. But what's the diff, right? Like I'm supposed to expect the Spermling to get it right.

"You used some pretty . . ." He's looking at his computer now, probably reading an e-mail from Miss Powell. "Some pretty foul language. We've talked about language before, Kyra."

And that's a total joke. I probably have one of the cleanest mouths at South Brook because I don't say the F-word. Anyone else here drops that bomb ten times in homeroom alone.

He sighs deep down in the fattest part of his fatty body and leans back in his chair, which groans and begs for the mercy of a quick death. I wait for it to break and send him sprawling back into the wall, but reality—as usual—disappoints me and the chair lives to suffer another day.

"So, do I have it, right, Kyra? You swore at her? You accused her of sex with a student? Do you have anything to say in your defense?"

I still say nothing. Which is a feat for me, I admit.

"Come on. I always let you have your say."

Still nothing. Giving him the opposite of what Miss Powell got. It doesn't matter what I say. He won't believe me anyway. And what's he going to do, tell Miss Powell to stop being a slut? He probably *likes* that she's a slut. He probably gets turned on by her—why should he be any different from any other guy? Even if it takes him an hour to find his own dick?

And besides, she'll never, ever try to talk to me again. So, really, I win.

"Fine, then. I have no choice but to let your father know what you did."

Oh, well.

He lets that sink in, like it's supposed to scare me or something.

"OK, get going." He starts to fill out a hall pass.

Whoa. No detention? No suspension? Nothing? Really? I can call a teacher a slut and I get nothing but a call home to Roger? Shit, I wish I'd known that *years* ago! I would have been calling teachers sluts back in middle school, man!

I guess my surprise shows because he says, "No, I'm not doing anything else to you. You've missed enough school and believe it or not, my primary concern is that you get an education. If you have a . . . a . . . a personality clash with Miss Powell, we'll see if you can't just resolve it like an adult. If not, we'll look into transferring you to another English class."

He tears the pass off his pad and holds it out to me. I jump up and grab it. He doesn't let go.

"You caught me on a good day, Miss Sellers. Don't think otherwise."

A billion comebacks fly through my brain. Sometimes I think God built my brain and then tuned it specifically for the cutting comeback, tweaking it like the geeks tweak their computers for maximum game performance, only I'm tweaked for maximum put-down performance.

But I like the silent vibe I've got going, so I swallow all those delicious insults, take the pass, and leave.

FIFTY-SEVEN

T KILLS ME, HOW CLUELESS adults are.

I mean, I get in trouble just for *talking*. For *talking*.

Do they realize that there are kids doing shit a million times worse in this school? Like Troy, for example. He supplies pot to all of the goths and sells it to some of the jocks, too, which is probably how any goths got invited to Pete Vesentine's party in the first place.

There are two freshmen who've had abortions. It's supposed to be a big secret, but there really aren't any secrets in high school. Someone tells someone, who tells someone, who tells someone . . .

And I know of a kid who does heroin and sells it to a couple of guys on the football team, but only during the off-season, which cracks my shit up.

Girls give guys blowjobs in the bathrooms between classes. Kids sneak in knives and drugs. All *kinds* of shit goes down, every day.

But, hey. I tell a teacher I can see her underwear and I get in trouble for it. What-the-hell-*ever*.

Roger is waiting for me at the end of the day. He's parked right in the bus circle, right out in front of everyone. I consider going to my bus anyway, pretending I don't see him, but he gets out of the car and stands there and then my phone rings and it's a text from Roger saying, *In the car—now.*

Shit.

So I get in, even though it's *way* embarrassing because my friends see it. Everyone sees it—everyone is getting on the buses.

As soon as the doors close, he starts in, going straight to Pissed Off:

"What the hell, Kyra? You couldn't go two days without getting in trouble?"

"I'm not in trouble. I don't have detention—"

"I got a call from your assistant principal—"

"—I'm not suspended—"

"—at work and you know I hate that, so, yeah, I'm sorry, but you *are* in trouble—"

"—I don't even have to write an essay or any shit like that—"

"—sort of the *definition* of trouble, Kyra—"

"—so how can you say I'm in trouble when they didn't even *do* anything—"

"—because when I get a phone call in the middle of the day that interrupts *me* at *my* job—"

"—*totally* blowing this *totally* out of proportion—"

"Enough!" he shouts. "Enough until we get home!"

I spend the drive figuring that I could tell him everything. I could tell him about Miss Powell and her underwear and the boys with their drool and their boners and how I called her a slut, which totally should *not* be an issue because you can't get pissed at someone for telling the truth, right? And I didn't even call her a slut, not really. I just sort of *compared* her to a slut. Which is different.

But then he'd want to know *why* I was talking to her in the first place and he'd want to know what she said and I would have to tell him how she was trying to "get through to me" and all that shit. And that would make *him* want to "get through to me" and talk about all that shit and I just don't want to. I have a system, you know? I've got Dr. Kennedy and I've got my letters to Neil and I do all right. I figure shit out on my own.

So by the time we're home, I'm ready to just go silent again and take my medicine. Which is what Roger has called getting punished since the beginning of time—taking my medicine.

"Tell me what this was all about," he demands as soon as we're out of the garage and in the house.

It worked for the Spermling; I shut my mouth.

"Come on, Kyra. You were talking plenty in the car just now. Spill it. Why did you go off on this teacher?"

I say nothing. I watch Roger go from Pissed Off to Sad, Tired to Pissed Off again.

"Fine. Fine. Go to your room."

Shit. Now I *have* to talk. "How long am I grounded for?"

"You're not grounded. I just want you out of my hair for a while so I can work."

Before I get to my room, he calls out, "And I can tell you *this* much—you're not getting that driver's license any time soon!"

Whatever. Like I even need one.

I go to my room and lie on the bed for a little while. I don't get it. Most of the time when my dad yells at me, I can sort of see his side of it. It's not like I *care* or anything, but at least I can see it.

But I don't think I did anything wrong this time. Miss Powell had no right to try to buddy up to me. I didn't ask for her to be my friend. She's a hypocrite. I hate hypocrites. I called her out on that. I told her the truth, right to her face. Why should I be punished for that?

But Roger wouldn't understand that. The Spermling wouldn't understand that.

I do my homework. I spend extra time on English because I once heard someone say, "The best revenge is living well." Which isn't as cool as *A little revenge and this, too, shall pass,* but it's still not bad. I figure that the best way to piss off Miss Powell at this point is to totally kick ass in her class.

After I finish my homework, it's probably time for dinner, but I don't want to remind Roger that I exist by going out to the kitchen. I have to walk past his little home office and God knows the sound of my *breathing* might disturb him or something.

But, hey—I have something else I can do, right?

I pull the envelope out of my messenger bag. The envelope with *Schemata,* Version 1 in it.

Oh, boy. I can't wait!

The scanner's in Roger's office, but I can still go through everything and figure out the best shots to use. I flop down on my bed and kick off my shoes and put the old stuff next to the new stuff and start paging through them, comparing.

But something weird happens. I can't focus. Well, no, that's not right. I can focus just fine. On *Schemata.* What I can't focus on is screwing over Fanboy. I should be looking for the best shots of Courteney, the most Dina-like shots. And then scan them in and make up posters and shit.

But instead I keep getting caught up in the story. I keep comparing the old stuff to the new stuff and . . . God, you know, it's not just the change in Courteney. It's not just that he's not drawing this grown-up fantasy version of Dina anymore. It's everything. I mean, he really made a big effort. The artwork is stronger and more mature. More detailed when it needs to be. But it's not like he's trying to cram every panel with as many lines as possible to impress the reader, like some guys do. He's got panels where he's completely removed the backgrounds, for example, because it makes the foreground stuff pop that much more. And in the old version, he had all these cool Photoshop effects for Courteney's powers, but he's toned them down. They're still there, but . . . I don't know. I thought it looked cool before, but now it's even better. It's more confident. It's like he doesn't need all that flash to impress you. He doesn't need to overwhelm you with a million filters and gradients and all that shit. He's just got the confidence to tell his story.

Damn. What the hell *happened* to him while I was gone?

I've got these two monsters inside me, playing tug-of-war with my gut. I want to buckle down and blow him away, but I also want to call him and tell him how totally amazing, how completely kick-ass this thing is now. How he's totally taken everything I suggested, but also added in his own shit and just . . . just, made something unreal.

I don't know what to do.

But I think about Miss Powell. How she shoveled shit at me and I just came back at her with the truth. I told her the truth.

And that's what I do, right? I mean, yeah, I lie. I lie a *lot*. I know that. But I tell the truth, too. About the important stuff. About stuff that matters.

So I have to tell him. I have to tell him the truth.

I call him. His mom answers the phone and I open my mouth and then I freak out and snap my phone shut because what if she recognizes my voice from my fake hospital call today?

I lie there staring at my phone. I didn't block Caller ID. She could call right back.

Shit.

Shit!

Shit!

After a few minutes, nothing happens. I have sweat on my head. It feels weird.

I fire up the computer instead. Luckily, Roger didn't block my 'net access. He does that sometimes when he's punishing me.

I wait. It takes forever for Fanboy to pop up online.

I notice Simone and Jecca are on, too. I block them real fast, hopefully before they notice I'm on. I don't want to be interrupted.

ONLINE

Promethea387: *Hey.*

XianWalker76: *Hi.*

Promethea387: *What's up?*

XianWalker76: *Not much. Did you look at that comic book?*

Promethea387: *Not yet.*

Promethea387: *You're not doing chat-speak anymore.*

XianWalker76: *Out of deference to you.* ☺

XianWalker76: *(Hope you don't mind the smiley, though.)*

Promethea387: *No, smileys are OK.*

XianWalker76: *You should read the comic. It's really cool.*

Promethea387: *Right.*

XianWalker76: *Seriously.*

Promethea387: *I will.*

XianWalker76: *u better*

XianWalker76: *I mean "You better."*

XianWalker76: ☺

Promethea387: *I've been reading Schemata and I have to be honest with you . . .*

XianWalker76: *brb*

Promethea387: *I think it's totally amazing.*

Promethea387: *Oops.*

Promethea387: *OK.*

XianWalker76: *I'm back. Sorry.*

XianWalker76: *And thanks!*

Promethea387: *Where did you go?*

XianWalker76: *I'm gonna have to get off soon. Mom wants the phone. And she's pissed.*

Promethea387: *Why?*

XianWalker76: *She thinks I have an STD or something.*

XianWalker76: *You still there?*

Promethea387: *Yeah.*

Promethea387: *Why does she think that?*

XianWalker76: *Someone called her today and said they were from the hospital and that I had test results or something.*

XianWalker76: *She was all freaked out when I got home.*

XianWalker76: *I've been spending all night trying to calm her down.*

XianWalker76: *But she's still not sure and she's pissed.*

XianWalker76: *She's like, "Why would someone call and say that if it's not true?"*

XianWalker76: *And I don't know what to tell her except that it's not true.*

XianWalker76: *You know?*

Promethea387: *Yeah. That really sucks.*

Promethea387: *I guess you should go.*

XianWalker76: *c-ya 2morrow*

FIFTY-EIGHT

I STARE AT THE EMPTY IM SCREEN for a little while. I feel proud. I feel like shit.

I feel like proud shit.

It worked. Simone's mean prank worked. Fanboy's mom is pissed at him. He's getting shit at home.

And now I should be on to the next step—sorting through the *Schemata* pages, plotting the world's most perfect, most embarrassing, most devastating revenge.

But when I look at the pages, I don't feel anger or that little thrilling tickle I get when I do something mean to someone who deserves it. I just feel sad.

Just remember, Kyra: A little revenge and this, too, shall pass.

My cell phone beeps. *i jst 8 half a pizza*

Jecca.

What the hell is it with her? What the hell is it with me? It's not like we're in love. What *are* we? What are we doing?

I stack up all the pages and crawl into bed. It's early and I'm not tired, but I am tired of thinking.

THE DREAMING

IT'S ALL A DREAM.

I know it's all a dream.

But I keep forgetting.

And then remembering.

It's called "lucid dreaming." I looked it up once. It's when you're dreaming and you know you're dreaming, so sometimes you can actually control the dream, if you really want to. And other times you just let it unfold, but even *that* is controlling the dream because you're deciding *not* to interfere. Which means you're telling the dream, "You keep doing what you're doing." Which is still some kind of control, right?

Right?

Dreams are confusing. Like, there's a scene in *Sandman*—I think it's in *Brief Lives*, but it might have been in *Season of Mists*—where Dream goes and meets up with Bast, who's this cat goddess. And she says to him, "Are we meeting or am I just dreaming that we're meeting?"

And Dream says, "We're meeting."

And Bast says, "Well, sure, but maybe I'm just dreaming that you said that."

The cool thing is that Dream doesn't deny it. He's just like, "Maybe."

So, you never know with dreams. Like, even in lucid dreaming. Are you really controlling it? Or are you just *dreaming* that you're controlling it? And is life like that? When we're awake? Are we really doing and thinking things, or are we just imagining that we're doing them? Maybe we're *always* asleep and that's why life doesn't make sense sometimes, why weird or bad things just happen out of nowhere. Maybe that's why we can't remember *everything* that's ever happened to us.

I don't know.

But I know I'm dreaming. And I'm at Jecca's house and she says

my rents rnt hme

And even though she's talking out loud, I hear her speaking in chat, somehow.

She's wearing all black again, like she used to, but she's wearing that white lipstick. She leads me out of the family room.

com w me

I let her take my hand and lead me away. For some reason, when we leave the family room we don't go into the little hallway that connects to the kitchen and the rest of the house. Instead, we're in the social studies hallway at school. There are kids all around and I pull my hand from Jecca's.

wut r u doing?

"I thought . . . We don't want people to know . . . right?"

But no one is paying attention to us. Jecca comes up to me and leans in and kisses me, and since it's a lucid dream, does that mean I *made* her kiss me? Or is that what would have happened anyway? Is this what I want? To kiss her in the middle of school and have no one notice? And is this what the dream means—that I *could* kiss her at school and no one would care?

u thnk 2 much, she says.

Now we're on the beach, which should be weird, but it's a dream. Jecca's still wearing the same black outfit. I think to look down at myself. I'm wearing black, too. Was I *always* wearing black, or did it just appear on me now because I decided to look?

"Where are we going, Jecca?"

2 my room

Right.

She grabs my hand again and we walk along the beach. We're the only ones here. The sun is bright, but I'm not worried about burning because it's just a dream.

"Are we like the chocolate raspberry lovers?" I ask her.

She looks at me like she doesn't know what I'm talking about, which she probably doesn't, even in real life. The sad thing is that it's not just dream-speak. I could explain what I meant, but I suddenly get one of those dream-moments, when your voice doesn't work. I should be able to get past that, right? Because I'm in control. But I can't. So, am I making myself *not* control my voice? Or is the dream out of my control now?

We're in a forest. Jecca dances, kicking up pine needles and leaves.

almost there

And then it's like I see an aerial map of the whole thing, and it makes perfect sense: I see Jecca's family room and then the school hallway and then the beach and then the forest and then Jecca's room, off to one side.

She opens a door and we're in her bedroom. She throws herself down on the bed.

do u luv me?

"No." I say it so fast that I don't even realize it's out of my mouth until a second later.

She doesn't even flinch. *will u have sex w me?*

I don't know what to say. I go over to the bed and sit down and then we're kissing, my eyes closed in ecstasy and her hands on me. I can't breathe. My body's on fire. I put a hand on her shoulder, then—I can't help it—I drag it down slowly, over her breast, down her side, down her hip and thigh, then over the thigh, between her legs and . . .

Something that shouldn't be there.

Hard.

I've never, ever touched a penis in my life. How can I be sure this is what one feels like? How can I know?

But somehow, I *do* know. My hand freezes there. Jecca keeps kissing and touching, but *is* it Jecca? Is it?

I don't want to open my eyes.

I don't want to open my eyes.

I don't want to open my eyes.

I don't want to open my eyes.

FIFTY-NINE

OPEN MY EYES.

The clock next to the bed tells me it's not even five in the morning. How long have I been asleep?

What the hell did *that* dream mean? Did it mean anything? Was it just my mind messing with me? Does it have some kind of significance?

I imagine a comic book panel: I'm standing with Dream, just like Bast did, and he says: *Maybe.*

Thanks a lot, Lord of Dreams.

I'm wide awake; no sense trying to get back to sleep when I just have to be up for school in another hour.

I ignore the *Schemata* pages because I'm just not ready for that yet. I don't feel like thinking at all, so I do something Simone does—I look in my closet and just stare at my clothes. Simone calls it "sartorial meditation." Whatever.

It's all black stuff, with the new white stuff all in one corner. I move things around and more colors appear. I *do* own stuff that's not black or white. My grandmother is always buying me outfits, hoping that maybe I'll change my mind someday. I can't bring myself to throw them away because my grandma is actually sort of OK. So I stick it all in the back of my closet and I tell myself that when she visits I'll wear one of her outfits, but I never manage to do that.

Sartorial meditation does nothing for me. I keep thinking about the dream. About the way it ended.

I bet if I told someone about that dream, they'd be all like, It's so obvious, Kyra. You think you want to make out with Jecca, but in reality, you totally want to be with a guy. Your dream is saying, "You're not gay, Kyra!"

But that's not it. I know it.

Because even though I didn't open my eyes . . .

It was a lucid dream, see? Lucid. I was in control.

And I know . . .

It's not just that Jecca had a dick. Or that she somehow magically turned into a guy. That's not it.

She turned into a *specific* guy.

I know that. Even though I never opened my eyes in the dream.

I know that she became Fanboy.

Christ.

And since I was lucid dreaming . . .

Does that mean I *made* her turn into Fanboy?

Either way, it doesn't matter, I guess. One way or the other, Jecca became Fanboy and I have to deal with that.

I don't *want* to deal with it.

I don't want to think about it.

But sometimes, the more you try *not* to think about something, the more you can't help thinking about it. So I'm standing here at my closet and I'm thinking, *What would it be like? To kiss him? To be with him? To have him as my boyfriend?*

Would we hang out all the time? Would I have dinner at his house? Would I have to hold his baby sister and pretend I thought babies were cute?

Would I help him with *Schemata*? Would it get even better because of me? Would we sneak down into his room and kiss and fool around a little bit (with the door open, of course, listening carefully for his mom's footsteps on the stairs)? Would we go places and hang out and talk about *Schemata* and his dad and my mom?

Would I . . .

I wonder.

I wonder what it would be like.

What would his friends think? What would *Cal* think? Would it be *Hey, check it out—Fanboy's slumming with the psycho goth chick?*

Or *Hey, dawg, Fanboy's gettin' some?*

Probably the first one. They all think I'm nuts. And ugly. And a freak with no hair and piercings who wears all one color all the time.

But . . .

But I don't *have* to be.

I could . . .

Stop it, Kyra.

But I *could!*

I look in my closet again. I could totally . . .

I could totally go a different way. I could wear a different bra, one that doesn't compress my boobs so much. And then if I wore a button-down shirt with some of the buttons undone . . . and a skirt with the waistband rolled up so that more of my legs show . . .

I don't even think about it; I just do it. I put on the outfit—white top with my least restrictive bra. I usually button it up to the last button, but this time I undo the top two. Then I undo a third one. Black skirt that usually comes almost to my knees, but I roll it and it's above the knees and when I put on my boots, you get this sexy six inches of leg between the top of the boots and the bottom of the skirt.

I take a step back and look at myself in the mirror.

Another new Kyra. We've had Goth Girl Kyra, White-Out Kyra, ElecTrick Sex Kyra, and now . . .

Sex Bomb Kyra?

I can't even describe how it makes me feel. This weird, delicious combination of horny, embarrassed, proud, and excited.

What would Fanboy do if he saw me like this?

Would he be like Billy Odenkirk with Simone? Would he *expect* things and then walk away if I gave them to him?

What would the *world* do?

Everyone would look. I know that. I have to deal with that. Everyone would look.

OK.

Fine.

Let them look. Whatever. Looking doesn't hurt, right?

So, we would go places. And people would look. At me. With him.

And they would be like . . .

I don't know.

I look really . . .

I turn in front of the mirror. Holy shit. My ass, in this skirt, like this . . .

Damn. I have a nice ass! Who knew?

People would look and think . . .

We would go to the comic book store together, maybe. And I would buy some cool Vertigo shit and some cool Top Shelf shit and he would buy, like, *The Delectable DildoMan* and I would tease him about it, but not in a mean way, and all of the fat, sweaty, pathetic virgins in their forties who work there and shop there would be staring at me and drooling, and they would all be so jealous of Fanboy, and I would be like, *Look all you want, you sad, sad effers. I'm not for you. I'll never be for you. I'm for—*

Shit. Shit!

What the hell is *happening* to me?

I don't know. But I know what it would be like. I know.

I stare in the mirror. I thought I'd gotten it down yesterday. When I looked at myself with the ElecTrick Sex lips, when Roger said I looked nice. I thought I'd hit the right combination: Ultimate Kyra.

But now I look pretty effing awesome.

Maybe there's more than one Ultimate Kyra? Is that possible?

My cell goes off. It's Simone: *want me 2 pick u up?*

God, yes. Better than riding the bus.

Back to the mirror. No way I'm ready for this yet. I get undressed and get a shower and all that. I feel like I'm washing away the night, the dream, all of it. And that's good because I need to get rid of it all. I need it all to go away because it's too much.

SIXTY

ONCE I'M OUT OF THE SHOWER, I feel a little bit better. Some of the confusion is gone and some of the anger is coming back, which is nice because anger is easier.

And I have a lot to be angry about, after all. I don't care *what* I dreamed—Fanboy still betrayed me. He just totally forgot about me while I was DCHH and then when I came back he acted all happy to see me and put that dedication in *Schemata* just because he felt guilty. So eff him.

And Simone wore all white, even though that was totally *my* thing.

And Jecca followed Simone and keeps acting all weird and won't even talk to me about what the hell we're doing and then talks about how she's got this big crush on Brad, so what the hell?

Oh, yeah! That feels *good!* A little righteous anger after your morning shower is good for the soul.

I start pulling stuff out of my closet—old stuff. *Black* stuff. We'll title this chapter "The Return of Goth Girl" or some shit like that.

Soon, I'm all in black again, except for one thing: a bright blue scarf that I tie over my head. It goes with the ElecTrick Sex. I look friggin' awesome. My reverse smiley face is pinned on the scarf, right above my ear, and it's perfect.

When I get into Simone's car, she stares at me. She's doing Slut in Virginal White again.

"I thought we were doing *white* now."

We weren't doing anything. I did something and you copied it. "I feel like mixing things up." I shrug.

She frowns, but then pulls out of the driveway and we're off. We both light up.

"You gotta go to the party tonight," she says.

Christ, not *this* again. "Whatev, Sim."

"Seriously. Jecca's going, I'm going, a whole mess of cool people are going. You gotta go."

"I hate that shit. God, Sim! You *know* that."

"You went to the party at Jecca's the other night."

"That was *different*. That was a *goth* party. A *quiet* party. That was all people I know. I hate being around all those douchebags I don't know, all those dumb-ass popular people."

"Fine, fine." She blows smoke.

I look at my cigarette. I've barely smoked it at all. I suck it deep, deep into my lungs. My head goes fuzzy and my lungs go orgasmic. Go ahead, lung cancer. Kill me. I dare you. Guess what? You can't. I'm stronger than my mom.

THE LAST TIME I SAW HER

the room the room the room is rosevomit because
roger left roses and
mom threw up before i came in
perfect timing

("Honey?" she said
In that clouded, confused way.)

cancer had eaten a path to her brain
yum—yum cancer loves brains
like zombies
eat her memory
she has trouble remembering   me
remembering the year

(When I was eight years old, I
Had the stomach flu
And threw up in the kitchen
And then in the hallway
And then twice in the bathroom
—Only hitting the sink once)

i should understand
but I can't
fluvomit does not equal rosevomit

dead already, to me
dead and gone
seventeen months of slow death
of hospitals and
hospices and
doctors and
radiation and
chemotherapy (latin for "poison")

("Honey, come close and let me see you.")

smell of death above the rosevomit
twelve and i had never smelled death before—
—but i knew
        (I knew)
I know

this is what death smells like

dead already
why won't this g host leave me alone?
and let me g et on with my life?

she touches me
once
on the arm

before her own arm becomes
too tired
and drops to her side

("Be strong,"
She said.)

i want to run
runscreamhide
get away
from the THING
in my mother's bed
the THING
that pretends to be her

SIXTY-ONE

A T SCHOOL, I JUST TRY to survive. I don't want to go to the office today. I don't want to talk to anyone and I don't want anyone to talk to me. I want to be more than just invisible—I want to be unhearable and untouchable and unsmellable.

Of course, Mrs. Reed has to comment the instant I walk into homeroom. "Back in black, Kyra?" She says it like a chirpy little bird and of course that means everyone has to turn around and look and confirm that, yes, I'm wearing all black again.

I take a huge breath and hold it as long as it takes me to get from the door to my desk. Mrs. Reed doesn't know what to do when I ignore her, so she goes back to looking at shit on her desk. I slowly let the breath out through my nose once I sit down.

Today is a wasted day, I realize. I should have spent the night working on the Fanboy Revenge Plan. But instead I got all weak and then went to bed early and had that seriously effed-up dream and all that. Today should have been Day One of Fanboy's Mortal Embarrassment. I need to get back on track.

So.

Posters: Definitely. I'll put them up all over the school. I'll have to be careful because I don't want to be caught doing it.

Website: Sure, why not? I can get some anonymous free site and put the stuff up there. I should be sure to put the web address on the poster.

Flyers: Ooh, I like this idea. I'll print up a million of them and leave them all over the place. I could just, like, walk past the bathrooms and throw a stack of them in there.

Best of all: Get copies of everything to Michelle Jurgens, with notes explaining it all. Yes, oh, yes. I don't know where her locker is or which homeroom she's in. Maybe I'll look her up and go to her house and put it all in her mailbox or something? Yeah, that would probably work . . .

The bell rings and everyone shuts up and the announcements start and I sit in my own little world and plan my revenge.

It's gonna be a good day . . .

SIXTY-TWO

MISS POWELL TOTALLY LEAVES ME ALONE in English. I mean, it's like I've got a disease that you can get just by looking at someone who's infected; she never even looks in my direction, even when some brainiac behind me is the only one raising his hand to answer a question.

And that's all good because I'm not really paying attention anyway. I'm just making plans. Figuring out the best ways to use the *Schemata* stuff, the best places for posters, what order to do it all in. I'll have to ditch some classes, but it's not like I've never done *that* before, right?

I'm putting more planning and effort into this than I did into trying to kill myself.

I give Miss Powell a little smile on my way out of her class. I just can't help it. She does nothing. Her face doesn't change at all.

I plan on sitting with the usual gang at lunch, but Fanboy starts calling out to me from his table and people start looking. I can't just diss him in public; it'll look suspicious. I'm supposed to be friends with him.

266

Shit.

I sit down across the table from Fanboy and next to Super-Cal. Oh, joy.

"Hey, Kyra."

"Hi."

Cal grins at me. It's the grin all the girls go crazy for, but it does nothing for me. "We need you as a beard," he says.

Fanboy rolls his eyes. "Cut it out."

"Just kiddin'."

"What do you mean?"

Fanboy just rolls his eyes again. Cal laughs. "There's these rumors going around that he's gay for me." He laughs again.

"Oh," I say as innocently as possible. Shit. They're *both* laughing about it now. Come on! That was a good idea! I got Simone to spread it and everything. They should be pissed about it, not laughing.

"It's weird," Fanboy says, "because it just started up all of a sudden, this week. I don't get it." He shrugs and looks at me. "Have you heard that?"

I swallow hard. Does he know? Does he know I started it?

"No. I haven't heard that."

"It hasn't spread to the goths," he tells Cal.

"Cool. I thought I was gonna have to mack on some mo' honeys to put this shit to rest." He says it all gangsta-tough, and he and Fanboy both crack up at it.

"Whatever." Fanboy waves his hand like he's waving away the rumors, like they're just stink in the air. He doesn't care. Shit!

"We're talking about *Sandman*," Cal tells me. "We both reread it over the summer."

"OK." I try to smile, but inside I'm seething. Fanboy's eating school pizza and I want to lean over and shove his face in it. And then dump his milk on his head for good measure. On the outside, I'm all nice, but inside I'm thinking, *Destroy you.* Over and over. I picture it like comic book panels:

Panel 1: KYRA, CAL, and FANBOY are sitting at a table in the South Brook High LUNCHROOM. There are kids in the background, acting up and doing the sort of stuff kids do in high school cafeterias. Kyra sits across from Fanboy and next to Cal. Fanboy and Cal are both eating. Kyra has nothing but a bottle of water. She's smiling at them both.

    CAL: So, is it true that you've only read it in TRADE?

    CAL: You NEVER read the single issues?

    KYRA: Yeah. So what?

    KYRA CAPTION: Destroy you. Destroy you. Destroy you.

Panel 2: Close in on Cal as he leans into the table, turned to talk to Kyra.

    CAL: But you HAVE to read it in single issues! That's the way he INTENDED for it to be read! Don't you get it?

    CAL: No one was even THINKING about trade paperbacks back then. You can only really understand it if you read it in its CONTEXT.

    KYRA CAPTION: Destroy you. Destroy you BOTH.

Panel 3: Kyra, shrugging.

 KYRA: It's the same story, right? What's the difference?

 KYRA CAPTION: God, I hate you. I will DESTROY you so bad . . .

Panel 4: Pull back a little bit. Now Fanboy is getting into the act.

 FANBOY: It's the same story, but you have to imagine the monthlong wait between each chapter.

 CAL: The anticipation.

 FANBOY: Right, the anticipation. And the letter columns, which add a whole new dimension to the story.

 CAL: But they were never reprinted.

 KYRA CAPTION: Destroy you. Destroy you. Destroy you.

"So you're missing a whole level of the story," Cal says. "Like a . . . a . . ." He snaps his fingers at Fanboy. "What did you call it the other night?"

"A meta-level," Fanboy says, like we're all supposed to understand *that*.

"Right!" Cal slaps the table and my bottle of water almost topples. "A *meta*-level."

Fanboy raises an eyebrow at me and I see a new expression on his face, one I've never seen before. Never.

It's pity.

Pity.

"See," he says, "a meta-level is when the story comments on itself."

My cheeks burn. I pray my white powder covers it. I can't stand the idea that he knows I'm embarrassed.

"It's like the old Sherlock Holmes stories," Fanboy goes on, and he sounds like the worst kind of teacher at this moment, and if I was pissed before, if I hated him before, I hate him *twice* as much now. Ten times as much, maybe. "See, those stories were mysteries, but they were really designed to teach you how to read them. You weren't just watching Holmes solve the mystery—you were also being taught how to solve the mystery of the story. See?"

He smiles a self-satisfied little smile. I want to lunge across the table and rip his throat out, but his bodyguard/boyfriend would probably stop me.

Treating me like an idiot.

Like an idiot.

"It's so cool," Cal orgasms. "When you read the whole thing, you see all these meta-levels that Gaiman put in there. Like, the whole thing in *Brief Lives*, where Dream has to go to see the oracle—"

"I know the story," I tell him. My voice sounds tight and coiled. They don't notice. *Brief Lives* is my favorite part of the *Sandman* series. How the hell can he try to tell me about it?

"Well, you know how he goes to the oracle at the end, right?" Cal goes on. "And it's like . . . He's going there to find what's-his-name . . ."

"Destruction," Fanboy and I say at the same time. He laughs.

"Destruction. Right. Anyway, it turns out that Destruction

270

is hiding out on the bluff right across from the oracle's temple! It's like he's living across the street. All the oracle had to do was look out the window." Cal is laughing his ass off now.

Fanboy shakes his head. "This part cracks him up."

"I don't think it's funny," I tell Cal. "It's *sad*. All that time, Destruction was so close."

"No, no," Cal says. "Dream owes the oracle a favor for telling him where Destruction is, right? And that favor is why Dream ultimately dies. But if Dream had just looked out the damn window at the oracle's temple, he never would have . . ." And he's off laughing again.

"It's funny *and* sad," Fanboy says. "It's ironic, Kyra. You go to an oracle and the oracle doesn't even need to look into the future or far away, just across the way a little bit. See, it's—"

"Stop it," I say. They're ruining my favorite story. "Just stop it, OK?"

"I'm just trying to explain—"

"Well, cut it out. I can figure it out myself. I'm not *stupid*, OK? I'm not a *genius*, like *some* people, but I'm not stupid, either."

The table goes quiet. I drink from my bottle.

Cal clears his throat. "So, uh, Kyra. Do you, uh, do you think that the whole series is a dream?"

"What?"

"Let's just drop it—" Fanboy starts.

"No." I turn to Cal. "What are you talking about?"

Cal looks over at Fanboy, then shrugs. "Just wondering . . . do you think the whole series, all of *Sandman,* is supposed to be a dream?"

"Why would I think *that*?"

"Something we . . . well, *he* noticed." He nods in Fanboy's direction.

Fanboy sighs and polishes off his pizza. "Maybe we should just not talk about this. It's upsetting Kyra—"

"I'm not a friggin' crystal goblet, Fanboy. I can talk about this shit."

He sighs. "OK. Fine. At the very end of the whole series, that guy Burgess wakes up. You remember Burgess?"

I'm not a dummy. Burgess was the guy at the very beginning of the series—he was the son of the guy who trapped Morpheus in the real world. Morpheus cursed him with "eternal waking," which is like where you dream and you keep dreaming that you're waking up, but you never do.

"Yeah, I remember him."

"Well, at the very end of the series, he finally wakes up for real. And he tells this guy that he's been having these weird dreams, and he even talks about cats. And there was that whole issue of *Sandman* that was about what cats dream about."

"So?"

"Oh, this is awesome . . ." Cal says.

"Well," Fanboy says, going into teacher mode again. I imagine this is what he sounded like when he fooled Mrs. Sawyer with the "Great Ecuadorian Tortoise Blight of 1928." She believed him and she ended up a complete laughingstock. So now I know how *she* felt when Fanboy psyched her out.

"Well," he goes on, "how could the cat story be a part of Burgess's dream unless the whole series was a dream? There's no other way for him to know about it. It's not like he could have read the comic book! So the whole series must be taking place in Burgess's head while he's dreaming."

"I don't believe that. The series is real."

"Then why does it end with *The Wake*?" Cal asks. "The whole thing's a dream and it ends because the dreamer wakes up."

I shake my head. "No. I don't believe that."

The bell rings. Thank God.

SIXTY-THREE

BUT I SPEND THE REST of the day out of sorts and pissed off. Are they right? Did I read the whole series and not get it at all? Is that possible?

I mean, I *love* that series. I adore it. I read it over and over and over again. I took it so seriously, and those two think it's all a dream and that all the sad parts are actually funny . . .

It makes me angrier and angrier as the day goes on and I keep thinking about it. Because even if they're right, who the hell are they to tell me I'm wrong? Who the hell are they to ruin something for me, to tell me that I'm stupid and that I didn't get it?

So maybe this morning I was a little . . . conflicted. Maybe I wasn't a hundred percent sure about wiping the floor with Fanboy, but now I am. I'm *two* hundred percent sure. And I'll have to think of a way to nail Cal, too. Just because.

Simone gives me a ride home. Jecca climbs into the back seat.

"I'm only gonna ask one last time," Simone says as we roll down the windows and smoke like crazy.

274

"Thank God for that."

"You sure you don't want to go to the party tonight?"

"Please please please pleasepleaseplease!" Jecca says from the back seat.

"No. I'm not going. Get off my back."

Simone shrugs and snorts smoke out her nose. I wish I could do that. "OK."

Jecca flounces against the seat and crosses her arms over her chest. "You suck."

"I know."

We all crack up.

"I bet *Katherine* would have come," Jecca says.

Simone coughs and chokes on her smoke. "Holy shit. I haven't thought about that in a *long* time."

Katherine.

Yeah.

KATHERINE

ATHERINE WAS MY MOM'S MIDDLE NAME. When she was in college, though, she used it as her first name. When I was little—like, in elementary school—I asked her why.

She sighed. "I don't know, honey. I was in college. People do weird things in college sometimes."

So she had all of this stuff with "K" monogrammed on it, and sometimes I would wear it or borrow it and pretend it was mine.

And then I invented my own Katherine. I don't know why. It was just one of those kid things that seems like a good, fun idea at the time for no particular reason.

I was maybe nine and I was hanging out with Sim and Jecca and I said, "I'm not Kyra. I'm Katherine, Kyra's sister."

It became a game. We all worked together and we invented this new persona. We decided that Katherine was three years older than Kyra. Her favorite color was plaid. (We thought this was really, really funny.) She liked old music and boys with blond hair. She wasn't afraid of anything except for ants.

When I was "in character" as Katherine, I would stand really tall and straight. I would walk a little differently, too, sort of like the models we saw on TV.

It was cool and fun. Simone or Jecca would call the house and talk to me and sometimes they would say, "Hey, put Katherine on," and I would put the phone down and pretend to go get Katherine and then pick it up and totally channel this different person and have a whole new conversation.

Katherine was fearless. She did everything I was afraid to do. She tried out Simone's brother's skateboard (and when she scraped her knee, she didn't cry or anything). She climbed trees like a boy. She was awesome.

Eventually, she went away. Jecca and Simone lost interest in her, and I guess I did, too, but I never *forgot* her. Whenever I would run into something tough or hard to deal with, I would say to myself, *OK, just be Katherine for this.*

Katherine died before my mom died. I guess I just stopped needing her. Or maybe I absorbed her into me. I don't know if it was suicide or homicide. I mean, I killed her, but she was me, so which one is it? I don't know.

And then—this part is where it gets a bit weird, but only a little bit—soon after Mom died, Katherine came back to life.

People were always asking me why I was so depressed or acting out and shit. And some of them knew about my mom and they still asked, like I was supposed to get over it right away. And some of them knew and just looked at me with pity.

That was bad enough, but then you had the people who didn't know about Mom, like new teachers and idiots at the grocery store or the mall. People who think it's their job in life to get into other people's business and be annoying like that.

They were all in my face about, like "Why don't you smile?" or "What's wrong with you?" or "You'd be so pretty if you weren't frowning all the time."

So I had to tell them *something*, just to shut them the hell up, but I'll be damned if I was going to tell them the truth. Because who the hell are they to deserve the truth? What makes people think they have the right to impose on you, to tell you how to live your life, to tell you to cheer up and be happy and all that shit? Who the eff gave them the right?

And that's when Katherine came back to life. She rose from the grave and this time she was mean and angry. At first she was just my annoying older sister. But then I started giving her all these other problems: The asshole boyfriend. The pregnancy. The miscarriage. The depression. It turned into a sort of game— how bad could I make things for Katherine and still have people believe it?

At some point, it stopped being a game. At some point—and this is the weird part—I started feeling sorry for Katherine. Which makes *no* sense, because I made her up, but there you go. I don't know what to say about that. I started feeling bad for her. She had a really shitty life, you know? Much worse than mine, because in addition to her mom dying of lung cancer, she had all this other shit to deal with, too.

In a way, I guess that made me feel better about what I was going through. It made things more tolerable, at least.

I told Dr. Kennedy about Katherine. He sort of did this little half frown thing that he would do sometimes. He said, "Do you hear Katherine speak to you?"

Now, if it had been anyone *but* Dr. Kennedy asking me that question, I totally would have said, "Oh, God, yes! She talks to me *all the time!* In fact, she's talking to me right now, and she's telling me that your beard conceals a microphone that you're using to broadcast my words to a crashed UFO under the Chrysler building in New York."

But it was Dr. Kennedy and he was the least assholish person in my world. So I said, "God, doc, how effing nuts do you think I am?"

He laughed. "Not all that effing nuts, Kyra. Just a *little* effing nuts."

Which was fine with me, because that sounded about right.

"She doesn't talk to me. She's just this . . . I don't know. She's like this extra part of me. Where I dump shit I don't want to deal with."

He nodded. "I get that. But you talk to other people about her. As if she were real."

"Well, yeah. But it's not like I *think* she's real. I know I'm lying when I do it."

"Why do you do it, though?"

"To get people off my back."

"Does it work?"

I shrugged. "Sometimes."

He sighed. "Well, I'd rather you not resort to lying to get around these issues. You really need to confront them head-on."

"My way is more fun."

"Oh, there's no doubt of that," he said, laughing some more. "I'm sure it is. But it's not really helping you, long term."

Long term was a big, uh, *term* in Dr. Kennedy's office. He was all about long term. He was always telling me that I had to learn to distinguish between short-term and long-term benefits, that

I could just blow someone off and that would solve my problem in the short term, but it would only make things worse in the long term.

I knew he was right. I just wasn't sure I cared.

I mean . . .

Look, the suicide option is always in the back of mind, OK? It's sort of like Katherine used to be—an escape route. A back door out of this crazy place, where "this crazy place" = "life." Walking up to Death and introducing myself to her.

And if you're gonna leave the show early, do you really need to worry about the long-term effects of your actions?

I never told Dr. Kennedy *that* particular theory. It's the only thing—the only thing, I swear to God—that I ever kept from him.

"You need to develop some . . . well, some *healthier* coping strategies."

I knew he was right. Assuming I decided not to check out of the Life Hotel early, I was going to have to figure some shit out. "Yeah, I know. But it's not like I even use her that much anymore."

"You used her quite a bit with this boy you told me about. The artist. Fanboy."

I giggled. It was a serious time and a serious topic and a serious session, but I always giggled hearing "Fanboy" come out Dr. Kennedy's highly educated, grown-up mouth.

He was used to it. He sighed. "I wouldn't have to call him that if you would tell me his name."

"His name isn't important. What's important is what he is. See?"

"I do. Kyra . . ." He leaned forward. There was a big-ass desk in his office, but most of the time we sat in chairs across from each other. "I want to send you home. Do you think you're ready for that?"

That was a tough one. Was I ready? I mean, I never wanted to go into the hospital in the first place. It wasn't my fault Daddy Couldn't Handle Her. It was *Daddy's* fault. But I have to admit—even though ninety-nine percent of the hospital was a complete effing waste, Dr. Kennedy wasn't. Dr. Kennedy was the only therapist I'd ever met who even came close to getting me . . . and believe me, I've had *plenty* of therapists to compare him to.

"I guess I'm ready . . ."

"But what?"

"I didn't say 'but' anything."

"I could tell. I could hear it in your voice, Kyra. That diploma on the wall isn't for shits and giggles. I'm actually minimally competent at my job."

I took a deep breath. Confessing things has never been my strong suit. Especially when they make me look weak. But I had no choice.

"Look . . . I'm fine with leaving. I mean, I hate this place, right? That's pretty effing obvious. I hate the orderlies and the patients and the psycho bitch roommate and I *really* hate Group and God knows I abso-effing-lutely *loathe* the nurses."

"Is there a point in here somewhere?"

"I *don't* hate you!" I blurted out, and then felt embarrassed and small and young.

"Believe me, I know exactly how exalted a position that is to be in. Believe me."

He waited. I guess I was hoping he would just get it and say what I wanted to hear, but I was going to have to do it. I think he knew what I wanted—he just wanted to make me say it. He was like that.

"I was just, uh, wondering . . . See, my normal therapist—"

"Ms. Webber."

"Yeah. Her. See, I don't like her at all. And I *do* like you."

He waited. He didn't move a muscle.

"So I guess . . . I guess I was wondering . . . See, the court . . . The judge says that I *have* to see a therapist. Because of these." I held up my scarred wrists. "So I was wondering if maybe . . . if maybe you could be my therapist. Out there. In the real world."

There. It was out. God, I hated *needing* someone, *asking* someone for help.

So weak.

"Well," he said, "I figured this was coming. I don't *usually* take on clients outside of the hospital, but I do make exceptions for certain cases. So why don't I talk to the judge and Ms. Webber and we'll see what we can do, OK?"

I nodded and that was that.

A couple of days later—just a few days ago now—I was released. Dr. Kennedy took over from the orderly and pushed my wheelchair to the door himself. I hated the stupid wheelchair policy, but Kennedy made it sort of fun.

Just before we got to the front door, he stopped. I could see Roger through the big glass double doors, waiting by the car. Kennedy waved to Roger and gave him the "hang on a minute" finger.

"So, Kyra. You ready for this?"

I nodded, even though I was worried. "I just want to feel normal. Out there. Does that ever happen?"

"For most people? Nah. No one ever feels normal. Some are less *abnormal* than others, is all. Look. I have another patient. Good kid. Little older than you. He went through a lot of . . . a lot of bad stuff when he was younger. He's got a lot of resentment and anger built up. A lot like you. He expresses it differently, but the two of you are very similar, OK? And he's getting better. Bit by bit. Day by day. I see it. I've been seeing him for five years now, and it's been a long, slow, painful process, but it *does* work. The road *does* lead somewhere." He looked down at me in my wheelchair. "Got it?"

I nodded. I felt very much like a little girl just then.

"Now get the hell out of my hospital. I have legitimately sick people to take care of. I'll see you for our first session in the real world in two weeks."

I was up and heading to the door when he called out to me. "Hey, Kyra."

I turned.

"Do me a favor, will you? See if you can leave Katherine in *here*."

Just like Dr. Kennedy to blow my mind in the last five seconds of my stay.

SIXTY-FOUR

"KATHERINE'S NOT GOING TO THE PARTY, either," I tell Jecca and Sim. "Sorry."

"Party pooper" floats in from the back seat.

"I have a shitload of work to do."

"Yeah, you have a lot of catching up to do," Simone admits. Sure. Let them think I mean schoolwork when what I *really* mean is the next step in the Downfall of Fanboy.

They drop me off at home with a couple of hours to go before Roger gets there, which means unfettered access to the scanner. I won't have him standing over my shoulder, asking questions like, "When will you be done?" and "Why are you scanning all of these comic books?" and "Is that a drawing of a naked woman? What the hell, Kyra?"

I make a sandwich and grab a bottle of water, then settle in at Roger's desk with a stack of *Schemata*: Version 2 (the Public Edition) and Version 1 (the Secret Dina Jurgens Edition).

I find the panels in the originals where Courteney looks the most like Dina. They're usually close-ups of her face, which is fine. I scan them in, along with the same panels from the *Literary Paws* version. When you put the two next to each other, you can tell that the same guy had drawn them. Perfect.

Unfortunately, there aren't any naked shots of Dina herself. Fanboy didn't give me any of those pages. Maybe they never existed. Maybe he just never got to those scenes before he changed how he drew Courteney. Or maybe he's not quite as clueless as I think he is; maybe he figured it wouldn't be all that smart to give me naked drawings of Dina Jurgens.

But it doesn't matter. Because the boy just can't help himself. There are plenty of full-body shots of Courteney/Dina where she's drawn very sexy, a total wet dream. So I scan those in, along with the new version that doesn't look at all like Dina. And then I scan in the naked shots that will be showing up in the next *Literary Paws* because I figure I'll show the matching artwork first and then show the naked images and say something like, "Now use your imagination. Who is this *really* supposed to be?"

I'm almost *tingling*, I'm so happy.

I burn it all to a CD and then delete everything from Roger's computer. I am a ninja at the fine art of Covering My Tracks.

Back in my room, it's time to kick ass. I plop down at my computer and load up the CD.

Sitting on my desk, right next to my keyboard, is a little reminder card I've had for a week now. It reads:

> You Have An Appointment
> With: Kennedy
> When: 11/25, 4p
> Where: B-dale ofc. (340B Iseman)
> Referral Needed? ☐

I push it around on my desk a little bit. What would Kennedy think of this? That's a stupid question. God, that's a *really* stupid question. I know exactly what he would say.

Are you sure you want to act out like this, Kyra? Think about it. What did this boy ever do to you?

He forgot about me, is what he did. I reached out to him. He was getting beat up in gym and I reached out to him. I never reach out to people. But I did that for him. And I helped him with his comic book. I taught him things. I told him the truth.

The truth? Really?

I told him the truth about the things that matter, OK? About women and girls. About the way the world treats people like him and me.

Like the two of you?

Outcasts, OK? People no one gives a shit about. I told him how to deal. I told him to be strong and to push through all the bullshit. I told him all of that. All of that. And then he . . .

He betrayed you.

No.

He called your father. Told him about the bullet . . .

That was . . . Yeah, I was pissed at first, but he was just trying to help. I get it. We talked about that in therapy and I get that.

So, what, then? What horrible sin did he commit?

He forgot about me! God, aren't you listening to me? He never called while I was away. Simone and Jecca called me. They got the hospital number from Roger and they called. They sent me letters and packages and stuff over the summer. But from him? Nothing. Not even an e-mail or a text message. I thought maybe there would be letters at home when I got there. But no. Nothing. He forgot me. He went ahead and he became, like, cooler, and then he didn't need me anymore, so he just tossed me aside.

Is that what you really think?

Eff yeah.

Are you sure?

Stop asking me. Yes, I'm sure.

Think about it, Kyra.

I push the appointment slip aside. Great. I left Katherine behind in the hospital, but now I have Kennedy in my head to make up for it.

I go through my messenger bag, dumping out most of the stuff in it. I plug my cell in to recharge and then go through my wallet until I find the business card I'm looking for:

Eugene <u>Kennedy</u>, Ph.D., M.D.
Asst. Dir. of Mental Health Services
Maryland Mental Health Unit
Lowe County General Hospital

And his phone number and fax and shit. On the back, he wrote another phone number. The emergency number.

If you feel like you're going to hurt yourself, I want you to call me. Anytime. I don't care if it's three in the morning on Christmas and you figure I'm busy playing Santa Claus. Call me. I'll answer.

Is this an emergency?

Nah.

I'm not hurting myself. I'm hurting someone else.

He would just tell me not to do it. He would tell me that hurting Fanboy will feel good in the short term, but won't do me any good in the long term. He would tell me that revenge isn't healthy.

And you know what? He's right. But I think I'd rather have my revenge than be healthy.

SIXTY-FIVE

AM NOT A COMPUTER WIZARD.

At all.

I thought this would be easy. I mean, on TV they just scan shit in and *click-click-clickety-click* with the mouse and shit moves around on screen. It takes, like, five seconds and they're done.

Me? I spend, like, an hour just trying to figure out which program is the best one to use. None of the stuff that came with my computer seems to do what I want it to do, which is just to put two effing pictures next to each other with some text there, too. But the pictures never seem to be the same size, even though they're both the same size on the pages I scanned. So I download some more programs and try them and then mess around on the Web reading dumb-ass tutorials that are written for hard-core geeks who speak fluent Brainiac.

Shit. I would tear my effing hair out, if I *had* any effing hair.

There's a knock at my door. Shit! I've been working so long, Roger's home and I didn't even realize it.

"Kyra?"

"Yeah, come in."

He opens the door and leans against the door frame, sort of half in and half out of my room. He nods at the computer and the papers and shit piled around it. "Homework?"

"Yeah."

"Good."

See how easy a little lie makes your life?

"I was thinking maybe pizza for dinner? Or I could run up to Hunan Palace if you want Chinese?"

My Dad-dar kicks into overdrive. Roger is being *way* too nice.

"I had something when I got home. I'm not hungry."

"Oh."

That was his cue to exit, stage right. But he's not going anywhere. He's giving me a variation of Sad, Tired—a hint of a little smile.

"I was thinking, maybe . . . maybe we could talk for a few minutes."

Oh, shit. That's never good.

"Would that be OK? And then you can get back to your homework."

I look at the screen. I'm nowhere *near* as far along as I want to be. I want this done tonight. Now. "I'm really busy, Dad."

The little smile goes big, but it's the kind of frozen smile adults give you when they're about to remind you that they're the ones in charge. "You'll have plenty of time to get caught up. We're overdue for a talk."

"We talk a lot."

"No. No, we don't. We yell a lot. We give each other crap a lot. But we don't talk."

"Fine." I lean back in my chair and cross my arms over my chest. "Fine. Go ahead. Talk."

He crosses *his* arms over *his* chest. I don't even think he realizes what he's doing.

"Can you drop the attitude for just, say, five minutes? Can you do that, Kyra?"

"God! I *said* go ahead!"

"That's what I mean. That. That attitude."

"*What* attitude? Jesus. You said you wanted to talk. I said talk."

He bangs the back of his head—lightly—against the door frame. "God. Why do you have to make everything so difficult?"

"God, Dad! Are you gonna *say* something or are you just gonna bitch at me?"

He takes a deep breath, which usually is a bad sign. I usually hear the words "You're grounded" after deep breaths.

He comes into the room and sits down on my bed, leans over with his arms on his knees, and stares at the floor.

I wait.

I wait some more. He's the one who started this. I don't have anything to say. Let *him* talk.

When he finally speaks, it's in a small, soft voice: "I don't know what to do, Kyra."

"Fine. Get pizza."

I expect him to give me crap for my sarcasm, but instead he just starts laughing his ass off. He falls back on my bed, laughing so hard, I think he might choke.

OK, I have no idea how to react to *that.* I thought I had him figured out. This is new.

He sits up, wiping his eyes. "Christ, Kyra. Christ. Sometimes you're just like her. Just like her. It kills me." He looks over at me, his face shiny with the tears he just rubbed into his skin. "Do you get that?"

"I guess."

"What you just said . . . Back in college, I was freaking out over a test. I had a paper due and I had this test coming up, too, and I didn't know which one to work on. They were both important and I was freaking out because I couldn't figure out which one was *more* important, so I was wasting all this time stressing about it, which just made it even *worse*. And then your mom said, 'Let's get pizza' and I was like, 'Are you nuts? I don't have time for pizza!' And she said, 'You have time to stress. So stress with pizza.'

"So we went and got pizza and by the time I was halfway through my second slice, I was already a lot calmer and I was able to figure out what to do."

"That's a nice story, Roger."

"Stop being so sarcastic. I'm trying to explain to you . . ." He leans forward again. "I miss her, too, Kyra."

"God, I *know* that! You tell me that all the time!"

"Well, maybe that's because I don't think you believe me. Or understand it. Do you know what it's like for me? You are so. Much. Like. Her. Do you know what that's like?"

I press my lips together real tight, so nothing can slip out.

"It's . . . You look like her. Beautiful like her. Your voice . . . It's hurts, Kyra. And I shouldn't take it out on you. I know that. I can't help it sometimes. I just can't. And I'm trying. I'm really trying. But it's tough. I don't have all the answers. I can't pretend that I have all the answers. And sometimes . . . God. I see you do this stuff to yourself. To your body. The piercings . . ."

He gestures around his face. "Poking holes in your beautiful face. It's like watching your mother get tortured. Shaving your head. Wearing all black. Or all white. Whatever. It's like I'm seeing it happen to you *and* to her. It's like adding insult to injury. Don't you get that?"

Well, hell. What am I supposed to say to *that*? I touch the stud in my nose, then the little ring in my lip. "I like my piercings."

He groans. "I know that. I'm not saying—"

"No, you *don't* know that. You think it's just, like, acting out or something. But I like my piercings. They make me *me*. I got each one for a different reason. I remember what I was thinking and feeling each time. And every time I look at them or feel them or touch them, I remember those times."

He looks surprised. I probably do, too. I've never told him anything like that.

"OK," he says. "I get that. But it's still tough for me. To see you do these things to yourself. Because it's like watching your mom, but it's also you. My daughter. My little girl. So I'm seeing the two women I love most in this world . . . I'm watching them fall apart. I'm watching them . . ." Tears spill down his face. "I'm watching *you* try to kill yourself. And watching *her* die. All over again."

"I'm not Mom. I'm *me*."

"You don't understand. You're too young."

"Stop saying that! You *always* say that! I'm not a little kid. I was there, too, y'know. I watched her dying, too. You think you're the only one who gets this shit? Huh? You think you're the only one?"

"Some things you just can't understand until you're older—"

"Stop it!" I'm shrieking. "Just stop saying that! I'm sick of it! I was old enough to watch her *die*, OK? I'm old enough to make my own decisions and shave my head if I want to and wear what I want and look how I want, OK? Stop telling me I'm a goddamn child because I'm not. Not anymore."

"You *are* a child. You're *my* child. And you'll be my child when you're forty years old. You'll *never* not be my child."

I hate it when he says stuff like that. I turn away from him in my chair.

"I will never stop worrying about you. Even if Webber and Kennedy and a whole platoon of shrinks and judges tell me that you're the sanest person on the planet and you would never in a million years ever again dream of trying to hurt yourself. I will still worry, Kyra. Because I'm your dad and you're my child, like it or not. I would worry about you getting hit by a bus or getting your heart broken or getting . . . getting cancer. That's how it is, and there's nothing you can do that will make me stop worrying about you or stop loving you."

I hear him get up from the bed. I grip the edge of my desk tight with both hands. Squeeze. My eyes are hot and itchy with tears. I squeeze them, too. I won't let the tears fall. I won't.

Hear his footsteps on the carpet. Right behind me.

Hands on my shoulders.

Hands on my shoulders and I go back in time, just like in a comic book. A panel transition:

Panel 1: We see KYRA from the front, sitting at her desk. She is SIXTEEN in this scene, with a nose stud and a fetching little ring piercing the corner of her mouth.

Her head is shaved, not quite smooth because it's been about a day and a half
since she last shaved it, and she's wearing
one of her old-style all-black Goth Girl
outfits. Her eyes are closed tight and her
face is screwed up in agony and rage.
Standing behind her—visible only from the
chest to the waist—is her FATHER, who is
resting both hands on her shoulders. He's
wearing a dress shirt and a tie that's
loosened around his neck.

Panel 2: Same angle, same players, only now
it's four years previous, so no piercings
and Kyra's hair is brown and long. It's actually sort of pretty. Kyra is standing now,
dressed in all black still, but this time
it's a dress—she's in mourning, standing at
her mother's graveside service. She is NOT
crying. She is looking down at the ground,
her hands clasped tightly in front of her.
DAD is behind her, in a black suit, his
hands resting on her shoulders.

    PRIEST (off-panel): . . . commit our sis-
ter, Patricia Katherine, to the hands of God
and of Jesus, His only begotten Son . . .

I freeze up at his touch. Back to the grave. It didn't rain, but
it was overcast and people kept talking about how it was a miracle that it didn't rain. Talk, talk, talk. That's all they did. Talk.

My mother was *dead* and all they could do was talk about the goddamn *weather*. Yeah, a miracle. Big effing miracle. No rain. What a waste of a goddamn miracle. Nice one, God. Let my mom die, but make sure it doesn't rain at her funeral. Where are your effing priorities?

I won't cry. I won't.

"You have to be strong," he said to me when she was dying. "Be strong for her. Don't let her see you upset. That will just make *her* upset."

So I listened. Because he was Dad and I believed him. I believed him when he said that if I was strong, she would be strong. If I was strong, she would be strong and she would live.

But he lied. Because she wasn't strong. She was weak. She died.

But I will still be strong. I will always be strong. I will *not* give him the satisfaction of seeing me cry.

I set my lips in a line. I crunch my eyelids even tighter, willing my tears away.

"Is that why you sent me away?"

His hands shake on my shoulders. "What did you say?"

And there are no tears now. No sadness. No grief. I've chased it away with anger, like I always do. Anger and sadness are like cats and dogs. One runs the other up into a tree and leaves it there.

"I *said*"—I pull forward and away from him, twisting around to face him—"is *that* why you sent me away? Because I remind you of her? Because you can't stand to look at me?"

"What? *What?* How could you even *think* that?"

"Because you just *told* me that, Roger. You just *told* me that. You can't stand seeing her everywhere, so you got rid of me."

He backs up. For the first time, I can't read the expression on his face. How did we get here? I don't care.

"I sent you away because you tried to *kill* yourself!"

"Really? You know what they called me in the hospital, Roger? DCHH. You know what that means? It means 'Daddy Couldn't Handle Her.' It means some rich phone company guy couldn't be bothered being a *parent*, so he just locked up his daughter and let a bunch of nurses and orderlies and doctors drug her up and handle her for him."

"*Handle* you? God, Kyra—*no one* can handle you! I certainly can't. I'm surprised anyone could! You think it's *easy* being a single parent?"

"I don't give a shit about how hard it is to be a goddamn single parent! It's your own goddamn *fault* you're a single parent! *You're* the one who should have died. I *wish* you died instead of her!"

"Oh? Oh? Really? Guess what? Guess what. I do, too, Kyra! I do, too! You think I don't know that? Don't you think I would trade my life for hers?"

"You *should*. You *should* feel that way. You're the one who *killed* her!"

And that's it. That's the end of it. That's the biggest gun I have, with the biggest possible bullet. We've danced around it for years. We've said everything else for years. That he was the one who should have died. That he was the one who wanted to die. All of it.

But we both knew the truth all along. We never said it, but we knew it, and it was time for someone to say it out loud—that Dad killed her. She got lung cancer from living with him, from breathing in his smoke every day for the thirteen years

297

they were married and the years before that when they dated. He killed her.

"You killed her." I say it again. It feels wonderful to say it out loud after so long. It feels awful. It tastes like cigarette ash on my tongue.

"Stop it," he whispers.

"You *killed* her."

"Shut up! Don't you *dare* say that!"

"It's the *truth*, Dad! Why can't I tell the truth? You killed her. You killed Mom."

"Shut! Up!" And his hands become fists and I'm pretty sure he's gonna hit me, but I don't care—I keep going:

"You smoked her to death. You killed her. You gave her cancer and killed her."

He spins around and screams, and when he turns back to me, his face is blood red. "Stop it, Kyra! Just stop it!"

He stomps to the door. "You're grounded. You're not going *anywhere*."

"Oh, yeah?" I jump up. "Oh, yeah? For how long?"

"Until I decide you're not!"

"Great! That's *great*, Roger. Why not just send me away again?"

"Maybe I will!" he yells, and slams my door on the way out.

SUICIDE

'M BLIND WITH ANGER. MY FINGERS are numb with it. I can't even see the computer screen. I can't feel the keyboard.

I don't know how long I sit at my desk. I don't know how much time passes. Roger's bedroom door slammed once, shaking the house, and then silence. It's been just dead silence in the house since.

It *was*. It *was* his fault. And he knows it.

And he takes it out on *me*. *His* fault. *My* punishment.

Like everyone else in my life. I tell them the truth, I tell them about themselves, and they punish me for it. Like Fanboy betraying me. Like Miss Powell getting pissed and whining to the Spermling.

I rest my hands on the desk, palms up. My scars shine in the light from the computer screen. Yeah, it hurt when I did it, but it also felt good and true.

Maybe that's my destiny. Maybe that's what I'm meant for. If this world doesn't want to listen to what I have to say, maybe it's time to leave it.

That makes sense, right? Doesn't it?

I think maybe that's the secret that suicides know. When people don't leave a note, I mean. You've got some people who do it because they're about to be caught doing something. Or people who do it because they *were* caught. But I think that all those people who kill themselves for "no reason," all of those people who do it and don't tell us why . . . I think it's because they know the truth. They know what I know, which is this:

We don't all fit in this world.

And for those of us who don't, we have a choice. We can stay and suffer, or we can go and meet that perky Goth Girl, Death, and let her take us by the hand and walk us into what Neil called "the sunless lands."

That doesn't sound so bad. Why do people have to make it sound so bad?

Staring down at my scars, I notice Kennedy's business card again.

If you feel like you're going to hurt yourself, I want you to call me. Anytime. I don't care if it's three in the morning on Christmas and you figure I'm busy playing Santa Claus. Call me. I'll answer.

Is *this* an emergency?

I know what he would say. Do I need to call him if I already know what he would say?

I want you to take some deep breaths, Kyra. Do that for me, will you? Good. And now I want you to do me a favor, OK? I want you to promise me—swear to me—that as long as we're on the phone together, you will not hurt yourself, OK? Will you do that?

And I would. Because it's Dr. Kennedy.

And then he would keep me on the phone. And if this number is a cell, he'd probably get in the car and he'd be talking to me the whole time and I'd be not hurting myself the whole time. And by the time he got here, honestly, he probably would have talked me out of killing myself because he really is pretty good at his job.

You've had arguments with your father before. What made this one worse than usual?

My father doesn't try to deal with me. He just tries to shut me up. And I won't let myself be shut up.

And Kennedy would tell me to chill out. He wouldn't say it *that* way because he's old, but that would be the point of it all. He would tell me the truths that other adults can't be bothered to tell: that, yeah, the world pretty much sucks most of the time. But the point of life isn't to live in a world that doesn't suck. The point is to try to make it suck a little bit less.

I get it. I really do. I even said to him once, "That's what I do. I tell people shit they need to know."

And he said, "I know that. You're not polite about it, but I know that's what you do. And that's fine. And someday, you'll find someone who appreciates not just *what* you do, but *how* you do it."

All the things he's said . . . All the things he *would* say . . .

I reach for my cell phone.

SIXTY-SIX

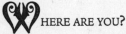HERE ARE YOU?

Jecca texts back: *on teh way to par-tay!!!!*

What am I doing? Dr. Kennedy talked me out of killing myself—for now—without saying a single word or even knowing what was going on. Which—I've decided—is the mark of a totally kick-ass therapist.

The party? I look at the time. Holy shit. It's eleven o'clock! How long was I arguing with Roger? How long was I sitting here like a zombie?

Why did I text her? What the hell is wrong with me?

Ugh. No. Be honest, Kyra. You're honest about other people's screwups. Maybe you should be honest about your own.

So. OK. You texted Jecca because . . . because you want to go over to her house. And kiss her. Feel that comfort, that warmth that you never get anywhere else. That makes you feel weak, but it's OK with Jecca because since you never talk about it, it's like it never really happened. Once it's over, it's like it never happened at all.

Now what? She's on her way to the party . . .

God, I can't stay in this house tonight I just can't. Not after all that shit. I don't even want to work on Operation: Destroy Fanboy.

Pick me up?

I wait. I wait. What's taking her so long to respond?

My phone chirps.

squee!!!!!!!!!

Good.

Top of street, I tell her. I'm grounded until parole, so I can't just have Sim pull up to the house.

I clean up around my desk, just in case Roger decides to come in here and look for shit. Which he totally would, that bastard.

I lock my door, not that that'll stop him. I stuff the usual bunch of clothes and pillows and shit under the sheets and then I turn out the light and grab my messenger bag and take advantage of living in a rancher and go out the window.

Friggin' fuh-*reezing* out! Almost Thanksgiving, and the air's like ice on my head, and I wonder what Roger'll get me for Christmas, ha-ha. Maybe a new batch of antidepressants.

I shiver and hug myself to stay warm. Even with the scarf on, my head still feels like a gallon of ice cream.

I walk up to where my street intersects with the main road. There are some house lights on and a big billboard lit up on the main road, so it's not totally dark, just colder than ass. I start dancing from one foot to the other, shivering and thinking that maybe this was a shitty idea because I don't really want to go to a party, but it's better than hanging out at home and *not* killing myself, right?

After ten friggin' *billion* years, Simone's car comes over the rise and pulls over to the curb. Jecca's bouncing in the passenger seat, waving, and when I get in the back, there's music play-ing so loud that I can barely hear Sim and Jecca shout, "Kather-ine's baaaaaack!" and then convulse with giggles.

"Turn up the effing heat!" I yell over the music. "I think my *ovaries* are frozen!"

Sim laughs and cranks up the heat. I lean back, clutching my bag to my chest, and let the hot air blast me back to life.

Jecca twists around to look at me. "What did you bring?"

"What?"

Sim adjusts the rearview so that she can look at me. "Yeah, what's with the bag? Are you camping out tonight? Doing homework at the party?"

I stare at Sim's eyes in the mirror, then move over to Jecca's, wondering what they mean, and then . . .

And then oh shit!

I'm an idiot! I'm a total effing idiot!

What the hell was I thinking? I grabbed my *messenger bag*, but not my purse. My house keys, my wallet . . . they're back home. So's my cell, still plugged into the charger.

I open my mouth to tell Sim to turn around, but then I shut up. It's too risky to go back. It's one thing to sneak out of the house and then sneak back in. That's two chances to get caught. But sneaking out, then back in, then back *out* again and then back *in* again . . . I don't like those odds.

Shit again.

I look in the bag, hoping that maybe I tossed something useful in there without thinking about it or remembering it. But no such luck. It's just the stuff that I didn't bother to dump out at the end of the day, which looks like maybe my math book and a copy of our English anthology and something crumpled up at the bottom of the bag.

Shit times three.

"Forget about my bag. Let's just have some fun tonight."

It's like the first time in my life they've ever heard me say *that,* so they both whoop and holler and we go speeding off into the night.

SIXTY-SEVEN

SIMONE IS TOTALLY GETTING LAID TONIGHT. I know this because as we get out of the car at Pete Vesentine's house, she says, "I'm totally getting laid tonight." When it comes to this sort of thing, Simone is rarely, if ever, wrong. She's like her own personal oracle; she's got a crystal ball for sex.

Actually, I'd be sort of surprised if Sim didn't get laid five minutes after walking through the door. She looks like something out of one of Fanboy's superjerk comic books—a total boy fantasy in all white. Probably wearing the white so she'll stand out at the dark party, but also because she just bought it and damn if she won't wear it, even though I've gone back to black (for now). I have to admit—she looks hot. Belly shirt that shows off her little navel ring and her tight abs, along with a plunging neckline. With the help of some Victoria's Secret engineering, her small boobs look enormous, like they're about to spill out of her shirt. Then a very short white skirt and brand-new white fishnets that she's already ripped up. The dragon tattoo threads its way through the net, like it's been caught and caged and is ready to burst free.

If I were a guy, I'd totally do her.

Jecca looks almost normal—hair still dyed black, but she's wearing it loose, not slicked or gelled. Black top, tight jeans, sneaks. She looks cute. If I were a guy, I don't know if I would do her, but I wouldn't *not* do her.

She's also the only one of us smart enough to have a jacket.

"I'm freezing my tits off," Sim says. "Let's get inside."

"Gotta have 'em to lose 'em," Jecca says.

"Someday . . ." Simone leads us to the door and we don't even knock because we can already hear the music and the talking inside.

As soon as I step inside, I regret it. What the eff am I doing here? I hate this shit. I hate these kinds of parties. Am I *that* desperate to be out of the house? I mean, please—Roger's asleep by now. What's the big deal about being in the same house when he's asleep?

I work up the guts to tell Sim to take me home, but she's already threading her away through the crowd, a slash of white in the dark. The house is lit only by a gigantic flat-screen TV, playing hip-hop videos, and some scattered lamps with weak bulbs. The whole place is a sea of bodies. I really don't want to plunge in.

Jecca takes my hand. "Come on," she says. "Let's look around."

I let her lead me. I see some other goths—Lauri and Troy and the rest. It's mostly juniors and seniors, but there are a few sophomores and even a couple of freshmen, mostly girls, and I want to warn them to get the hell out.

My ass gets grabbed a couple of times as we push into the crowd. I bring my arms up to protect my boobs. My ass is one thing, but you touch my boobs and I'll kill you.

We make it through the living room and down a hall of dancing bodies into the kitchen. A bag of chips has exploded—there are chips and chip fragments and chip dust everywhere. Jecca experiments with something red from a punch bowl.

"Whoa. Oh. Oh, God. That's *strong*." She holds her cup out to me and I sip from it. Holy shit.

Jecca downs the rest of it. I look around for something to put out the flames, but there's only beer and some bottles of booze. After a minute of looking, I find mixers and the remains of mixers—bottles of Coke and sour mix, a carton of OJ. I drink some of the OJ and pour a rum and Coke, minus the rum. Date rape victim, I've decided, is not going to be an item on my résumé.

I look around, but Jecca's gone. Great. Sim can take care of herself—sort of—but I wanted to keep an eye on Jecca. Shit.

I look around again. Maybe I missed her. It's a big kitchen and there are a lot of people in here.

A girl pushes past me, sloshing me with her drink. "Sorry," she says.

Yeah, right, whatever.

"I said, 'sorry'!" she shouts, like I didn't hear her or something.

"Yeah, OK," I tell her, planning my escape route out of the kitchen and back into the hell of the house.

"I'm Leah," she says, and holds out her hand, like we're at a friggin' cocktail party or something. Her eyes are glazed and she's unsteady, and she slurred her *sorry*s a little.

I really don't want to shake her hand, but I go ahead and do it, just to make her go away.

It doesn't work. "I'm a shophomore," she manages to say.

Oh, God. Like I even care. "Yeah, that's great. Keep killing your brain cells and you might make it back to freshman by Christmas break."

She laughs much harder than I deserve for that one. "You are *shoooo* funny!" She hiccups and her drink sloshes me again and she goes away.

Before I can move, though, someone else comes plowing right through me, not even apologizing. It's some little skinny guy, *fantastically* ugly and covered in zits, and just to prove that all types come to these parties, he's actually got his *backpack* with him, and he's carrying it on his hip, like it's a baby or a basket of laundry. Weird. At least I was smart enough to leave my bag in the car.

I can't help staring at him. He's just *so* ugly that he's almost good-looking. I decide his superhero name is Backpack Boy.

I shake it off.

Time to find Jecca. Shit. I wish I had my cell. I'm such an idiot.

There are three ways out of the kitchen—the way I came in, a hallway that looks like it leads to bedrooms, and a door that goes outside to a deck, where people have gathered already, including Drunk Leah at one end and Backpack Boy lounging right near the door so that I can't see anything. I poke my head outside and try to lean around him so that I can look for Jecca. Someone pushes past me and "accidentally" brushes my boob. I kick him in the shin.

"Hey! What the hell was *that* for?" He spins around and glares.

"You know, asswipe. Keep moving." And then, as if to prove something (I don't know what), I whip off my scarf and show him my bald head. He shrugs and goes out onto the deck.

Jecca's nowhere to be seen . . .

"Hey, can you *move?*" I shove at Backpack Boy. "I'm looking for something."

He cradles his backpack like it's filled with glass. "Sure. Sure. Don't shove."

I step outside and I finally get a lungful of air that doesn't taste like beer or sour mix. It's cold outside, but better than the body heat inside. Jecca's not out here, but I give myself a little break and just drink my Coke and breathe in the cold air. Backpack Boy stands off a few feet, still cradling his backpack. God, this world is just jam-packed with weird assholes, isn't it?

Eventually I'm done with the Coke and the deck, so I go back into the kitchen. The idea of going down toward the bedrooms is frightening. I do *not* want to see what's going on in there.

As I fight my way back to the living room, I can't help wondering: *Is there a chance Fanboy is here?* I mean, probably not. He's not the party hardy type. Still . . .

He *did* tell me that he came to a party here just before summer break. Just before I went away. Yeah. This is where . . .

This is where he made out with Dina Jurgens.

It makes me angrier than it should. Why do I even care, other than that it's just stupid? He got to make out with what was, at the time, the hottest girl in the school. Good for him. Hooray. Let's throw a parade for the Geek Done Good. His whole life just took right off after that, didn't it? He made more friends, got his shit published, got people paying attention to him . . .

And I went away. That was probably the best part for him. Who needed *me* after all that shit, right? Who'd need me after he got the chance to eff around with Dina Jurgens?

I shove—*shove hard*—my way through the crowd in the hall-way. People yell and complain and someone even throws a (mostly) empty cup at my head, but I don't care. I need to get mad, so I take it out on the crowd and push through until I emerge in the living room.

Fanboy. It's always Fanboy. God, I have to stop thinking about him, just for a little while. So what if he made out with Dina? So what if he doesn't need me? Who cares? Why do *I* care?

"Kyra! Hey, Kyra!"

I don't recognize the voice at first, but as Cal makes his way over to me, I make the connection.

"Holy shit," he says as he sidles up to me, "you should try out for the football team, girl! You broke through that crowd like"—and then he spits out some football crap that I have no way in the world of understanding—"know what I mean?"

Not a chance.

But if he's here, then maybe . . .

"Hey, is, uh . . ." I don't want to seem too eager or too *any-thing*. "Is what's-his-face here?"

"Nah. This really isn't his scene. I'm kinda surprised to see *you* here."

"I came with some friends."

"Cool. Cool." He drinks from a red cup and looks around the room. We just stand there for a while and then he says, "Hey, can I tell you something?"

I hate when people do that. Because if you said no, would they really just forget all about it and walk away?

I give it a shot: "No."

He laughs. "God, you're funny! Anyway, no, really, look—I think it's so cool that you, you know, look out for him, you know? He's a great guy, but sometimes he needs someone to kick him in the butt a little bit. And he gets distracted so easily . . . So thanks for doing that. And for—you know, last year—telling me about *Schemata*."

Oh my God and then he does it—he totally puts an arm around me and hugs me.

"What the hell are you drinking?" I ask him. Because that's the only explanation I can think of.

He steps back and grins a big, broad grin filled with dazzling white teeth and for a half a second I understand why all the girls go weak in the knees for him. He passes his cup under my nose.

"Nothin' but Coke," he says. "I'm in season. Football."

"So are half the people here."

"I do my own thing. But, y'know, I don't judge . . . Whoa."

I follow his gaze. Simone—of course it would be Simone—is dancing on a table with another girl, one I don't recognize. All the guys are cheering and hollering. Every single one of them right now is imagining what it would be like to be with Simone, or with the other girl, or with both of them. Another Simone prediction about to come true—she is definitely getting laid tonight.

Cal has disappeared. Good. I didn't feel like dealing with him anyway.

I don't see Jecca anywhere in the living room. Great. I'm gonna have to brave the Dark Hallway of Sex and the Bedrooms of Death to look for her. Hopefully she isn't passed out and being gang-raped. Because that could *totally* happen in a place like this.

If someone is hurting her, I'll kill him. That's all there is to it. Simone's different. Simone wants it. Simone deliberately puts herself in positions where guys get to take advantage of her and she usually doesn't regret it. Jecca's not like that. She's not a virgin, but she's not a slut, either, and I won't let people treat her like one.

Then something hits me right there in the midst of the booze and the hollers and the grinding, even as I watch Drunk Leah stagger past me. It doesn't *literally* hit me like the cup a couple of minutes ago. It's just a thought. That I treat Jecca the same way I treated Fanboy. I never kissed Fanboy, but I *understood* him and I gave him courage and I pushed him. And with Jecca, I understand her and I try to help her make the right decisions.

So, you know, eff everyone. All these people think I'm some terrible person because I smoke and I cuss and I'm sarcastic and there's shit I can't be bothered with, but you know what? I'm a *good* person. I take care of my friends.

And then—as if that revelation makes me glow in the dark—Jecca suddenly appears, stumbling over to me. She's what we call Drunk Enough. Like, it's not totally drunk, just Drunk Enough that you feel good and sometimes say and do stupid things. She flops to my side and wraps her arms around me.

"Kyyyyyyrrrraaaa!" she says. "I *love* you, Kyyyyyyyrrrrra!"

Drunk Enough.

"Yeah, OK, Jecca." I'm just glad her clothes are still in order and she doesn't look like anyone's abused her.

She lays her head on my shoulder and sighs a long sigh. We stand there for a million years.

"Will you do me a favor?" she singsongs.

"What?"

She looks around quickly, then leans over to whisper in my ear. She's Drunk Enough, so she misjudges the distance and her lips brush against my ear—they're slick with lip gloss, and for a second I almost turn to intercept them with my own. But I don't.

"Kiss me," she whispers, her lips flicking at my ear.

SIXTY-EIGHT

'VE GOT A BOWLING BALL in my throat. It takes four tries to swallow it down. I've gone rigid and sweat starts to gather in my pits and along the back of my naked skull.

"*What* did you say?" I whisper back. I know damn well what she said, but for some reason I have to pretend I didn't hear it. I have to give her a chance to back out.

"*Kiss* me," she says, a tiny bit louder, almost groaning it in my ear.

"Here? Right here?" We're surrounded by people. No one's really paying attention to us, but it's not like people are *avoiding* looking at us, either. If we kissed right now, someone would see. And point it out to other people and then everyone would see. Everyone would know.

My stomach twists and turns. I can't tell if it's the idea of being seen or the idea of kissing her.

"Yeah," she says, then suddenly pulls away from me. She pouts. "Come on, Kyra." She looks around quickly. "We have to hurry."

"What?"

She smiles at me. "Look. See?"

She points. Brad—*teh HOTTEST junior @ sb!!!*—is standing with a group of guys at the other end of the room. They're all watching us. Brad tips his beer bottle in our direction, like he's saluting.

"Come on, Kyra. He won't wait forever. Kiss me."

"What the hell? What the hell are you talking about?"

But I know. Even as I ask the question, I know.

Still, Jecca's Drunk Enough, and she answers the question in a jumble of endless sentences without breathing:

"It would be better if you still had hair, I think, and maybe if you wore something so your boobs were, I don't know, *out there* a little, but it's OK. It's OK. See, I was hanging out over there and I was totally trying to get Brad to pay attention to me, you know, and he was, like, *not*. Not paying attention. And they were all watching Sim and that sophomore girl and I was like, oh my God, this is my chance, and I said that I could do more than that. They're not even really *touching* each other, right, and I saw you and I said—"

Don't say it, Jecca. Please. Don't say it.

"—that I would go *kiss* a girl and Brad *finally* paid attention to me! He paid attention, Kyra!" She's still smiling and there are tears in her eyes and she drinks from a nearly empty beer bottle. "I've liked him, like, all *year*. Since the summer. And I never thought he'd notice me, but he noticed me when I said that, so come on. Kiss me."

I am . . .

I am

so

angry

at her in this moment. So angry that I could put my hands around her throat and squeeze, squeeze so hard that her eyes bug out and then *pop* out, squeeze until she chokes, her tongue going all swollen and hanging out of her mouth, squeeze until her head actually *comes off*.

The room spins and swims around me. All I hear is a high-pitched whine. I'm still sweating, but now I'm somehow cold, too.

I think I'm gonna pass out.

That would be so weak. That would be *so* weak.

I focus on that. It would be *weak* to pass out. I focus on it and it doesn't happen.

"Come *on*, Kyra. He's still watching." She leans toward me, and oh, God—those lips. I've always loved leaning up into those lips, feeling them against mine, then the soft, wet moment when they part, and her tongue . . .

I take a step back from her.

"Come on, Kyra!" She glares at me. "I *told* you. I told you, like, a million times. How much I liked him. I e-mailed you. I told you. I didn't tell you on the phone because you never know who's listening at the hospital, but I sent you those e-mails all summer long about how much I liked him. And, like, you never answered me, but that's OK because I know you were away and stuff, but come *on*, Kyra. You *know*. You *know*."

"I don't know what the hell you're talking about. First time I heard about this shit was a couple of days ago."

"What the hell's wrong with you? What's the big deal? We do it all the time."

"But . . ." I don't know how to explain it to her. No, wait,

that's a lie. I *do* know how to explain it to her. Here's the thing—
what Jecca and I do . . . it's for *us*. Whatever it is, whatever it
means or doesn't mean, it's for *us*. It's *about* us. It's not to show
off. Or to turn on some jack-ass Ryan Seacrest look-alike.

I step back some more. I'm disgusted. I can't do it. I *won't*
do it.

But if I *have to* explain it to her . . . then I guess it didn't
mean anything at all. I guess it was all just bullshit, like *everything* is bullshit.

I don't know which is worse: the idea that Jecca doesn't take
it seriously, or that she *does* and is willing to cheapen it and use
it anyway.

"I have to go," I tell her. "I have to go."

"No, wait."

But I've already turned. I'm already going. Her fingers brush
my back, trying to grab my shirt and pull me back, but I keep
pushing forward through the crowd. I bump against Cal and
Drunk Leah and Backpack Boy and other people, but I don't
care. I'm out of here. I'm gone. I can't stay here anymore. It was
stupid to come in the first place. What was I thinking?

I finally get through to the front hallway and then I get the
door open and I'm outside, like being born after labor. It's cold
outside, but I don't care. The cold feels good. My sweat could
freeze and I could die from the shock, but I don't care.

What is wrong with me? Why is it that everyone I . . . uh,
everyone I care about, you know, *betrays* me? My mom. My dad.
Fanboy. Jecca.

I always thought it was *them*. I thought it *had* to be them.
It couldn't be me, right? But maybe it is. Maybe it's been me
all along.

And if that's the case . . .

If that's the case, then maybe I don't belong. Maybe I'll never belong.

If that's the case, then maybe I *should* just check out of this world after all. Maybe in that case, there's no reason for me to stick around.

There's certainly no reason for me to stick around *here*.

SIXTY-NINE

I GRAB MY BAG FROM SIMONE'S CAR. There's no way I'm going back in there to ask her to give me a ride home. No way. She would want to know why. Besides, she's not Drunk Enough. She's *drunk*.

It's too risky to try to steal one of the many, many cars parked here. Some people are milling around outside, even though it's cold, and I could get caught way too easily.

So I sling the bag over my shoulder and I start to walk.

I walk up the street Vesentine lives on. It connects to another residential street, like a plus sign. I stand at the intersection and try to remember—did we turn on to Vesentine's street or just go straight?

Times like this I wish I said the F-word. Because it would be very appropriate and feel *really* good.

I turn left. I think I remember us making a last right-hand turn.

Roger used to hang out with this guy from work, Dave. They stopped around the time Roger got promoted to management. Anyway, Dave had this expression he used to use: *colder than a witch's tit*. I hated that expression. I still hate it, but I can't help it—it pops into my head and just runs there on an endless loop: *Colder than a witch's tit. Witch's tit. Witch's tit.*

And it *is*. It's colder than anything in the whole world out here. It must be a million below zero. With my luck, I made the wrong turn and I'll end up in a cul-de-sac and I'll have to turn around.

Or maybe I wouldn't turn around. Maybe I'll just find a little spot somewhere and sit down and then lie down and curl up in a ball and just . . . go to sleep. That's what it's like. I read it somewhere. Freezing to death feels like going to sleep, and apparently you feel real warm right before it happens. That would be nice.

Like I'm a trained dog or something, thinking about suicide immediately makes me think of Kennedy. Ha! I don't have his number with me. And even if I did, I don't have a phone. Sorry, doc. I know I promised to call you if I was going to try to off myself, but I literally *can't* keep that promise. So sorry for you.

When I tried to kill myself the first time (ooh, and Kennedy would be pissed at me for *that*—he always called it "the last time"), I thought I would really do it. But, honestly, it didn't matter if I succeeded or not. That's what I told myself as the blood started to flow and I stared at it in amazement. It didn't really matter because even if I didn't actually *die*, I would at least get to see how people reacted.

But then Fanboy went and ruined that. Because I swear to God, I didn't know that you couldn't kill yourself the way I slashed my wrists. I didn't know. It's sort of humiliating, really. Because I bet people assumed I *did* know. And they all weren't thinking, *Wow, she tried to die!* or *Poor girl* or *Good riddance.* No. They were all thinking, *What a poseur* or *She's looking for attention—how pathetic* or *Gee, look at this—I bet Daddy Couldn't Handle Her.*

I sort of feel like I should go and find the emergency room people who took care of me that night. Go to them and say, "Hey! Hey, I really *was* trying to kill myself! I really *did* want to die! I'm not a wannabe! I'm not like the pathetic girls who cut themselves up. I really wanted to die."

Too late. But when they find me frozen to death on the side of the road, they'll . . .

Ah, shit. They'll figure it was an accident. Right? Because who commits suicide by lying down in the cold?

I guess I should keep going, then.

THE LAST TIME I SAW HER

the room the room the room is rosevomit because
roger left roses and
mom threw up before i came in
perfect timing

("Honey?" she said
In that clouded, confused way.)

cancer had eaten a path to her brain
yum—yum cancer loves brains
like zombies
eat her memory
she has trouble remembering   me
remembering   the year

(When I was eight years old, I
Had the stomach flu
And threw up in the kitchen
And then in the hallway
And then twice in the bathroom
—Only hitting the sink once)

i should understand.
but I can't
fluvomit does not equal rosevomit

dead already, to me
dead and gone
seventeen months of slow death
of hospitals and
hospices and
doctors and
radiation and
chemotherapy (latin for "poison")

("Honey, come close and let me see you.")

smell of death above the rosevomit
twelve and i had never smelled death before—
—but i knew
        (I knew)
I know

this is what death smells like

dead already
why won't this g host leave me alone?
and let me g et on with my life?

she touches me
once
on the arm

before her own arm becomes
too tired
and drops to her side

("Be strong,"
She said.)

i want to run
runscreamhide
get away
from the THING
in my mother's bed
the THING
that pretends to be her

("Be strong
And don't be afraid
And be good
For your father.")

for the father who
KILLED ME
she means
Be Good because
because "Being Good"
will protect you.
rig ht, mom?
Being Good
Will make everything ok,
right, mom?

Being Good
will mop up the puke
and wipe it from your lips.
right, mom?

(Tears in my eyes.
"Don't cry,"
She said.
I hated her
For it.
I could cry
I could cry
No one could
Stop me.
I had the *right*.)

("Honey?"
Weak and confused.
"Come closer."
I had stepped back.
"Honey?"
Weak and confused.)

not my mother
my mother was not weak and confused
i will not let that be my mother
and i leave i walk away
from the rosevomit.
but i turn to her
one last time
and I say:

SEVENTY

AND AS I WALK, I think of Mom, of course. And I think of Kennedy, of course. Suicidal thoughts = Mom + Kennedy. All the time. It's like I can't help it.

I think of what I said to Mom the last time I saw her. I think of how I told Dr. Kennedy that I tell people shit they need to know. And how he said . . .

"I know that. You're not polite about it, but I know that's what you do. And that's fine. And someday, you'll find someone who appreciates not just *what* you do, but *how* you do it."

And he's right. That's the person I need. And it *isn't* Jecca.

That's a big realization for me. It's what Kennedy would call a breakthrough, and I'm sort of sad that it's happened here, on a dark, empty, cold street, with me all alone. It seems like the kind of thing you should celebrate with someone.

Ha. Celebrate. Celebrate figuring out that the one person I felt warm and safe with in the world isn't the person for me? Ha.

I guess I should have known, though. It's not Jecca's fault. She was probably just looking for the same things I was looking for. We both needed a warm body that made us feel good, and we got lucky that we had each other. I think I've known, deep down, that this wasn't anything permanent or real. Because I've always known that I'm not gay. And maybe I could be bi or something, but that didn't seem right either. Mainly because there were no other girls I was interested in. You'd think if I was really, truly bi that there would be at least *one* other girl, right?

So, sorry, Kyra—you're straight. How boring.

I see some lights up ahead. I guess I went the right way. Yay for me.

It's the sign for the Narc. All-night grocery store. Yes! Sweet!

It's past midnight, but there are maybe a dozen cars in the parking lot. I scope them carefully. Late-night shopping runs are a *bonanza* for car thieves. People are groggy and tired and out of it. They do stupid things, like leave their cars unlocked. Like leave the keys in the ignition. Or sometimes they just leave them sitting on the seat because they're grabbing their shopping list or purse or whatever and they just forget about them.

Excellent.

I wander the parking lot sort of casually. There's a little Toyota sitting the farthest from any sort of light—the nearest lamppost is burned out.

I watch it. This is a mistake. The longer I stand here and watch it, the better the chances that the owner will come out of the store and drive away.

That thought—and the sub-witch's-tit cold—drives me toward the car. I toss one last look over my shoulder, just in case, and then I just *commit* and go for it.

FAILURE

TUG THE HANDLE on the driver's side. The heavens open and God smiles down on me—the door opens.

I slide into the seat quickly, reach up, and turn off the dome light. Last thing I need is someone seeing me in here.

OK. Check the ignition. No key. No such luck. That's all right.

Scan the passenger seat. Nothing.

Calm down, Kyra. Don't panic. People sometimes leave spare keys in their cars.

I check the cup holders and the pull-out ashtray and the pockets on the doors. I go through the glove compartment.

Shit.

Shit!

OK, calm down, Kyra. Think. Can you hot-wire it?

I've hot-wired cars before, but I had tools then. And they were older cars. This one's about five years old, I guess. Is it even possible to hot-wire a car that new? How long do I have until the owner comes out?

I check the steering column. Is there a place where I can break it open? Or maybe . . . I found a pair of nail clippers in the glove compartment. Can I pry something open with them?

And then it happens.

Someone taps on the window.

I freeze.

Shit.

Shit shit shit shit *shit!*

The owner is back. Goddamn it!

OK, Kyra. Calm down. You'll open the door. You'll say, "Gee, I'm sorry." And then you'll get out like a good girl and then you'll run like hell.

I turn to say I'm sorry.

A cop.

It's a *cop.*

Busted.

SEVENTY-ONE

H E'S GOT HIS FLASHLIGHT OUT—that's what he used to tap the window. He grins at me, but it's not a happy grin.

I don't know what to do. I just totally freeze. Should I say it's my car and I lost my keys? Would that work?

"Step out of the car," he says, like we're just talking like old friends. And then: "Now."

I get out. He takes a step back. He flicks on the flashlight and shines it in my eyes. I put my hands up to shield them and he says, "Put your hands down."

I put them down and close my eyes against the light.

"Hand me the bag. Slowly."

I hand it to him. Slowly. I don't know what else to do.

"Anything dangerous in here? Any weapons?"

Unless you consider algebra a weapon, no. I giggle at the thought.

"This isn't funny, miss." He takes my bag and then I hear him take a step closer to me. A step and a sniff. "Are you drunk?"

"No." Still have my eyes closed. He lowers the flashlight, I guess, because the bright red of my eyelids goes black and I open my eyes. The light is pointed toward the ground. "This is a misunderstanding," I tell him. "I lost my keys and—"

"Don't even try it." He shakes his head. "Do you think I'm stupid?"

Well, not much to say to that. So I say nothing.

"Close your eyes again."

"Why?"

"Because I'm a cop and I *said* so, smart-ass."

Not the best reason in the world, but he's armed and I'm not. I close my eyes.

"Now touch your nose with your right index finger."

"What? Why?"

"Because you reek of booze. Now touch your nose."

I do it easily. "I'm not drunk. Someone spilled—"

"Now touch your nose with your *left* index finger."

Again, I do it easily. I also walk a straight line for him and do some jumping jacks, which I don't mind because they warm me up a little bit.

We're out here just long enough that a guy comes walking over to the car.

"Something wrong here?" he asks.

The cop turns to talk to him. I consider running. But I don't think I'd get very far. I don't think the cop would shoot me, but he's in pretty decent shape—he could probably catch me.

"Found this young lady in your car, sir. Do you know her?"

He squints at me. He's got beard stubble and his eyes are bloodshot and he's carrying a big thing of diapers. "Nope. Don't know her."

"Did you leave your door unlocked?"

"Uh, probably. This is my fault, I guess?"

"No, no, not at all. I'm taking her into custody."

The guy sighs. "Look, can we just forget this? No harm, no foul, right?"

Yes! Yes, let's just forget this!

"I just have to get home," the guy says, hefting the diapers, "and it's really late and all, and I don't want to have to go to the police station and press charges and—"

"You don't have to do any of that," the cop says. "I rolled up on her in the commission of a crime, so you don't have to press charges at all. We'll take it from here."

"Oh." The guy seems surprised. I *know* I am. Shit.

So I get put in the back seat of a Brookdale police car and the cop puts my bag on the front seat next to him and he radios in something that is half numbers and half cop-talk and then we're off.

SEVENTY-TWO

I'T'S NOT A LONG TRIP from the Narc to the police station. Brookdale's a small town.

At least I'm warm. The cop has the heat on in the car.

Here's something I never knew: In police cars, there are no lock buttons or door handles in the back. Which makes sense, I guess. You don't want tough, hardened criminals like me jumping out of the car, right?

Oh, God, Kyra. Focus! You're being *arrested!* You are truly effed. Effed beyond belief.

At least he didn't handcuff me. I've got that going for me. Which is nice.

We pull into the police station and he grabs my pack, then lets me out of the back and grabs my elbow with his free hand and guides me into the station.

I've never been here before. I don't know what I expected. I guess I thought it would be like on TV, with people running all over the place and a million cops and maybe some skanky hookers handcuffed to a bench.

But it actually just looks like an office. There are some cubicles and a receptionist's desk, where a woman sits, bored and yawning.

"Hey, Luce," the cop says.

The receptionist—Luce—says, "What have we got here?"

The cop rattles off some numbers.

"Ah," Luce says, raising her eyebrows. "A car thief. How nice for you."

"It's bullshit," the cop says. He sits me down in a chair near a desk and then—I swear to God—he handcuffs me to the desk!

"Hey!" I pull at the chain. "What the hell, man! You don't have to do this."

"Shut up," the cop says very pleasantly, without even looking at me. He's still talking to Luce. "I've got serious shit to be doing. Heroin deals in the Narc parking lot and all that. And what do I find? Junior car thief. Give me a break. Owner didn't even want to press charges. And she's probably a minor, so . . ." He turns to me. "Hey, kid? How old are you?"

I've decided I'm not talking anymore. That's what they tell people on TV, right? There's always some lawyer saying, "Don't say anything to anyone!"

So I'm not saying anything to anyone.

"C'mon, kid. How old are you? If you're a minor, this is gonna be nothing. You'll go to Juvenile Justice and . . ." A light comes on in his eyes. "Unless . . ."

He opens my bag and starts pawing through it. "If you have contraband . . ."

I laugh. Contraband. Yeah, right.

"Shit." He looks so disappointed, I almost feel sorry for him. Almost. "Nothing."

"Nothing?" Luce asks.

"Nothing. No ID, even. Just some schoolbooks and a comic

book." He tosses the bag on the desk and sits down. "All right, kid. Let's get this done and over with. I'll call your parents, you go home, a court date's set, et cetera, et cetera." He types on his keyboard. "All right. Name?"

I say nothing. Maybe if I don't say anything, they'll just let me go. He's got more important things to do, right?

"Name!"

Nice job, asshole. Like saying it louder is gonna make me answer.

"Kid! Give me your name."

I just stare at my shoes.

He leans toward me and I realize that he has absolutely beautiful blue eyes and *gorgeous* lashes. Why do guys always have great lashes? "Look, kid, I know you're scared. I get it. Trust me, as long as this is your first offense, this is *not* the end of the world. You look maybe sixteen to me, right? Am I right?"

I say nothing.

"I think I'm right. Look, you're a minor. You've never been arrested before because otherwise you'd know the drill. So you're not going into the adult system. Juvenile, first-time offense, you're looking at probation. Scout's honor, kid. I'm not bullshitting you. I call your mom and dad and they pick you up tonight. You don't go to jail. Not tonight. Not at all. You go home and your parents yell, but then you go to court in a few weeks and the judge gives you probation and as long as you keep your nose clean, when you turn eighteen, this whole thing goes away like it never happened.

"So give me your name."

I take a deep breath.

And I say nothing.

SEVENTY-THREE

AFTER A WHILE, HE GETS TIRED of trying to get anything out of me. As he keeps reminding me and Luce and the walls and the air, he has more important shit to deal with.

"Let next shift handle her," he says, and gets up. "Fine, kid. Stay here all night for all I care."

He rummages through my bag again. "You'll need something to do while I'm gone . . ." He holds up the algebra book. "Not hardly." He shows me the English anthology.

I don't say anything, but my expression says it all.

"Then you've got exactly one option, kiddo." He reaches in, pulls something out, and tosses it to me. It lands in my lap.

"If she has to use the john, let her, but keep an eye on her," he says to Luce, who nods and yawns.

And then the cop leaves and I'm left here with Luce and a bent, twisted comic book in my lap.

Great.

Great.

This is the best thing ever. Shackled to a chair in a police station in the middle of the night. No one knows where I am. It's not like this is a heist movie and I've got a posse out there ready to bust me out of jail. And sure, Luce doesn't look all that tough, but I totally bet she could still tackle me if I tried the old "Let me go to the bathroom—oops, look, I'm running!" trick.

So I either give them my name and make things worse with Roger, or . . .

Or I sit here all friggin' night and when Roger wakes up in the morning, he sees that I'm not home and . . . and he calls the police looking for me.

Shit. I'm busted no matter what I do.

OK, so what do I so when I'm in a situation like this? Well, usually I tell someone off or run away from the situation or try to kill myself, but none of those are options right now.

The only option I have right now is in my lap.

Ugh.

I hate superheroes.

CAPTAIN ATOM

PEEL OPEN THE MYLAR SLEEVE and pull the comic book out. *Captain Atom* is the title. Right. Because that's totally a name that makes sense.

The cover's still as stupid as it ever was: I guess the guy on the cover is, in fact, Captain Atom himself. Because usually superhero comics aren't *that* clever, and besides, he has this symbol on his chest that I guess is supposed to be a stylized atomic symbol. Anyway, he's sort of tiny at the bottom, holding up the massive block of stone that's crumbling around him.

The first time I saw it, I thought it looked like a million other dumb superhero covers, but now that I'm actually studying it, it's sort of different. For one thing, he really looks like he's straining, which is kind of cool. And for another thing, he's *so* tiny compared to the stone and the whole cover. Usually superjerks are huge and bigger than life. This guy looks almost insignificant on the cover.

All right. I hold my breath to avoid the stink and open the comic and read it.

It doesn't suck. Not totally. Like Fanboy said, it's got Death in it, but . . .

I have to read it again. I flip back to the beginning and read it again. Slowly, this time. Paying a lot of attention.

And then I read it a third time.

OK. OK, I have to take a second and think about this. I have to gather my thoughts. Because . . . wow.

I hate to admit it, but it's not bad. It's not *great*, but there's a lot going on here. And there are only a couple of pages of stupid fight scenes, but even they sort of make sense in the overall story.

I look at the credit box. The first name is usually the writer, and in this case, that's a guy named Cary Bates. I've never heard of him. I bet Cal knows everything in the world about him. Fanboy, too.

Anyway. It's about this guy called Captain Atom (duh!), and that name isn't as totally idiotic as I thought because it turns out that his *real* name is Nathaniel Adam and he's a captain in the air force, so the Captain Atom thing is almost like a pun. That's already much cleverer than I would expect. When he's superheroing, he has this really shiny silver skin, but he's not the Silver Surfer, duh. Even I know that the Silver Surfer is a Marvel character and this is a DC comic.

So right away I was sort of impressed because they tell you that Captain Atom just turned fifty, which is cool. Superheroes are usually these young guys, but Captain Atom is old. So that's different.

I was a little lost because this is issue 42, so I've missed a lot, but Bates does a pretty good job of catching you up. So apparently it's Captain Atom's birthday and he wants to do something special: He wants to—and this is where it's a little weird—he wants to go to some astral plane and, like, build a clone of his dead wife there and talk to her about his problems. This guy in the story makes a joke that it would be quicker than therapy.

And you know what? I totally identify with that. Not the part about making a clone or whatever, but the part about . . .

I guess if you could talk to someone who's dead, it would make things a lot easier.

Anyway, something goes wrong with the plan to visit the astral plane and instead Captain Atom dies. Which, in superhero comics, is no big deal because people get better from death like they get better from a cold. But it was still really well done. And Captain Atom ends up in a little boat somewhere with Death. Gaiman's Death. The cool goth girl from *Sandman*.

But that's not all. There's this *other* guy there, too. A black guy in funky armor and—I swear to God—these *skis*. And Death says that the black guy is *also* Death!

Now, this sort of blew my mind. She explains that there are different *versions* of Death. That *she* is Death as Comforting Release. And that the black guy with the skis is Death as the Race Everyone Runs . . . and loses.

I never thought of that before. I mean, I loved the way Gaiman wrote Death as this friendly presence, this comfort, this big relaxing *sigh* at the end of life. But it never occurred to me that Death is also something inevitable. Something everyone faces, no matter what. And that's what the black skier represents.

So then Death (the girl version) takes Captain Atom to Purgatory. Because he has to work out his sins if he wants to go to Heaven and see his wife. And that totally blew me away, because for one thing, it's a superhero comic and it's saying that super-heroes are sinners. That sort of surprised me.

And the other thing was that I realized this whole thing was about a guy who missed his dead wife and just wanted to see her. And he was willing to die and go through Purgatory to do it.

Would Roger do that? Would Roger be willing to go through all of that to see Mom again?

What if . . .

What if *I'm* the only thing keeping him here? What if he really *does* miss Mom, but he can't join her—*won't* join her—because he . . .

OK. So, anyway:

Captain Atom goes through all these levels of Purgatory. It's pretty cool because he actually meets *Destiny,* the oldest of the Endless, the big brother to Dream and Death from *Sandman.* And Destiny tells him that he has to work off his sins and Captain Atom goes to do it.

Anyway, eventually he works off his sins and he gets to Heaven, where he sees his wife. And I have to admit that the more I looked at those panels, the more I got into the book because I couldn't help seeing my dad and my mom there, even though I tried not to. I tried really hard.

And then there's some kind of mystical mumbo jumbo about how Captain Atom can't stay and then Death and the black skier show up again and reveal that Captain Atom has to return to life to fight *another* version of Death: This one is called Nekron (which is a stupid name, but whatever) and he's "Death as the ultimate opponent."

That's where it ends. Captain Atom has to return to life and fight this Nekron guy.

So, like I said, I read it a bunch of times. It took like an hour to read it three or four times.

I feel like my head's been messed with.

I mean, yeah, it's got some *Sandman* characters in it, even though it's a superhero comic. But it's not like what you normally expect from a superhero comic. And it's nothing like a *Sandman* comic, either. It's this different thing, this different way of looking at the same characters and ideas.

I always thought that superhero comics couldn't do that kind of stuff.

But, you know, *Sandman* is all about Morpheus needing to change. Right? The whole series is about how he has to evolve. But he won't. So he dies. But death is a change, so maybe he *does* change, finally.

And this Captain Atom comic . . . it's all about change, too. Captain Atom has to admit his sins and overcome them. That's change. And *he* has to die in order to change, too.

And now Death is so different. I mean the character, but also the idea—little-*d* death. I guess they're the same thing. They're supposed to be.

I was never afraid of death. Death made sense to me. Death was like Neil said: comforting. When Mom was sick—toward the end, especially—I always heard people saying that death would be a blessing. She could finally rest, they would say.

If it was good for her, why not for everyone? Why shouldn't I slit my wrists and get some blessing of my own? I couldn't find any here on earth—that much I knew for sure.

But . . .

But what if Death *isn't* a comfort? Or at least, what if it's not *just* comfort? What if Death is a bunch of different things, depending? Like sometimes it's comfort and sometimes it's just this inevitable conclusion and sometimes it's "Nekron, Lord of the Unliving!"

I don't know.

I don't know what it means.

SEVENTY-FOUR

"CHANGE YOUR MIND YET?"

I almost jump out of my skin. I've been staring at the last page of the comic book (a huge splash panel of Nekron himself, a really gross skeletal-looking guy) for, like, forever. The cop has come back.

"How long have I been here?" I ask, and then remember that I'm not supposed to be talking.

He grins. "Talking, are we? Ready to give me your name and cut the crap?" He checks his watch. "And an hour, maybe hour and a half."

Yeah, it's like two in the morning. And I'm all messed up. It's not just lack of sleep. Or stressing over being arrested. It's more than that.

It's Jecca. It's Captain Atom. It's Death and Nekron and Morpheus and all of it.

It's Mom. It's Dad.

I don't know to put it into words. All those people, all of those characters . . . Connecting. Interacting. Some for real. Some in my head.

Look, maybe in life there are certain people . . . like Captain Atom and his wife. They matched up. So maybe we match up with people. And maybe we don't forget about those people. Maybe we can't forget about them.

"Someday," Kennedy said, "you'll find someone who appreciates not just *what* you do, but *how* you do it."

And if I do? What if I did already? What if I already found that person and he's as far away from me now as Mom is from Dad, as far away as Captain Atom's wife is?

Would I be willing to go through Purgatory? Confront my sins?

Could I do that?

"I go off-shift in a half-hour, kid," the cop says, "so you better—"

I interrupt him before I can think too hard about it. "My name is Kyra Sellers."

SEVENTY-FIVE

Y HEART RACES AS HE takes down my information—name, address, phone number, all of that. Is this what "being responsible" or "taking responsibility for your actions" feels like? Yuck.

I'm not a *total* idiot, by the way. I give him my cell number instead of the house number.

"Go ahead and call your dad to pick you up," he says, nodding to the phone between us on his desk. He's still typing in the computer. I'm no longer handcuffed.

"I can't," I say, and it's the best kind of lie—the kind that spills out so easily that most people assume it's true. "He's on vacation."

The cop snorts laughter. "Hey, Kyra, you've been a real kick tonight and all, but if you think I'm gonna let you walk out that door without parental supervision, you're nuts."

"No, no, I know. I'm staying with a friend. Can I call him instead?"

He laughs some more. "You're not having your boyfriend come and get you."

"It'll be his mom." I hope.

His eyes narrow in suspicion. "Give me a name."

Oh, crap. I can't remember . . . Fanboy's last name, sure, I know *that*, but I can't remember his *mom's*—

Ah. Wait. "Marchetti," I say.

"Like the park?"

I never realized that. "Yeah, like the park."

He looks up the name in the phone book and then calls the number. I know it by heart, but I guess he wants to be sure I'm not trying to pull a fast one.

He frowns into the phone and holds out the receiver so I can hear. "Busy signal. We'll try again later."

But I know there's only one reason for a busy signal at two in the morning: Fanboy's up and on the 'net. It could be busy until the sun comes up if he's really working hard.

"Can I use your computer?" I ask.

It takes some convincing, but he finally lets me at the computer. I don't have my buddy list, but I have Fanboy's username memorized anyway. I fire up a chat program, log in, and, sure enough, XianWalker76 is online.

Promethea387: *Hi. I have sort of a HUGE favor to ask you . . .*

GOTH PURGATORY

I'T'S NOT THE EASIEST THING in the world to explain that you're under arrest and you need to be picked up at the police station *please please please* while you're in chat and there's a cop looking over your shoulder, but I somehow get Fanboy to agree to get his mom and come get me.

The cop (whose name—I swear to God—is *Roger.* Can you believe it? *I* barely believe it) sits with me on the front steps of the police station and waits with me. Now that he's got me in his computer, he seems much more relaxed and almost vaguely cool.

"Sorry if I stopped you from catching bigtime drug smugglers," I tell him.

"Nothing going on tonight. Another time." He looks over at me. "You don't do any of that shit, do you?"

"Dude, I don't even *drink.*" I think about it. "I smoke, though. Just cigarettes."

"That shit'll kill you, too. Lung cancer and all."

"Yeah, I know."

He shrugs. "I smoke, too. Stupid. But there you go."

Shit. I just remembered. "Are you gonna arrest me for smoking?"

"No. I didn't *see* you smoke. I didn't find cigarettes on you."

"OK."

Headlights flash out on the road and then a car turns into the police station parking lot.

"Watch yourself," Roger the Cop says. "Don't do stupid shit."

"I'm trying."

He squints at the car, sees an adult, and goes inside after patting me on the shoulder.

I watch the car come to a stop a little ways away from me. I can make out Fanboy's mom in the front seat. Fanboy gets out from the back seat and comes over to me.

He has this walk . . . This weird way of walking. Hands in his pocket. He walks like he doesn't know where he's going. Like each step could lead him somewhere terrible or somewhere wonderful. And he's OK with it either way because at least he'll get to see something amazing. He's all bundled up against the cold, with a hat and a heavy coat, and the coat makes him look ten times bigger up top than down below, which is sort of funny, but I just smile. I don't laugh; I just smile.

I'm all messed up, just seeing him. I'm still so angry at him. So hurt. Hurt that I was replaced.

But there's something else, too. Something that might be bigger than the anger. I'm not going to call it love. That's not my word. I don't know *what* to call it, but I know that it's the feeling I got in my drug haze in the hospital, the wanting for him to come rescue me, the tug, the pull. Wanting him to lend me a jacket when I'm cold.

"Hey," he says.

"Hey. Uh, thanks." I look over at the car. "How pissed is your mom?"

He looks over his shoulder at the car. "Not nearly as pissed as you'd think, if you want to know the truth. Betta was keeping her up anyway. And sometimes only a car ride will get her to sleep. So in a weird way, it sort of worked out."

"Oh. That's good."

I don't know what else to say.

"I asked her to let me talk to you a little bit before we left," he says. He's not sitting down. Just standing in front of me, his hands still in his pockets. He's bundled up against the cold and then, suddenly, miraculously, he does it. He does the magical thing:

No, he doesn't strip off his jacket and put it over my shoulders. It's like negative ten million degrees out here and he doesn't want to die. No, he takes off his *hat,* and—before I can move—he jams it over my head, right over my scarf.

"Your head must get cold," he says.

So, he surprises me and then I go ahead and surprise both of us because I start crying.

I don't mean to. I don't want to. It just happens. It catches both of us off-guard and I'm too shocked to cover it up or anything, so I just sit there, crying.

"Hey, uh, Kyra? Kyra, it's gonna be OK. I can . . . Do you want me to talk to your dad? Like, I could go in first or something?"

Shit. That just makes it worse. Why does he have to be nice to me sometimes? At the worst times?

I shake my head. "No. No. Don't do that. This is my crap and I have to deal with it. I have to take my medicine."

He shuts up and lets me cry a little bit. The car door opens and I figure, like, great. Great. Now it's over. I don't even get a chance to talk to him and even though I have no idea what to say . . .

Another door opens and then his mom walks by, holding the baby, who's fussing. "I'm going inside to borrow their bathroom and change her," she says to Fanboy. "So wrap it up in ten minutes or so, OK?"

He tells her that's fine and she disappears inside. Ten minutes. I have ten minutes. I don't know what to say.

So I do what I always do—I stop thinking about it. I just let it come out.

I wipe away the tears and I glare at him. "I was so damn angry at you. I hated you so much."

He just stands there, his lips pressed together. I can't tell what he's thinking. He watches me.

"I was so pissed. I . . . I'm the one who left that note on your car." Am I confessing? Or showing off how mean I can be? I don't know.

"Yeah. I actually figured that."

What?

"I mean," he goes on, "Dina wouldn't have written that. And she's away at college; why would she come back and leave me a note like that anyway?"

"And I'm the one who called and pretended to be from the hospital." Oh, God, it feels good to say it. Good and bad. That's Purgatory for you.

He sucks in a breath. "I sort of figured . . . I wasn't sure, but . . . Well, I knew *some*thing was going on. But I didn't know why."

"Why? Why? I'll tell you why. Because . . . because you forgot me!" Rage. It's back. Thank God. I almost didn't know how to live with myself without it. Being all lachrymose. Anger is better. Anger is always better than sadness.

"I was gone for six months, Fanboy. Six months! And you never called. You never wrote to me. You didn't send me a single e-mail or a text message or *anything*. It's like I didn't exist. And I come back and you're this whole different person. You have new friends and shit and it's like I never existed and you just went ahead and tossed me on the trash heap and forgot all about me and went off and did your own shit. So *that's* why. *That's* why, all right?"

I'm sort of breathing hard by the time I've got it all out. It feels *good* to let it all out. Finally.

He stares at me like I've slapped him, which I could have, which I *should* have. Maybe it's not too late. Maybe I could stand up and smack him right now.

"I called," he says, his voice low and small. "A lot. Your dad wouldn't talk to me."

And that stops me cold. Because the whole time I was in the hospital, I would ask Roger, "Has anyone called for me?" And he would say no. Well, he gave Simone and Jecca my number at the hospital, but other than that . . .

"I don't believe you," I tell him, but I'm not sure.

"I called and said I was your friend and he wouldn't tell me where you were. Because I couldn't tell him who I was. I thought he'd recognize my voice from the bullet thing."

The tears start to come back. My vision blurs. Shit! Why? Why are they here? He's lying. I don't believe him.

Or do my tears know something I don't know?

"And I e-mailed you every single day. Every day you were gone. You never answered."

And that is *total* bullshit because when I came back from the hospital, the first thing I did was check my e-mail and there was nothing from him at all. Not a single e-mail for six months. So *there.*

I'm about to give him an entire boatload of shit for lying to me when his mom comes out carrying the baby and says, "All right, guys, let's get going."

Out of Purgatory. Into hell, no doubt.

SEVENTY-SIX

SHE MAKES HIM SIT IN the back, to keep an eye on the baby. Which means I get to sit up front with Fanboy's mom, who does *not* look at me with anything remotely resembling kindness or pity.

So I stare straight ahead at the dark roads of Brookdale and try not to think of how many blood vessels Roger is going to bust when I tell him what happened to me. Because Roger the Cop has my name and shit, so I really can't avoid this anymore.

Crap.

To take my mind off it, I think about Fanboy's lies, which makes me angrier and, therefore, better.

E-mailed me every day. Yeah, right. What a load of bullshit.

I had no e-mails from him. None. Does he think I'm stupid?

If he does, he's not the only one. Jecca must think I'm stupid, too. Telling me she e-mailed me about Brad all summer long when she never did.

Wow. *Two* people think I'm stupid! And not just a little bit stupid, either. Really, hugely stupid. Because you would have to be an enormous moron to miss all those e-mails. If they really e-mailed me all the time, there would be so many e-mails that you'd have to be blind to miss them.

Wait.

Wait a second.

Does Jecca even know Fanboy? Do they know each other at all?

Because it would be really stupid for them to both use the same lie. And Fanboy is actually a really good liar, so he wouldn't screw up like that.

So, no. They can't know each other. It's not like they planned this or something.

But then . . . Hang on . . .

So if they didn't plan it, then it's just a coincidence? It's just a coincidence that they both decided to tell the exact same lie?

Does that make sense?

No. Not really.

Jecca . . . Jecca kept insisting that she'd sent me e-mails about Brad over the summer . . . She really didn't sound like she was lying. With Fanboy I can't always tell, but Jecca, she's not the world's greatest liar. I can usually tell with her. I can—

It hits me like a truck on the highway: Roger. Roger wiped my e-mail account while I was gone.

He tiptoed through my account, deleting anything he thought would upset me . . .

("Someone has to protect you from yourself. From all the crap out in the world." That's what he said to me when I came home from the hospital.)

Leaving some spam and some boring, innocent stuff so I wouldn't get suspicious.

I don't know *why*, but I get it. He went into *my* computer and screwed around with *my* files and erased *my* e-mails!

Goddamn!

That means that . . .

That means that maybe Fanboy *did* e-mail me every day.

Maybe he was telling the truth.

Oh, shit.

What . . .

What does *that* mean?

Every day.

Who e-mails someone every day for six months? When they never get a single response?

God, this is *seriously* messing with my head! I was . . . I was going to *destroy* him. The stuff I did already was bad enough, but then . . . The flyers. The posters. The website.

My stomach goes all lurchy, like I'm on a boat on a rough sea. God. If I had actually *done* that . . .

I would have wrecked him. I would have ruined him for the rest of high school. I would have destroyed not just him, but also *Schemata*. No one would have taken it seriously after that.

And I would have done it for no reason.

Because he didn't forget me.

Oh, God.

He didn't forget me.

SEVENTY-SEVEN

WE PULL INTO MY NEIGHBORHOOD and I hear my own voice—low and croaky and sick—tell Mrs. Marchetti which house is mine.

She pulls alongside the curb by the driveway. This is the part where I get out of the car, but I don't want to. It's not just that it's warm in the car. It's that once I get out of the car and go inside, I'm probably going to end up right back in a hospital for another million months because Roger will overreact *again.* And I'll never be able to tell Fanboy . . .

Tell him . . .

How sorry . . .

"Hey, Mom?" he says from the back seat. "Can we have a couple of minutes?"

It's like the boy can read my mind.

"Betta's still wide awake," he says quickly, "so maybe you could drive around a little more until she falls asleep?"

She twists to look back at the baby. "Yeah. Yeah, OK. But . . ." She faces front again, takes a deep breath, then turns to me. "You need to understand something, Kyra. I'm not leaving here tonight until I see your father in that doorway. You understand? You're not sneaking into the house and trying to avoid this. I need to know that your father sees you tonight and knows what happened."

The usual Kyra stuff bubbles up in my throat and fills my mouth. But instead I just say, "I understand."

Fanboy and I get out of the car and she drives off.

So.

Here we stand at the foot of my driveway in the freezing cold.

"I really wrote to you every—"

"I know you did," I tell him. "I know. My dad must have wiped stuff from my computer, I think."

He just nods, like that makes all the sense in the world.

"That asshole." God, I still can't believe it! "That effing *asshole*. Who does he think he *is*?"

"He's your *dad*."

"So? That doesn't give him the right to—"

"I'm not saying it gives him any rights. I'm saying . . ." He stops and sighs, the sigh a dissolving cloud on the cold November night.

"Look, let me tell you a story, OK?"

"You're always telling me stories, Fanboy."

"Well, what can I say? That's, like, the only thing I'm halfway good at in this world, you know?" He grins, and I want to fling myself at him and kiss that grin, but I hold back.

"Anyway, when Betta was born, my mom had all of these toys and things, right? Stuff you buy for babies. And I really . . . When we brought her home from the hospital, I was like, you know, she's not that bad. I mean, I was really dreading her be-ing born . . ."

"I remember."

"Yeah, but I was wrong. Because I love her. I really do. So when we got her home, I wanted to do something for her. So I was in my room and I looked around and I rummaged through my closet and I found . . . Man, this is weird . . . I found my old teddy bear. I couldn't believe I still had it. It was in a box way in the back. And I said to my mom, 'Can I give her this?'

"And my mom sort of laughed. Because, see, when I was real little, she gave me that teddy bear. And it turns out that it was *her* teddy bear, when *she* was a kid. And I was like four when she gave it to me. I don't even remember. But apparently she gave it to me and she was like, 'This was Mommy's when Mommy was little. And I saved it all these years to give it to *you*.'

"And, like, I said, 'I don't remember any of this,' but Mom says that I started to cry. And she couldn't figure out why. And apparently I said to her, 'I don't ever want to have kids!' And when she asked me why, I said, 'Because I don't want to have to give away my stuffed animals!'"

I wait for a punch line, but he just stands there, grinning at me like he's revealed something amazing.

"I, uh, think I missed the point of that story, Fanboy."

"Look, Kyra. Look. Here's the thing. She was doing some-thing nice for me, right? She couldn't know that in my little four-year-old brain, I would somehow twist it into something *bad*, right?"

"So?" This has got *nothing* to do with me and Roger and deleted e-mails.

"*So*, the point is this: Parents screw up no matter what. If you fix one thing, you just screw up another one, is all. Even if your dad had let those e-mails go through, he would have messed up something else. Or maybe one of those e-mails would have said something that would have hurt you even *worse* than never getting all of the other ones. That's just the way it is, you know? You can never know for sure. *They* never know. You're the one who told me adults were idiots, remember?"

Yeah. Yeah, I remember. "They're idiots. They're just grown-up kids with more money who listen to shitty music . . ." That's what I told him.

"They don't know what the hell they're doing. They're just trying." He shrugs. "That's just the way it is."

"What, you're saying I should *forgive* him? For violating my privacy? For making me think that . . . *people* forgot about me while I was gone?"

"Forgive? I don't know. Understand, maybe."

We both start shivering at the same time, which makes us laugh, which makes us a little warmer.

"I think we're both gonna be blue soon," he says.

"That's fine. If I freeze to death out here, I don't have to confront my dad."

He nods like he knows. But he's never really been in trouble. So he can't know.

"My mom should be back soon . . ."

"Right. Look . . ." God. Look, Kyra, you just need to *do* this, OK? Just get it all out. After Roger finds out you were arrested, you might never see him again, for all you know. So say it.

"I'm the one who spread the rumors that you were gay."

He just laughs. "Wow, you really *were* pissed at me, huh?"

"Aren't you angry?"

"Nah. Like that's so terrible? Besides, I don't care what other people think. Isn't that what you taught me? And I'm not a complete idiot. I sort of figured that out. I mean, it was a hell of a coincidence—you come back to school and then all this weird stuff starts happening to me."

"I don't get it. If you knew I was doing all of that, if you knew, then why are you even here? Why were you nice to me? Why are you still my friend?"

"Jeez, Kyra. I know that you . . . Look, when my parents got divorced, I went through a lot, OK? Not saying it was the same thing as your mom dying, but I went through a lot. I mean, for a while there I thought I was going nuts. Even worse than when you met me. So I mean, I know that you're having a tough time. And I want to help you. Because I like you. And because . . . I don't know. I guess I feel guilty. About calling your dad last year. And getting you sent away to the hospital."

"That was my dad's decision. Not yours."

"Yeah, but . . ." He sighs. "I don't know. I feel bad about it. So, I figured I'd make it up to you. Somehow."

And wow. Wow. This is so much better than him lending me his hat.

"What the hell happened to you while I was gone?" I ask, but not in a tough way. In a totally admiring way.

"What do you mean?"

"You're different. More confident. It's like you're a grownup or something. What happened?"

He stares at me like I've just asked him to perform brain surgery on me. Then, slowly, he smiles, and it's this open, honest smile that just kills me. It's this smile that says, *Hey, right now? This very moment? This is a great moment. This is a really awesome moment.*

"*You* happened, Kyra."

"I was away—"

"No. You weren't. Because I kept thinking about you. All the time."

And yes. Yes, this is *definitely* better than his hat.

SEVENTY-EIGHT

I'T'S A GREAT MOMENT. ONE OF the greatest in my life, and I feel like it might get even better, but then I hear a car and see headlights, and Mrs. Marchetti's SUV comes down the street.

He hears it, too. "Let me walk you to the door," he says.

He doesn't grab my hand or anything. He just walks up the driveway with me. I feel like, as long as he's next to me, maybe I can handle this. Maybe I can.

I take off his hat and hold it out to him, but he shakes his head. "Keep it for now. For the next time you decide to escape when it's, like, absolute zero out."

It makes me way, *way* too happy to put his hat back on my head. Even through the scarf, I can feel it on my bald dome and it's so nice and so cool to have something of his touching me like that.

His mom stops at the foot of the driveway and waits there, watching. I don't have my keys. I'll have to ring the doorbell. Roger will get up. He'll stumble out of bed. Put on a robe. The porch lights will come on and then the door will open and then I'll have to take my medicine.

We stand there at the front door. "Want me to ring the bell?" he asks.

"No. That's OK." But I can't move my arm. I can't raise my hand to do it. It's not that I'm afraid of Roger or of what will follow. It's just that I don't want *now* to end. I don't want *now* to become *then*. I want it to stay *now* forever. Even though it's so damn cold.

"Here." He takes my hand, and it's not cold out anymore. "We'll do it together." And he lifts my hand to the button. Yes. I can do it. We can do it together.

"Wait." I pull my hand away from the button, gripping *his* hand tighter. "Wait."

He tosses a worried glance down the driveway. "What?"

"One thing, first. You have to tell me something."

"What?"

"The third thing. Your third thing."

He pulls out of my grasp and goes all . . . withdrawn. I feel like he's running away from me even though he's standing still.

So I reach out and grab him. Grab the hand that held mine just a second ago. "Come on."

"Kyra. No."

"Why not?"

He looks away. Looks at the sky. Looks at the road. Anything but me. "I told you. I told you before. If I tell, I'll . . . I'll never get it."

"That's not true. That's not . . . That's like superstition. Magic bullshit. Just tell me. I won't tell anyone else. I promise."

He shakes his head.

"Please," I say. I've said the word to him before, but never like this. Never the way it was supposed to be said. Asking for something. Not being sarcastic. It's the first time I've said it to him for real.

"Please," I say again, and it's easier the second time.

He sighs and leans into me, our hands still touching, now the fingers intertwining like they were meant to, like it's the most natural thing in the world.

He puts his lips close to my ear, so close I want to turn my head just a little bit, just enough to feel them. But I stay still and I let him whisper it to me. The third thing.

Then he pulls back a little bit and looks at me like he expects me to laugh. Or to snort. And a little while ago maybe I would have. But not now.

Because you know what? It makes perfect sense. It really does.

"Me, too," I tell him. "Me, too."

He grins at me. "You ready?"

Not really. But all good things must come to an end.

But . . .

I want . . .

Oh, just do it, Kyra. Give him a kiss. He's dying for it. *You're* dying for it. Just lean in so that we're as close as before . . .

No. No. I want it and *he* wants it, but not now. Maybe another time. When there's less going on. When his mother isn't watching.

"I'm ready," I tell him, and I'm surprised that it's the truth.

Together, we reach out for the doorbell, our hands tight. I unfurl my index finger and he unfurls his and we both push the button. Through the door, I hear the muted chime.

"Thanks," I tell him.

"Thanks to you, too," he says, then lets go of my hand and

stands there for just a second—hug her? kiss her? no, not yet—and starts to walk down the drive.

He's halfway down when I call out to him in a loud whisper.

"What?" he asks, turning around.

"Hey. So, uh, I know that you hate 'Donnie' and all that, but I was thinking . . . Maybe it would be cool if I called you Donald. Or just Don."

He chuckles. "I don't know. I was kinda getting used to Fanboy."

I flip him the bird, but I'm smiling. "In that case, I'm *definitely* switching to Don."

He laughs and goes to the car and I hear footsteps inside and the outside lights come on and I turn to the door and steel myself to take my medicine.

THE LAST TIME I SAW HER

the room the room the room is rosevomit because
roger left roses and
mom threw up before i came in
perfect timing

("Honey?" she said
In that clouded, confused way.)

cancer had eaten a path to her brain
yum—yum cancer loves brains
like zombies
eat her memory
she has trouble remembering me
remembering the year

(When I was eight years old, I
Had the stomach flu
And threw up in the kitchen
And then in the hallway
And then twice in the bathroom
—Only hitting the sink once)

i should understand
but I can't
fluvomit does not equal rosevomit

dead already, to me
dead and gone
seventeen months of slow death
of hospitals and
hospices and
doctors and
radiation and
chemotherapy (latin for "poison")

("Honey, come close and let me see you.")

smell of death above the rosevomit
twelve and i had never smelled death before—
—but i knew
        (I knew)
I know

this is what death smells like

dead already
why won't this g host leave me alone?
and let me g et on with my life?

she touches me

once
on the arm
before her own arm becomes
too tired
and drops to her side

("Be strong,"
She said.)

i want to run
runscreamhide
get away
from the THING
in my mother's bed
the THING
that pretends to be her

("Be strong
And don't be afraid
And be good
For your father.")

for the father who
KILLED ME
she means
Be Good because
because "Being Good"
will protect you.
right, mom?
Being Good

WIII make everything OK
right, mom?
Being Good
will mop up the puke
and wipe it from your lips.
right, Mom?

(Tears in my eyes.
"Don't cry,"
She said.
I hated her
For it.
I could cry
I could cry
No one could
Stop me.
I had the *right*.)

("Honey?"
Weak and confused.
"Come closer."
I had stepped back
"Honey?"
Weak and confused.)

not my mother
my mother was not weak and confused
i will not let that be my mother
and i leave i walk away
from the rosevomit.

371

but i turn to her
one last time
and i say:

"Fuck off and die."

SEVENTY-NINE

AND SHE DID. THAT NIGHT.

Dear Neil,

I have a secret to tell you.

I haven't sent any of these letters to you.

You don't know that because, well, I haven't sent them. So you don't know they exist, so you can't miss them.

Which is weird, because you would think that the opposite of *you* not knowing I didn't send them would be you *knowing* I didn't send them. But it isn't in this case. And that's strange.

So why did I write these letters if I never sent any of them? Wow. That's a long story, but I'll tell it anyway.

It all started in the hospital, when I was DCHH. In my first session with Dr. Kennedy. It was a long session.

Time is a funny thing in the hospital. In the mental ward. You lose track of it easily. I mean, they keep things pretty regimented, but you still lose track of time. Because every day is the same, pretty much. And between the drugs and the sameness, it's easy to forget the hour, the day, the month.

That first session was a couple of hours. Dr. Kennedy had talked to Ms. Webber, who was my usual, court-appointed therapist, the woman I'd been seeing for years, ever since I tried to kill myself by slitting my wrists the wrong way. I didn't like Webber. She was too cheery. She was too upbeat.

Kennedy, though . . . Right from the moment I met him, I could tell he was different. He was no-nonsense. He wasn't upbeat. He wasn't downbeat, either. I wish there was a word for what he was. I guess the word *should* be *beat* (ha, ha), but that's not it.

He was a realist, I guess, even though that doesn't say it all.

So partway through that first session, Kennedy suddenly says, "You hate your mother."

And I was like, "Shut the eff up. I don't hate my mother. I hate my *father*. And she's dead anyway."

And he dropped it, but he kept coming back to it, circling it like . . . Like . . . You know how you can have something in, say, the bathtub? Like a sponge? And you pull the plug and the water starts to drain out and you figure the sponge would head straight for the drain, but instead it takes its time getting there and when it *does* get there, it circles for a while before finally hitting the drain? You know what I mean?

That's how Kennedy was. He took his time. And eventually he got there.

"I don't hate my mom," I told him again.

"I think you do. That's what I'm hearing. A lot of anger. And that's perfectly fine. It's OK to be angry. It's OK to hate."

He was the first adult—hell, the first *person*—in my life who told me that it was OK to feel those emotions. The first person who didn't try to get me to swallow them or purge them. That was when I knew—that was *how* I knew—that I'd been right, that Kennedy really was different.

"So you hate her," he went on.

And I had to admit it. "Yeah. I guess." It felt bad and good at the same time to say it. I wasn't sure if God existed or not (still not sure, if you want to know the truth), but I figured that there was a pretty good chance he'd strike me dead right there for saying that.

"Why do you have trouble saying it?" he asked me.

And, like, duh! "Because it's bad. It's wrong."

"Because she left you," he said. "I'm not saying you *always* hated her. Just when she got sick. Right when you needed her the most."

"It's not like she had a choice," I told him. And I felt like complete shit, because he was right. He was right, it was true, and the truth made me look like such a weak, pathetic, self-absorbed, selfish bitch.

"She didn't have a choice," I said again. "Roger's the one who smoked. She just got cancer."

"But you blame her for it."

"No."

"Then why do you hate her? Why are you so angry?"

"I don't know. I don't want to talk about this." I still had the Bangs of Doom at that point, so I sort of flipped them over my eyes and sank down into my chair, and I figured that was that.

But he just leaned back in his chair and said, "I have an idea, Kyra. It's going to sound a little bit strange, but I'd like you to play along, OK?"

So, here's *another* secret. I'm just full of secrets today, huh?

The other secret is what Dr. Kennedy said next. His big idea.

See, I wasn't supposed to be writing letters to you in the first place anyway.

Kennedy wanted me to write letters to my *mom*. He's a pretty smart guy, but you know what? I thought that was a pretty stupid idea. Especially for such a smart guy. Because my mom is dead.

"The letters aren't for her, Kyra. They're for you."

Well, that's fine and all, but it's still stupid. What's the point of writing a letter to someone who will never, ever get to read it?

So I thought about it. Because he asked nicely. When we finished up that session, I went back to my room and blocked out the psycho-bitch roommate and thought about it. I'm not dumb, you know. I know that I'm not the smartest person in the world, but I'm not an idiot either. I just don't like school. I don't like sitting there all day while people who think they're smarter than me blather on and on and on. It's not that my teachers are smarter than me. They've just memorized more. Which is no big deal, especially because they're older and they've been to college and stuff, and you have to memorize all kinds of shit in college.

So I thought about it. (Huh. I started two paragraphs the same way.) And I got the point of the letters—it's supposed to help me work shit out, sort of like therapy, only with just me talking.

I was OK with the idea of writing letters. I don't mind writing. I used to write really bad, really shitty poetry, right around when Mom died. So writing is fine.

But I decided that I couldn't write to Mom. And I sure as hell wouldn't write to my dad, because he's alive and if I wanted to say something to him, I would just go say it, you know?

And I thought about you, Neil. About your work. About how much I love it. Because it's like you only have your own life, you know, but it's like you understand other people's lives. That's just amazing.

So I thought and I thought, and I thought, I'll write to Neil

Gaiman. That's what I'll do. Because if anyone in the world could understand what I'm thinking and feeling, I bet it would be him.

Originally, I was going to write e-mails even though Dr. Kennedy said I should write actual letters. He's old school, I guess. I wasn't going to do that, though. E-mail is fine. But they only let us use the computer for, like, an hour a day in the hospital and there's always someone looking over your shoulder and there's no e-mail anyway, so I decided I would have to do actual letters. And since I was going to do that, I figured I might as well go all the way and actually write them by hand, with pen and paper, like in the old days.

Whew. Now that I'm home, I write these on my computer, but it's still tiring. Especially this one, which is really, really long.

I didn't believe in this letter-writing idea at first, but I have to admit—it's helped me think about things. It's helped me organize my thoughts.

When I first read *Sandman* and I first saw the whole goth thing, something about it *spoke* to me and I couldn't help it. I thought that if I did it and did it *my* way, then it would mean something different from what it does for the rest of the world. But it didn't matter. Everyone just saw the black and they thought goth and they didn't get it. So now I've done something more extreme. Something my *own*.

And then, of course, other people copy me.

But, you know what? That's OK. Because I've realized that maybe I don't care about that. And that they can't copy me if they don't know what to expect.

It's weird, Neil. Because your work has meant so much to me ever since I discovered it. It was like a special herb or bandage I found right when I was hurt and sick and needing it the most. And I loved it. It helped me. And now I wonder if I ever really understood it. Part of it is Fanboy and Cal talking about it, I guess. Like, did you really mean to end *Sandman* sooner than you did? What stories would we not have gotten if you'd stuck to your original plan? *Dream Country*? *A Game of You*? What would have gone away and never been told?

Or would you have told all the same stories, just shorter? In that case, which *details* would have been lost?

But the more I think about that, the more I realize it doesn't matter. Because the lesson I get from all of this is that you didn't have it all figured out from the start. You rolled with the punches.

And maybe that's what *I* need to do.

I learned a lot from reading your comics. From thinking about them.

But it's weird, because tonight I learned a lot from another comic book. It wasn't one of yours, but it had some of your characters in it.

Here's the thing: In your comics, Death (you know, the big *D*, like my cup-size, LOL) is comforting and cool. And that's great.

But that's just Death herself. It's not death (with a little *d*), the actual, you know, *event*. You made her up and she's the person or the thing or the whatever that helps us get through the door from being alive to being dead, right? She isn't actually *being* dead, right? I think I've got this straight.

That Captain Atom comic made me realize that actually being dead might not be all comforting and calm, you know? Even if a nice person with a perky smile and a cool outfit greets you. Being dead might actually suck. It might be a lot of work. And if that's the case, then maybe . . . maybe I should do the work here and now, while I'm alive, so that maybe someday—like a million years from now—I can relax and enjoy being dead.

That's sort of what I learned tonight.

Oh. One last secret:

This will be the last time I write to you.

I'm not sending this one, either.

Dear Mom,

It's been a while. Sorry I haven't written until now.

It's so late at night that it's early in the morning. I did something pretty stupid tonight (or last night, I guess) and I got caught. Don't worry. It's all going to work out.

Still, I was up for hours talking to Dad and then I did some writing to someone else and now I'm writing to you. I'm going to have to get some sleep soon, but I wanted to write this while I was thinking it.

And wow. Now that I'm actually sitting here at the computer, typing, I don't know what to say. Dr. Kennedy was right—it's a good idea to write to you. But it's also scary. Because there's so much to say. And I don't want to get it wrong, which is weird because you're dead, so it's not like I can really send this to you. It's not like you can really read it.

But maybe you can. I feel like you can. Like you can read it while I write it. Is that weird? Probably.

I'm OK with weird, though. If you've been watching over me since you died, you know that I'm OK with weird.

I'm sorry, Mom.

I'm crying while I'm typing this. I want to tell you that so you'll understand if there are any typos.

I'm sorry.

Not just for saying what I said the last time I saw you. Not just for that.

I'm sorry for hating you.

I hated you before you died and then you died and I *really* hated you after that.

I'm sorry.

One time you told me that the opposite of love isn't hate. And I didn't understand that, but I think I do now. Because if you hate someone, you must still care, right? You have to care a little bit; otherwise you would just ignore them and forget they even live. Or lived.

So maybe . . . Look, I'm sorry I hated you, but maybe—once you died—maybe that was my way of keeping you alive.

I think it was *easier* to hate you. Like, if I hated you, then I didn't have to be so sad. And that was better for me.

But even though I hated you, I still loved you. So I guess it's possible to love and loathe at the same time. It's like when you were dying, I was all, "Thank God she's dying" and "What am I going to do without her?" at the same time.

Does that make any sense?

It makes a weird sort of sense to me.

I only let myself think of the bad things. The times you criticized me. The times you made me change clothes when I liked my outfit the way it was. The times you made me do things I didn't want to do, things I didn't see any sense in doing. It was easier to think of *those* things and hate you.

So when I sat down to write this letter, I forced myself to think of my favorite memory of you. I wouldn't let myself start until I had that memory, until it was strong and bright and bold in my mind.

I thought it would take a long time, but it didn't. Once I let it, it popped right into my head.

It was brushing your hair, Mom.

Do you remember? When I was a little girl, you would sit on the edge of the bed at night and I would get up on the bed on my knees behind you and brush your hair with the big paddle brush. Fifty strokes on the right, then fifty on the left. We would count them together.

I loved those times. When did we stop doing that?

I don't remember.

Why did we stop?

I don't know that, either.

But I remember this: I remember your hair falling out from the chemo. And I remember those memories of brushing your hair each night hitting me suddenly, powerfully, like bullets in my mind, in my soul, in my heart. I had forgotten about brushing your hair until suddenly there was no hair to brush anymore.

And then I wished for it to come back. I wished for me to be a little girl on her knees behind her mommy, brushing her hair and counting to fifty . . .

And then I hated you.

You were so sick. And I was growing up and I needed you, but you were dying. So I hated you. And I hated you even more when you died, when you left me, left me all alone. Yes, alone, because Dad wasn't even alive at that point. It's like he died when you died, and by the time he came back to life, it was too late.

Am I a terrible person for thinking these things? I don't

know. I hope not. Because it feels good to finally write them down, to say them to you.

God, Dr. Kennedy is a *genius*.

I promised myself that I would be honest with you in this letter, so there are some things I need to tell you. Three things. Three things that I need to tell you more than anything.

First of all: There's this girl. Jecca. You remember Jecca. She used to come over to the house. She was just plain old Jessica back then. We started calling her Jecca after you died.

Anyway, for a little while there I thought maybe I was falling in love with her. But I wasn't. It wasn't that at all. Because in writing this letter, I realized where this whole thing with Jecca started, *how* it started.

It started with me brushing her hair.

We used to have math together. We sat in the back of the room, me behind her. And back then she wore her hair long and I would spend math period brushing her hair, counting to fifty in my head . . . Sometimes she would forget her brush, so I would use my fingers, just combing through her hair, over and over, touching her hair, feeling how warm and soft it was.

Somehow that turned into more. I don't know how. It doesn't really matter anymore, because I finally get it. I was confused about Jecca because with her it was never about sex or even love. It was about *need*. About needing someone and wanting someone and wanting to be held, but knowing—deep down—that you were needing and wanting and being held by the wrong person. But still thinking that the substitute was good enough. Because the truth was too tough.

And for a while there, I thought that maybe I was using her as a substitute for *you*, but now I know that that's not true, that that's not what I was doing.

Which brings me to my second thing.

I want you to know: I'm going to try. I'm really going to try. I can't make any promises. I'm still Kyra. People still piss me off and you can bet I'm going to tell them when they do. But I'll try to watch my mouth. And I'll try to be nicer to Dad. Maybe I'll even start calling him Dad. (But maybe not—let's not get *too* carried away!)

I don't know if you know this or not, Mom, but I tried to kill myself a while back. And then a few months ago I had a bullet and I was gonna try to do it again, but I didn't.

It's not that I was trying to see you again. I'm not sure *what* it was anymore. It's weird, because just a day ago, I felt like I understood it. And now I feel like it's something that happened to another person, a long time ago, something I heard about from a friend of a friend.

So what changed in the meantime? Well, I know a little bit of what changed. But I think for the most part, I just realized some things.

Like, life isn't perfect. Hell, life is shit most of the time. But it's my life. I get to do what I want with it. And getting rid of it would be like throwing away an outfit just because you're not entirely sure you'll ever wear it. Why not just keep it, just in case? You never know what you might do with it. Just like my clothes. I could have thrown out all of those outfits that Grandma bought me, but I kept them, way in the back of the closet. I even wore the scarf. I could have thrown out all of my black clothes when I started wearing white. But I kept them. And now I'm going to wear them again. Because I've realized: I'm not just White, ElecTrick Sex Kyra. I'm also Black, Post-Goth Kyra. And maybe a bunch of other Kyras, too. Who knows?

And Ultimate Kyra? What about her?

Well, I figure Ultimate Kyra is *all* the Kyras.

That's what I figure, and maybe I'm right or maybe I'm wrong, but the only way to find out for sure is to keep going and keep looking and find out someday.

So some days I'll be one. And some days I'll be the other. And some days I'll try something new.

And sometimes I'll let my hair grow out. And sometimes I'll shave it off. People will wonder about me, but I don't care.

I don't care because . . .

Well, because of my third thing.

I've met a boy.

I know. I know you're worried. I remember when you sat me down and talked to me about sex. And you told me that I wasn't old enough for it yet, and I was curious, so I said, "When will I be old enough?" and you sort of sighed and you said, "Too soon. No matter when it is, it'll be too soon. But there's nothing I can do about that."

I never understood that. I don't know if I understand it now.

I'm not going to be like Simone and sleep with a guy just because I like him and I think it'll make him like me. That just cheapens what's really going on because he's the one. He's the guy Dr. Kennedy was talking about, the person who doesn't just appreciate what I do, but appreciates why I do it and how I do it.

When I shaved my head, he liked it. Simone and Jecca just went along with it.

Fanboy liked my new look. Sim and Jecca just used it for themselves.

And I've been thinking about what you told me, about how the opposite of love isn't hate. So if I hated Fanboy because I thought he'd forgotten me . . . If I was able to be that angry at him, doesn't it mean I've cared about him all along?

I don't know how he feels about me. I mean, I think I have a pretty good idea, but I'm not a hundred percent sure and you can't *assume* things when it comes to stuff like this. But that's OK. I have time to work it out.

I always thought love made you weak, Mom. And I thought that love made everyone weak.

You know what? I was *right*. Love *does* make you weak. So there.

But . . .

Maybe it's OK to be weak or needy for one person. Maybe that's all right. Maybe I don't have to change for the whole world; just for him. Is that OK? I think it has to be. I don't think I can be different for everyone else. I don't think I can let them in or clue them in. But for him, maybe I can. Maybe that's what life is about—one person. Maybe it's about finding that one person. I don't know.

I don't know.

But I know this: I can't be alone anymore. I can't sit in the dark while other people fumble around in the quiet and the murk, trying to find me, trying to locate me, while I huddle in the pantry, hiding, hoping no one finds me, not opening my mouth, not speaking, waiting for Jecca to come along and make me warm and alive for a few minutes at a time.

I need to be out there.

Living.

Looking for my own life. My own kisses.

I need to open my mouth.

I need to be heard.

I need to live.

You're gone, Mom.
I'm not.

ACKNOWLEDGMENTS

THANKS, AS ALWAYS, TO EVERYONE at Houghton, especially Lisa DiSarro, Jenn Taber, Betsy Groban, Linda Magram, and Alison Kerr Miller, to say nothing of the poor folks in Design who had to format that one chat transcript... round of applause, please.

Also to: Robin Brande, who read multiple drafts; Alexandra Heyser, my secret (oops) teen girl connection, connoisseur of dirty tricks; Eric Lyga, who read the early draft; and Margaret Raymo, who believed in Kyra's voice... and found the perfect cover photo.

Special thanks to Kathy Anderson, who believed in the book from the start and who loves Kyra almost as much as I do. When the website fanboyandgothgirl.com launched, it had blogs from Cal and Fanboy. Kathy insisted that there had to be something from Kyra as well, so I hit on the idea of some letters she could write to Neil Gaiman, a device that I was thrilled to be able to expand and exploit in this book.

Sincere thanks, too, to Officer Stacey Gaegler of the Hampstead (MD) Police Department, who answered my questions about arresting car thieves with patience and good humor. As always, anything I got right is her influence; anything I got wrong is my fault.

I have to offer deep, deep public thanks to Molly Krichten, whose influence on this book is quite impossible to overestimate. You have no idea. She might understand Kyra better than I do.

Last but certainly not least: My thanks to the legions of *Fanboy and Goth Girl* fans who deluged my e-mail inbox with requests for a sequel. This book was never part of the plan. I'm glad the plan changed and I hope you are, too.